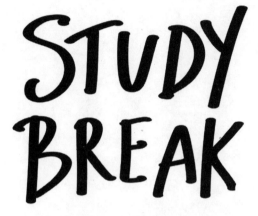

STUDY BREAK

11 College Tales from
Orientation to Graduation

STUDY BREAK

11 College Tales from
Orientation to Graduation

EDITED BY
AASHNA AVACHAT

WITH STORIES BY
Jake Maia Arlow • Arushi Avachat • Boon Carmen
Ananya Devarajan • Camryn Garrett • Christina Li
Racquel Marie • Oyin • Laila Sabreen • Michael Waters
Joelle Wellington

FEIWEL AND FRIENDS
New York

A Feiwel and Friends Book
An imprint of Macmillan Publishing Group, LLC
120 Broadway, New York, NY 10271 • fiercereads.com

Our books may be purchased in bulk for promotional, educational, or business use. Please contact your local bookseller or the Macmillan Corporate and Premium Sales Department at (800) 221-7945 ext. 5442 or by email at MacmillanSpecialMarkets@macmillan.com.

Library of Congress Cataloging-in-Publication Data

Names: Avachat, Aashna, editor.
Title: Study break : 11 college tales from orientation to graduation /
    edited by Aashna Avachat.
Description: First edition. | New York : Feiwel & Friends, 2023. |
    Audience: Ages 14 and up. | Audience: Grades 10–12. | Summary: "This
    collection of interconnected contemporary YA short stories, written by
    Gen Z authors, explores different parts of 'the college experience,'
    from questioning your major to questioning your identity" —Provided by
    publisher.
Identifiers: LCCN 2022034727 (print) | LCCN 2022034728 (ebook) |
    ISBN 9781250848055 (hardcover) | ISBN 9781250848048 (ebook)
Subjects: CYAC: Universities and colleges—Fiction. | Short stories. |
    LCGFT: Short stories.
Classification: LCC PZ5 .S8979 2023 (print) | LCC PZ5 (ebook) |
    DDC [Fic]—dc23
LC record available at https://lccn.loc.gov/2022034727
LC ebook record available at https://lccn.loc.gov/2022034728

First edition, 2023
Book design by Michelle Gengaro-Kokmen
Feiwel and Friends logo designed by Filomena Tuosto
Printed in the United States of America

ISBN 978-1-250-84805-5 (hardcover)
1 3 5 7 9 10 8 6 4 2

Dear reader,

All books begin with an idea, and this book had a particularly unique conception. *Study Break* began in perhaps one of the most Gen-Z ways possible: from a tweet, a quote retweet, and a ton of DMs. In the spring of 2021, Camryn Garrett sent off a tweet wishing there would be more space for novels set in college in the Young Adult category. Ananya Devarajan quote retweeted it: "Imagine . . . an anthology of diverse college stories that all connect by the end. If this does become a thing, PLEASE LET ME WRITE IT."

And so, it began.

Now, this book is a time capsule: All twelve authors in this anthology were either in college or recently graduated at the time we wrote these stories. Those moments in time and in our lives are preserved in this collection.

Space for college-based stories in YA is increasing, and we are proud to contribute to that goal. It has been an honor to work to bring something that started as a series of tweets into book form for you to read. Shaping this collection as editor has been a great privilege of my life, and the authors of *Study Break* have made the work so fulfilling.

Thank you to Camryn and Ananya for lighting the spark, and to you, reader, for keeping the fire going.

Welcome to the University of Milbridge. We are so excited to have you.

STUDY BREAK

11 College Tales from
Orientation to Graduation

FALL SEMESTER

Catch You on the Quad

By Oyin

I.

Imagine, for a moment, lazy summer
days falling
crisp; oranges browns olives reigning
on August's parade; a campus
beaming with buildings
that hold answers, dorms that house
questions; wishes dropped
into a creek with the tiniest bridge;
manicured lawns teeming with magnolia
trees, bursting with bodies dancing

about its grounds, shimmying
with overstuffed boxes and suitcases
to Desai, to Greathouse;
the buzz of voices coasting above
eager fields and streets with instructions

to call every day, focus
in class, attend club
meetings, feast in fabled Café,
get sorted in financial
aid, throw (pity) parties;

imagine: the rookies
just out of high school
classes and clubs, homecoming,
payments for this and that and that and this,
deadlines, prom, graduation, homeleaving;

there's a newness: in their eyes,
in shiny not-yet-swiped ID cards,
in secret trips, in nerves floating
around Polaroids freshly placed on plaster
walls and fairy lights illuminating;

imagine, veterans returning
from summer spent battling
heat-induced fatigue, fighting
hometown friends (or ex-friends),
strategizing with lovers
(or those soon-to-be), dueling
parents (or the ones who stepped up)
for approvals on transfers and altars to
uncommon saviors—

only to hear the rallying call
of former classmates and former roommates
wheeling borrowed blue bins almost as old
as the universe seeing the birth of Milbridge,

only to realign with the campus itself:
its bronzed moose guard still, in anticipation
of high fives and fist bumps and double taps
for luck, its Last Drop openmouthed
to offer coffee-fueled confidence
during late-night cramming sessions
and meet-cutes forever memorialized
on cement walls;

imagine, for a moment, the feet that will
tickle the grass months from now, when
rookies and veterans sit with each other
in the quad;

Until then—the campus sighing in relief,
settling into itself, into fall, and thinking:
they are

here.

AUGUST

The Ultimate Guide to Orientation
By Ananya Devarajan

A **Revised** Guide by ~~Anushka~~ **Aarti** Chandran

Rule One: The key to becoming valedictorian at the University of Milbridge is a competitive course load. Set yourself up for success by declaring ~~a minor in Informatics~~ ***a double major in economics and psychology*** *on Day One.*

Aarti Chandran stepped into the August sunlight, where she stood beneath the watchful eyes of the UMB school mascot: a friendly moose rendered in bronze. She watched as hordes of cooler-than-her upperclassmen passed by, standing up on their tiptoes to give him a fist bump or a high five as if it were second nature.

Her older sister, Anushka, placed a hand on her shoulder and squeezed. "What do you think?" she asked, a hint of nostalgia in her voice. "Does it feel like home?"

Aarti knew what the right answer was—*yes, Anushka, I have the same gut feeling that you did five years ago*—but if she was being honest, she wasn't so sure yet. UMB was her sister's home before it was ever hers, and the threads of her legacy were still present throughout campus, a distinct feeling that drifted from the depths of Pitfall Lake, where Anushka had her first kiss, to the bustling dorms at Desai Hall.

"Of course it does. It's everything we've ever dreamed of."

Anushka let out a squeal and grabbed Aarti's hand, dragging her through the magnificent gates at the front of the school. "Oh, I'm so excited for you! I'll have Mom, Dad, and Ishaan bring in your boxes, and we can get you checked in for orientation in the meantime."

The mention of Ishaan, Anushka's college-sweetheart turned fiancé, sent a nervous rumble through the pit of Aarti's stomach. His existence in their lives was a constant reminder of Anushka's successes at UMB, all of which had roots in her orientation— dozens of doting friends, the perfect roommates, and an instantaneous boyfriend, to boot. Flash forward to five years later, and Aarti donned a fresh set of mehendi on her hands from Anushka and Ishaan's engagement ceremony.

"Why don't you help with the boxes, too? I want to see if I can do this on my own." Aarti tore her eyes away from her sister and analyzed the architecture surrounding them—blue-windowed science laboratories stood along the sidewalk, complemented by the swaying magnolia trees in the center of campus. A group of professors swapped stories outside the brick humanities building next door, identical lanyards around their necks. Despite the lack of a clear architectural theme, the university was unified by its spirit, thanks to the community who'd decided to call this place their home.

Anushka blinked at her. "Are you sure?"

Aarti patted her back pocket, where her sister's personal guide to surviving orientation resided patiently, and flashed her a knowing smile. "Even if you're not physically here, I'll still have your advice with me. That's more than enough."

"I trust you." Anushka pressed a kiss to Aarti's cheek. "You're going to love it here. Don't let your anxious brain get to you, okay?"

"I won't." Aarti waved goodbye as her sister ran off to find the rest of their family. In the corner of her eye, she saw Anushka turn around for another glance at UMB, and Aarti hoped she would one day find the same attachment to her welcoming, but unfamiliar new home.

Once she was alone, Aarti pulled "The Ultimate Guide to Orientation at the University of Milbridge" out of her pocket. It was a stack of crinkled papers bound together by a thick gold thread. With the utmost care for her sister's handiwork, Aarti flipped past the cardstock cover in search of Rule One as she walked through campus. Whereas Anushka had declared a minor in addition to her pre-admitted major on the first day of orientation, Aarti planned to take her education one step further with a double major.

Her attention snapped away from the handbook when the doors of the Office of Academic Advising swung open. An Indian boy with a smile that matched the glint of the gold chain around his neck, neatly tucked into the collar of his sweatshirt, exited the building. A bell rang above his head, its sound fading as he held the door open for her with the base of his heel. Their shoulders brushed when Aarti stepped forward, and a powerful spark of heat erupted in her chest, unleashing a cage of butterflies in her stomach.

"After you," the boy said, voice smooth like the Madras filter coffee she drank with her father every morning before school. His dark eyes locked onto hers, and she couldn't bring herself to look away now that she'd fallen into his trap.

It was almost as if her intuition knew that this boy meant

something, that he was important in ways mere logic could not begin to describe.

Aarti hated to copy Anushka's meet-cute right down to the alluring Indian love interest and quaint university setting, but the thought that she might be at the beginning of a similar destiny was reassuring. The downside was that Aarti was now acutely aware of her off-brand black leggings and basic UMB maroon sweatshirt, the loose tendrils of her curtain-bangs escaping her ponytail in a not-so-styled, not-so-trendy way. The sole redeeming factor was her sharp, winged eyeliner, but there was only so much makeup could do for her now.

"Uh . . . thank you?" Aarti meant to phrase it as a statement, but something about the boy and the sheer potential he represented rendered her useless.

The boy just looked at her, eyebrows lifted, expression amused. "My pleasure," he replied. "See you around." With a laugh, he left the building, leaving Aarti to stew in her embarrassment alone, just the way she liked it.

So much for a perfect meet-cute.

A counselor waved at her from what seemed to be the only empty desk in the room. Her hair fell into curled waves, and she was likely no more than a few years older than Anushka—twenty-five at best. "You lost, sweetheart?"

Aarti's eyes flicked to the crowd of students lining up behind her, and she quickly made her way to the back of the room. "I actually had a few questions about my course schedule."

The counselor exchanged a not-very-subtle look with her colleague, who was helping another student at the desk beside them, before returning her attention to Aarti. "Why don't you have a seat? If you give me your name and student ID number, we can get started on answering your questions as quickly as possible. I wouldn't want you missing out on the fun of orientation!"

"Thank you." Aarti slid into the cushioned chair, reciting her identification details from memory. She tried to hide her awkwardness, her fear that she didn't quite belong and that everyone in the room knew it as much as she did. On the surface, Aarti was the typical legacy student—poised to succeed from the very first day, armed with a step-by-step guide that could only be learned from the mistakes of those that came before her. It was a privilege, of course, but Aarti couldn't help but wonder if she'd been set up to fail the moment she'd committed to the same university as her sister. "I was wondering if I could declare a double major. I know what I want to study, and I really would love to get a jump on that if possible."

Aarti heard her request echo through the room despite the chattering voices surrounding them in every direction, and she sank deeper into her chair to avoid being perceived any more than she already was. The counselor bit her bottom lip, rouged in dark purple, and Aarti wasn't sure if she was deep in thought or trying to restrain her amusement. "While I do love your determination, I'm afraid we cannot allow such requests for freshmen."

"Can you make an exception?" Aarti pleaded, her heart growing heavy upon seeing the counselor frown slightly and shake her head. If immediate failure wasn't the most on-brand way to start her orientation, she didn't know what was. Aarti had always been the last-one-picked-for-teams-in-gym, never-been-asked-to-a-school-dance, straight-3's-on-her-AP-exams kind of girl. She wasn't sure why she'd thought university would be any different. "When my sister was a freshman here five years ago, she was able to declare a minor on the first day. Can I do that?"

The counselor shook her head again. "Sadly, I don't think I can offer that option. Our rules have changed since your sister enrolled here." When Aarti remained frozen in her chair, the counselor stole a quick look at the clock. "I know academics matter, but that doesn't mean you can't enjoy yourself too. Don't be afraid to take your time, sweetheart."

Aarti flinched at the term "sweetheart" and the way it was thrown at her in such a condescending manner. It was one thing to not accomplish the very first rule of her sister's handbook, and it was another to be teased for it.

"Thank you for your time." Aarti pushed her chair back with a purposeful screech, and offered the counselor a smile that barely reached her eyes. "I appreciate your help."

"It's my pleasure. Feel free to visit again next year if you're still interested in adding a major, but until then, have a great time at orientation! I hope you know how lucky we are to have you with us." The counselor returned her smile before turning back to her computer, oblivious to the string of curses Aarti was whispering to herself for letting her academic dreams go so easily.

"One rule failed, another nine to go," she mumbled under her breath as she left the Office of Academic Advising. The door swung to a close, and seconds before Aarti stepped away to approach her orientation group in front of Desai Hall, she heard a pitying laugh and a sentence along the lines of *I admire the poor kid's spirit, but . . .*

As if the disappointment of fumbling the easiest rule in the handbook wasn't enough, Aarti now had to come to terms with the fact that her counselor didn't even believe in her. She had never been more humiliated in her entire life, and she had no idea how she'd recover from it in time to leave behind a legacy great enough to rival her sister's, especially if the only way for her to do it was to rely on socialization—a skill she'd yet to develop—instead of academics.

Before she could hatch a new plan for how to spontaneously become an extrovert as outlined in Rule Six, Aarti stumbled into a girl who looked as lost in thought as she was. They were wearing the exact same outfit, but the girl pulled it off ten times better, with elegant silver hoops that mirrored the sparkle of the crescent moon ring on her finger. She was magnetic in every sense of the word, and in that moment, Aarti was convinced that their meeting was a powerful act of fate.

She would be a fool to let this opportunity go to waste.

*Rule Two: Find your forever family, the friends and mentors that will stand by you throughout your time at the University of Milbridge, **and never let them go.***

"I am so sorry," the girl exclaimed, a horrified expression on her face, the polar opposite to the charming boy Aarti had met earlier. "I didn't mean to bump into you like that, but I—"

"Don't even worry about it. It's more my fault than it is yours." The girl softened as Aarti spoke, her eyes crinkling ever so slightly at the corners. Something about her set Aarti at ease, so she extended a hand. "In the spirit of awkward introductions . . . Hi. I'm Aarti Chandran."

"Arisha Rahim." She clasped her palm around Aarti's. "I feel like I haven't had the chance to talk to the other students yet, so I'm really glad that we could meet, even if it was an oddly physical encounter."

"Tell me about it. Outside of meeting you, I've only really interacted with an academic counselor, and that was not a fun experience at all."

"I'm so sorry to hear that. Hopefully, the rest of your orientation is so amazing that you forget all about that counselor." Arisha offered her a sympathetic smile. "And, hey, maybe our meeting doesn't have to end so soon. What orientation group are you in?"

Aarti checked her email, scrolling through a handful of notifications regarding orientation that her sister had neatly sorted into a folder for her on their drive to campus. When she found the email with her move-in time and group designation, she showed Arisha. "Group twelve."

Her eyes lit up. "Those are some crazy odds. Twenty-five possible orientation groups, and the random girl I bumped into outside of Advising just so happens to be in mine."

"It's almost like it was meant to be," Aarti said. She thought back to when she was practically laughed out of the Office of Academic Advising, fully convinced that she'd never come close to achieving the perfect orientation the way her sister had, only for Arisha to stumble into her life a few minutes later. It couldn't possibly be a coincidence. "Shall we?"

"We shall."

The two girls made their way to the front of Desai Hall to meet the rest of their orientation group, and for once, Aarti wasn't fretting over her earlier failure. Instead, she was captivated by the young couple sharing a gyro in front of the dining commons, the moose plush toys that waved from the Roman-inspired windows of Godfrey Library, the gentle hint of fresh water in the air, wafting over the groves of trees near Pitfall Lake a few miles over.

Was this what her sister had meant by the campus feeling like home?

"How are we feeling about the undeniably awesome University of Milbridge?" their orientation leader, a girl with bright pink hair and a sleeve of tattoos up her left arm, shouted from the revolving glass doors of Desai Hall. A group of twenty or so freshman stood in a circle around her, and Aarti felt a wave of infectious excitement wash over her as she joined them. Their orientation leader continued once the group, Aarti and Arisha included, responded with a smattering of cheers. "That's what I like to hear! Now, for a quick introduction before we head back over to Godfrey Library to grab your official UMB student ID cards: My name is Lily, I go by she/her pronouns, and I'm your go-to source for all your orientation needs. We're going to have some time to get to know each other better as the day goes on, but until then, follow me to pit stop number one."

Arisha looped her arm with Aarti's as they followed Lily to Godfrey Library. Back in high school, Aarti might've laughed at such a gesture—no teenager looped arms with another teenager unless they were straight out of an early 2000s Disney Channel Original Movie—but in college, it was like a form of approval.

"What are your thoughts on a rapid-fire round of small talk?" Arisha asked, with a curious glint in her eyes.

Small talk, especially of the rapid variety, wasn't exactly Aarti's idea of a good time, but she couldn't bring herself to say no. She reminded herself that she was at orientation, that this was the time, if any, to finally step out of her comfort zone. She couldn't let herself pass up the opportunity to make a friend simply because she was scared.

"That's a great idea. Should I start?"

When Arisha made a sweeping motion with her free hand that Aarti took as a nonverbal yes, Aarti cleared her throat, buying time to remind herself of how to build friendships from the bottom up. Perhaps it was best to go big, rather than go home.

"What were you like in high school, and is that similar to who you want to be at UMB?"

Arisha's lips formed a small circle, as if she hadn't expected to face a question with so much weight at noon. Her expression evened out after the surprise faded, and she grinned at Aarti. "That's a good question. Honestly, I think I'm still deciding who I want to be, but I can promise you that the Arisha you're meeting today is the Arisha I enjoy existing as the most."

"I completely get that." Aarti squeezed her arm in solidarity. "Everyone expects us to have it all figured out the moment we turn eighteen, but we were never even given the chance to explore ourselves until now."

"Yeah, and it's not like we had a guide or something to figure it out earlier," Arisha said, and Aarti shifted her gaze away, ears burning red. The guidebook sitting in her pocket suddenly felt heavier. "Sometimes I feel like I'm the only one who still has no clue who she is."

"Trust me, you're not alone on that." Aarti sighed. "Back in high school, I was never Aarti Chandran, but Anushka Chandran's little sister. I thought the pressure to live up to her legacy would ease when I finally made it to college, but I ended up at UMB just like she did. I don't know if I should continue to try to be like her, or if I should take a risk and try to be me."

Arisha paused as if a lightbulb had clicked on in her mind, her foot hovering midair above the stone staircase leading to Godfrey Library. The library was constructed in two halves, split by a walkway lined with eucalyptus trees, with entrances on either side. "Maybe it doesn't have to be like high school. We finally have the chance to make our college experience all about us, so why don't we try it out? It's not like we have anything to lose, right?"

Before Aarti could respond to her very valid point, Lily showed them to the line outside of the ID photo booth. A trio of tired-looking upperclassmen stood at an iMac desktop, pointing back and forth between the screen and the printer. An administrative staff member handed out the freshly laminated ID cards to each student in line, most of whom seemed engaged in deeper conversations than when they had first met. It was interesting to see how quickly the freshmen bonded with each other, their relationships laced with nothing short of magic. Aarti didn't think something so special happened often in the real world, and it made her want to hold on to Arisha tighter.

"Next!" a member of the trio called out, his eyes narrowing at Aarti as if he recognized her features, but couldn't quite place them. She quickly averted her gaze from him before she got the *Are you related to Anushka Chandran, by any chance?* comment, and approached the booth.

She wasn't sure where to look—at the other upperclassmen behind the computer or straight ahead at the plaster wall or at a higher angle in case the camera was swinging from the ceiling—nor did she know if her heat-strung hair needed a touch-up before being captured in a photo that would define her next four years.

A flash of light went off in her face, and the printer began to whir loudly.

"Enjoy the rest of your orientation!" the staff member chirped as she handed the ID card to Aarti and ushered her to the side. The plastic was smooth beneath her fingertips, and she flipped it over in her hand, her heart racing with anticipation.

"What the hell?" Aarti muttered under her breath when she saw her face in the rectangle in the corner of the card. Her T-zone was covered in greasy splotches that would make her dermatologist mother scream, and her hair was stuck to her forehead like a bowl of sad, limp Maggi noodles. Not to mention her cross-eyes, which were now forever immortalized in the shiny laminate. "This doesn't even *look* like me!"

A boy snickered behind her, and Aarti's chest filled with rage. She spun on her heel to confront the person who'd made fun of her, only to falter when it was the same boy from earlier. He seemed to recognize her, too, because the smug expression on his face was fading, and quickly at that.

"Do you have something to say about my photo, buddy?"

"The name's Rohan Patel, and no, I don't have anything to say."

A tendril of curly black hair fell into his eyes, and Aarti remembered Ishaan and his iconic meet-cute with Anushka. She'd tripped over a University of Milbridge moose plush toy that Ishaan had dropped on his way out of the campus store—her sister would never admit that she'd fallen on purpose, but Aarti could see the truth in the roaring blush on her cheeks every time she told their story—and like a modern Prince Charming, Ishaan caught Anushka and whispered the sweetest apology in her ear. They'd been inseparable ever since.

Normally, Aarti would feign disgust at the thought of their meet-cute, but she was much too engrossed in dissecting the meaning behind Rohan's reappearance in her life. Was this history repeating itself? After all, there had to be a reason why she was meeting a very attractive Indian boy on her move-in day, almost exactly like her sister had during *her* orientation.

"Did I scare it out of you?"

"Definitely not." His grin returned to his heart-shaped face, all rounded edges and soft corners. If Aarti stared for even a second longer, she'd see the crescent indents on his cheeks, two friendly dimples to counteract the teasing lilt to his voice. "You know, I'd feel a lot better if I could put a name to the face I accidentally made fun of."

"Aarti Chandran." She could barely keep up with his banter, but she had to try, if only to see what she could make out of their relationship. "You know, some people might consider this impression of yours to be quite rude."

Arisha joined them with a playful bump to Aarti's hip. "What did I miss?"

"You're actually right in time for me to apologize to your friend." Rohan offered Arisha a polite smile before he crossed his arms and tugged on his earlobes, asking for her forgiveness in traditional Hindu fashion. Aarti's heart melted at the sight. "I promise I didn't mean to laugh at your photo, and I'm sorry if I hurt your feelings."

"You made fun of her photo? How bad is it?" Arisha snatched the card out of her hand, and a soft laugh left her lips as soon as she flipped it over. "Oh, they really did you dirty with this, Aarti."

"I know." Aarti bared her teeth in a grimace. "But thank you for the apology, Rohan. I appreciate it." The silence between them continued for a second longer than she was comfortable with, and she took it upon herself to shift the conversation. "How's your orientation been? Have you made any friends yet?"

"Not too many friends yet." He exchanged a glance with Aarti as if he knew she'd understand the vulnerability behind his simple statement. A shiver raced up her spine when his eyes locked onto hers. "I don't know about you, but I'd rather ditch whatever this orientation is and explore campus on my own. I think it'd be more fun that way."

"Someone as *sweet* as you without a million friends? I find that hard to believe." Aarti teased, and Rohan threw his head back, laughing like a little kid. She congratulated herself on unknowingly speaking his language, which seemed to consist of lame jokes and witty banter. "Not to crash your solo date or anything, but I'd be down to sneak out of orientation and create some memories on our own terms. Arisha, are you in?"

Arisha stole a glance at their orientation leader, who was deeply involved in a conversation with one of the upperclassmen taking the ID photos, before turning back to them. "Are we really doing this?"

"I think we are." Rohan flashed them a smile, but underneath that charm, Aarti saw the silent *thank you* playing on his lips. Whether he'd admit it out loud or not, Aarti had a feeling that Rohan's original plan to explore campus by himself was somewhat of a defense mechanism, a last resort for if he really did end up with no friends at all.

Aarti wanted nothing more than to prove his fears wrong.

She beamed at him. "Come on, Rohan. You're one of us now."

Rule Three: The University of Milbridge is full of potential, but it is only what you make of it. Give yourself the chance to do all the things that scare you. **No one will judge you here.**

Hundreds of constellations shone above Pitfall Lake, and Aarti could've lost herself in counting them for the remainder of the night. In the cusp of Orion's belt, she saw the soft smile of her older sister, a twisting memory of shared birthday parties at Sky Zone and bunk beds where Aarti was always forced to sleep on the bottom. Back then, Aarti and Anushka were so much more than sisters—they were best friends.

Until one day when, without any warning, everything changed.

Anushka moved out. She started her new life at UMB, where

she found a new family, new friends, new love, and suddenly Aarti was demoted to being nothing more than her little sister again. The secrets they once shared were replaced with unsolicited advice and unnecessary fights and the constant expectation of living up to the legacy of a girl she no longer recognized.

And now Anushka was all grown up while Aarti was here—dreaming about the life her sister had already achieved, wishing on every star as if it would bring her the same destiny. However, even at such different stages in their lives, Aarti considered Anushka to be her person. No matter how far they strayed, she knew they'd always find a way back to each other.

"Aarti? You in there?" Arisha waved a hand in front of her face as she pushed herself off the grass, stretching her arms out with a satisfied sigh.

"Yeah, are you all right?" Rohan added. His concern was palpable, a complete 360 from the boyish grin he sported for the majority of the day as they climbed to the roof of Desai Hall and ran through the sprinklers in the park behind The Last Drop coffee shop and took Polaroid photos with the iconic moose at the head of campus. She could still feel the weight of Rohan's hand lingering on her waist after the photo was captured.

"I'm here," Aarti said. "I was a bit lost in my thoughts, but I'm back to earth now."

"Phew, that's a relief." Arisha swiped an imaginary bead of sweat off her temple. "I was just telling Rohan that I think I'm going to head back to the dorms now. I can't miss out on my beauty sleep, you know."

"And what a travesty that would be." Aarti grinned, reaching out to squeeze Arisha's hand goodbye. "I won't keep you up, but I hope we can see each other again soon."

"How about tomorrow? We can do lunch." Arisha turned to Rohan, who flipped a silver coin into Pitfall Lake. Instead of the coin skipping like the rock Arisha had expertly thrown earlier that night, it fell into the water with a satisfying *thunk*. "You're invited too, by the way."

Rohan visibly brightened. "Really?"

"Of course." Arisha chuckled. "Good night, you two. Don't stay up too late."

"We won't." Aarti waved as Arisha walked away, hands in her pockets and her head up high as if she were watching a replay in the night sky of the memories they'd made together. Aarti turned back to Rohan, who flipped another coin into the lake. He let out a low whistle as this one sank too, and he flashed her a butterfly-inducing smile afterward.

"Penny for those thoughts of yours?"

"Only if you can return them with a thought of your own." Aarti lifted a neatly threaded eyebrow at him.

"Done deal." Rohan sat up a little straighter, leaning against an old tree with roots larger than the area surrounding Desai Hall. The moon shone behind him, and he looked almost angelic in the light. "What's on your mind?"

"My sister," she said after a beat of hesitation. "I miss how we used to be before she went to college and got engaged and made the perfect life for herself. I guess what I'm trying to say is that I'm not sure if there's still space for me in her dreams anymore."

"Have you told her that?"

"What? That I miss her? No." Aarti hadn't thought of doing that, not even when Anushka and she were saying their goodbyes that afternoon. The majority of it was Anushka rattling off last-minute reminders and Aarti tucking away each word for safekeeping, but there was one moment at the end that Aarti wished she could bottle up and remember forever—her sister pulling her into the tightest hug, *I love you and I believe in you* whispered into her ear with so much pride. Aarti should've told Anushka how she felt then, but she was too scared of her sister seeing her as anything other than the effortless sequel to her timeless debut. And now, Aarti couldn't help but wonder if that exact insecurity played a hand in the distance between them now. "What if she doesn't understand how I'm feeling?"

"I think you're forgetting that she went through university too. She might've felt the same way you're feeling now but could never tell you since she's the older one." Rohan shrugged. "Then again, this advice is coming from me, an older sibling, so I am a bit biased."

Aarti chuckled, her body growing warm despite the wind drifting over the lake. There was something special about this boy, and it'd be a shame if she didn't try to figure it out before orientation ended. The time she'd spent with him, stealing glances when she was sure he wasn't looking and brushing shoulders accidentally-on-purpose, wasn't nearly enough.

"Your turn," she said. "What's your story?"

"Where do I even start?"

"Any dark secrets or rickety skeletons in the closet? Unforgettable memories or adventures? First loves or heartbreaks?" When his face went slack, Aarti silently cursed herself. "Let's pretend I didn't say that last sentence. Sometimes I talk before I finish thinking and—"

Rohan reached across the grass and pulled her hand into his. A surge of electricity coursed through her skin, unlike any touch she'd ever received before. She wondered if it was an act of friendship, of the solidarity and trust that came with a vulnerable conversation like theirs, but a small voice in her head disagreed.

"I had a girlfriend in high school, and it didn't end well." Rohan sucked in a deep breath, and she ran her thumb over the back of his hand without thinking. In response, his voice grew calm. "Don't get me wrong, I'm grateful to have had the opportunity to fall in love like that—the all-encompassing, end-of-the-world-and-it's-just-us kind of love. But when it inevitably ends . . . that's another kind of pain entirely."

"I'm sorry. I can't even imagine what that feels like."

"It's all right. Like all things, it's a part of life that I had the privilege of experiencing." Rohan gestured around him with a crooked smile. "It's like our time at UMB. There will be days when we wonder if we'd have been better off elsewhere, but I've heard that the potential this place holds makes all the sacrifice worth it. And that's how I view love too. High risk, even higher reward."

With every word Rohan spoke, Aarti felt her mind expand past all the boundaries she'd put on herself because of fear—fear of falling short of the great expectations her sister had set for her, of never being understood for who she really was, rather than the person she had the potential to be. She wouldn't have even noticed the emotional paralysis that consumed her if it wasn't for Rohan's words.

For a boy that had laughed at her ID photo only eight hours ago, he'd surprised her in the best possible way.

She shifted so that she was sitting closer to him, their shoulders connecting with confidence as they watched a single cloud move past the stars. "Do you think you'll ever fall in love again?"

In her periphery, Aarti noticed Rohan looking over at her, and she fought the magnetic urge to make eye contact. "One day." Something about the way he said the simple phrase made it seem like a promise, and although she couldn't decipher what he meant by it, her pulse skyrocketed. She could feel it ticking against the crook of her jawline like a time bomb seconds from detonation. "When I'm ready to take that risk again."

She turned to face him now, their fingers still laced together like the threads of an intricately designed salwar kameez. "Thank you for trusting me."

"It's easy to trust you, Aarti." With his free hand, Rohan raised an imaginary glass of champagne to the air. "To many more nights like this in the future."

"To us," she corrected, thinking back to Rule Three, scribbled in Anushka's handwriting. It was the only rule that was explicitly in her control.

Do all the things that scare you. No one will judge you here.

In that moment, Aarti realized that what scared her the most wasn't declaring a double major or making new friends. It was the towering legacy she'd confined herself to. Maybe that was why she decided to pull the handbook out of her pocket, replacing Anushka's name on the cover with her own. Maybe that was why she began revising each rule with a UMB-red pen, crossing out every phrase that didn't feel true to who she was and who she wanted to be.

"What are you doing?" Rohan asked, his voice drifting through the air like a gentle breeze. She looked up at him, and suddenly, the boy with endless potential was nothing more than a boy. A boy who might not be everything to her in the future, but was hers in the present.

Aarti passed the handbook to him so that he could see the improvements she'd made. "I'm redefining my legacy."

He flipped through each page with an awestruck expression, his finger tracing over the loops in Aarti's handwriting, distinct from her sister's block lettering. "What made you decide to do that?"

The last of the Ishaan-tinted rose hue that once surrounded Rohan's frame had faded by now, and despite the frightening permanence of her words, Aarti chose to finally express how she felt when she was with him—the real him.

"It's not every day you meet your best friends on the first day of orientation, and I wanted the handbook to reflect that, the memories we're making together and the lessons I'm learning in the process." Aarti raised an imaginary glass of her own and repeated herself, this time with greater confidence. "To us."

The corners of Rohan's lips quirked upward as if he understood exactly what she meant. He echoed the unspoken sentiment back to her in his sweet-coffee voice. "To us."

Even if her friendship with Arisha didn't last forever, even if she didn't find the love of her life in Rohan by the end of their four years here, Aarti would always remember how their connection felt nothing short of infinite when they were together. As she rested her head on the crook of Rohan's shoulder, the handbook happily forgotten on the grass beside them, she watched the sparkling Milbridge skyline beyond Pitfall Lake.

"To our new home," she whispered, and Aarti meant it with her whole heart.

SEPTEMBER

Shofar, So Good
By Jake Maia Arlow

I rip off my tenth outfit attempt, adding to the pile of clothes scattered across the floor of my dorm.

At first glance, it looks like the discarded attire from some raucous heterosexual orgy. Half the clothes are from the women's section—crop tops and skirts and flower-print dresses—and the other half are from the men's—oversized sweatshirts and button-downs and jeans with unfathomably deep pockets.

I can't decide how I want the world to see me today.

It doesn't help that I'm dressing for formal Shabbat dinner at Hillel, an activity that I would gladly skip if I hadn't received a text from my mom telling me that she had reserved me a seat.

Telling me, mind you, not asking, which shouldn't surprise me at this point after nineteen years of dealing with her I'm-just-doing-what-I-know-is-best-for-you Jewish Mother Energy (JME, if you will). At this point, I'm just trying to do everything in my power to not disappoint her like I did last year.

I finally decide on a loose but sturdy pair of high-waisted jeans and a black turtleneck. Not exactly Shabbat-dinner-chic, but it's what they're getting. I slip on a tight sports bra and then throw on the shirt and pants, before realizing that I look like Dwayne "the Rock" Johnson in that old photo where he's leaning against the staircase.

It's better than nothing.

My whole vibe is gender-confused-fancy-toddler, with my unkempt chin-length hair and gangly limbs that I still don't have full control over, nineteen years post-birth.

It's good enough, I remind myself.

It has to be.

· · · · ·

"Are you new?" a girl whose curly hair has been flat-ironed into submission asks me as I try to find a seat at Shabbat dinner.

"Yeah," I tell her. "Just transferred."

She gives me a pitying look. "Did UMB not let you in the first time? I heard it can be super competitive for some people."

I would fight her if I hadn't heard the same thing from my mom—I lived with her all of last year while I went to community college. She wouldn't let up on the fact that I was "wasting my potential." But I would've been happy to stay at my old school for both years and get my associate's if I hadn't needed to get far, far away from her. A scholarship to UMB didn't hurt, either.

"My first school just wasn't the right fit," I tell the girl through clenched teeth.

"Well, I hope you like it better here!" She waves too cheerfully and then runs off to join a table of girls who look like the ones who bullied me at Hebrew school for not wearing a dress to my bat mitzvah. (I wore a fitted navy pant suit, and honestly, I looked as good as someone actively going through puberty possibly could, so fuck them.)

I grab a plate of rubbery chicken and find a seat at a table full of pimply first-year boys. I nod at them, and they nod back. It's something like solidarity.

Even though I wouldn't quite call this "finding Jewish community," like my mother so firmly insisted on when I transferred, it's still closer to it than what I had at my old school.

The whole dinner is awkward and tedious—with a number of speakers talking to us about Hillel and its mission—but at least there's challah.

Then a middle-aged man with too much exposed chest under his button-down takes the mic and smiles around the room.

He starts by doing a bit of crowd work—which gives me second-hand embarrassment so strong that I want to pass out—then clears his throat, his face turning serious. "I just wanted to say that this is a safe space." I try not to snort into my chicken as he continues. "And it's *especially* a safe space for people who agree with our core value that young Jews having a positive relationship to Israel is essential to the health and well-being of Judaism." He grins again, trying to hold eye contact with all of us in the drafty event space. "But of course, it doesn't matter what you believe politically, what matters is that you're here, with us."

I stiffen in my seat, not knowing how to react to this. I'm deeply relieved when the dinner is over.

A girl with an ASK ME ABOUT JEWISH LIFE AT UMB pin on her dress accosts me as I'm leaving. "Are you interested in attending Shabbat dinner in the future?"

"Maybe?" I tell her, halfway out the door.

"Okay, well if you are, you should sign up now, because slots go FAST!"

"Um, I'm all right, then," I say. I can see my mom's face so clearly: the scowl when she finds out I'm not even *trying* to participate in Jewish life here. That was the whole reason she let me transfer, anyway. I told her there were no opportunities to find the Jewish community that she wanted for me back at my old school.

And the thing is, I really do *want* Jewish community, just not the same kind that my mom wants for me. She's told me for my whole life that she has my best interests in mind, but really, I don't know how she could possibly know my "best interests" when she's only ever done things for other people's approval.

Thankfully, my roommate's not in our dorm room when I get back, so I toss my carefully selected clothes aside in favor of a ratty T-shirt and shorts.

I flip open my computer and ignore the thousand tabs I have up for an essay about ekphrasis in my Romantic poetry elective. I don't know what ekphrasis means, and at this point I'm too afraid to ask.

I open YouTube, where, as my "Block Sites, Save Time!" Chrome extension reminds me, I spend "At Least Six Hours a Day on This Website—Would You Like Me to Block?" I click *No, thank you*, and then proceed to watch genderfluid TikTok compilations for a full hour.

That is, until the fire alarm goes off, and I jolt out of bed and slam my feet on the cold, hard tile floor of my dorm.

It's chaos. Every single person in the dorm stumbles, haggard, out onto the field in front of Desai Hall. Most people thought ahead and brought sweaters, but I'm exposed to the elements in my T-shirt and shorts with—oh, yup, there's a hole in the ass. Cool cool cool.

"EVERYONE STAY CALM!" an RA shouts at no one in particular, which has the opposite of the desired effect.

"Do you think it's a drill?"

I turn around to see who asked this. They're half concealed by their comforter, which is wrapped around their head like a blanket cocoon.

At first, I'm certain they weren't talking to me, but I become less convinced as they continue to meet my gaze expectantly.

"Um, probably." I wrap my arms around my waist, the early fall breeze that had felt crisp earlier feeling cruel now. "It's pretty much always a drill."

"Until it isn't," they say ominously, eyebrows raised.

I smile a little. "I guess so."

"Gali." They reach a hand out of their comforter-cocoon to wave.

"Fray," I tell them.

"GALLLLLLL," someone shouts from across the lawn. A tall girl in pajama bottoms and a blazer jogs across the field. "So, drill or fire? What do we think?"

I turn away from Gali and their friend after that, not wanting to intrude. The first few weeks of school have been filled with near-misses on friendship. Not that I thought this comforter-ensconced person could be a friend, but I don't know, would that really be too much to ask?

"Are you going to the meeting tomorrow?" Gali asks the girl who ran over here, after they discuss whether or not it's a real fire (they settled on drill, or microwave popcorn incident).

"I don't know," the girl says. "I have a problem set due the day after tomorrow, and I haven't worked on it at all."

"There'll be doughnuts . . ." Gali says.

I'm turned away from their conversation, so I don't see the look on the girl's face when she relents. "Fine," she says. "Oh, and also, I saw someone from Hillel tabling for Birthright. Are we going to do any countertabling?"

I almost stop breathing. *Countertabling.* Whatever club they're talking about, it's anti-Hillel, which might be the right club for me. If I have to follow my mother's instructions for what to do with my Friday night and eat rubbery chicken again, I might scream.

"Yeah, I think we're doing Return the Birthright stuff," Gali says. "JVP national sent us some brochures and shit."

Fuck.

These are the people my mom went out of her way to warn me about when I went to college. JVP—Jewish Voice for Peace—is the pro-Palestine Jewish organization that my mom's spent half of my life demonizing. "Self-hating Jews," she calls them.

Which only makes me more interested.

My mom is a Zionist. She's supported Israel for as long as I can remember, just like everyone else at my synagogue, and apparently at UMB's Hillel. Sometimes, at my shul back at home, the rabbi will have us pray for Israel, and I never know what to do. Because I don't know if I believe the same thing they do, if I want to be praying for a country to which I have no connection.

All I know is that I'm a Jew, and my mom's a Jew *and* a Zionist, and those two things aren't the same.

I've never gone any further than thinking these thoughts in my head, though, because I've never wanted to oppose my mom or disappoint her. She's been there my whole life, a steady but commanding presence. She's loved me, fed me, clothed me. All I've ever wanted is to live up to her expectations. I got bat mitzvahed for her, even when I was getting bullied in Hebrew school. I went to Hillel today for her.

At my old school, I was trying to get away from Judaism, from those expectations my mom laid on me over the years, of being the perfect "daughter" and making her and the congregation proud.

But now . . . I don't know. I really *do* want Jewish community again, especially here at UMB. I want to break bread with people, I want to sing with them, pray with them.

Unfortunately, though, the only thing I know for certain is that I don't want Jewish community like the one at Hillel. It's too much like what I grew up with. I don't want rubbery chicken. I don't want to have to explain myself to people. I want them to understand *every* part of me, for something more than Judaism to connect us.

And maybe this cute person and their friend are my ticket back in, even if it would disappoint my mom.

It's not like I'm living with her anymore; she doesn't have to know every little thing I do.

This can be my secret.

· · · · ·

One Year Ago, at My Old School™

There are twenty thousand students at my local community college but, somehow, only five Jews.

At least, that's how many show up to the sad little "Knishes and Kvetching" event that the local synagogue puts on for Jewish students.

"Knish?" one of the other four Jews asks me.

I shake my head. "I'm okay, thanks."

I'm in my usual Shabbat services outfit: a maroon dress my mom bought me in eleventh grade that somehow still fits, even if it feels all wrong on my skin.

"Actually, where's the bathroom?" I ask after a few minutes of knish-eating silence.

Someone tells me, and I rush in and grab the sides of the sink. I've been avoiding mirrors since the beginning of the semester, but I hazard a glance at this one.

And I almost vomit. I look like a bad imitation of a nice Jewish girl you'd see at a Saturday morning service.

Before this moment, I'd been having inklings that maybe I wasn't a girl, but seeing myself like this, it seals the deal. I can't look at myself, in this dress my mom bought me, in this synagogue with people I have nothing in common with other than being Jewish.

I leave the event without saying goodbye. I don't owe these people anything. I only went because my mom begged me.

Later that night, I open a browser on my computer and start filling out transfer applications.

· · · · ·

Transferring was for the best. A week after I filled out the UMB application, someone in my public speaking class at my old school gave a speech about how Jews are the original Christians, and I had to excuse myself because I was laughing too hard . . . until I started crying about how I had gotten myself into that situation in the first place.

It's better here, at UMB, where there are more Jews and fewer reasons to hate myself.

"Hey, aren't you from the fire drill?"

"Oh, uh, yeah," I tell Gali as I walk into the stuffy classroom where this week's JVP meeting is being held.

Did I maybe search for them on every form of social media to find out exactly what their deal was and where the JVP meeting was going to be this week?

Sure, fine, yes.

But, looking around, I'm glad to be here for more reasons than just seeing Gali again.

Everyone at the meeting is infinitely cooler than me. They all have shaved, dyed heads or floral inner arm tattoos or both. I didn't get the memo—I'm in my clean-cut synagogue outfit.

I look like a fucking dweeb.

"Since we have a new face," Gali starts after a few minutes of idle chatter (during which I stood in the corner eating half a powdered doughnut, so my "new face" is covered in sugar), "why don't we do a quick round of icebreakers?"

In my experience, college so far has been at least 70 percent icebreakers.

"I'll go first," Gali says. "Hi! I'm Gali"—a few people laugh at this, in the way you do when you're hearing someone you know very well break the ice—"I'm a history major, my pronouns are they or she, and I'm the president of JVP this year!"

The five other people in the room go after Gali, introducing themselves as the vice president, the secretary, the treasurer, and the class representatives. There are so few people in the club that everyone's on the board.

"I'm Jonah, I'm a bio major," the secretary tells me. "My pronouns are they/them." They turn to me. "And I think we might be in environmental science together?"

I nod and smile at them, happy to get to know someone outside of class when I've thus far failed completely at that.

The girl from the fire drill is Rose (she/her, poly sci), and now that she's wearing a T-shirt I can see that she has a half-sleeve of floral tattoos. Of course.

Then, it's my turn. Everyone turns their shaved head toward me and waits for me to say something, anything.

"Um, I'm Frayda," I tell them, looking down at my hands. "But you can call me Fray. I'm an English major with an environmental science minor." I take a deep breath; I've never said my pronouns out loud before, or if I have, it's been the wrong ones in an attempt to make other people comfortable. "And my pronouns are they/them," I manage to spit out. "And I'm not . . . anything. Just interested in the club, I guess."

Everyone laughs at that, and I glance up long enough to see Gali grinning at me.

"We're super glad you're here, Fray," they say, and it takes everything in me not to say something unhinged like, *No, I'm the one who's super glad to be here.*

So instead I just nod, and they go on to talk about JVP's mission. "I'm sure most of you know this already, but since we have a new person, I figured we should go over the basics." Gali grins at me again, but this time I can't meet their eye.

This is the most rebellious thing I have ever done. My mom would be more disappointed about this than she would about me showing up at home drunk off my ass or totaling her car or something like that. I almost don't want Gali to talk about JVP's mission, because then it'll be official: I'm no longer my mom's obedient little "daughter."

"So we're a pro-Palestine organization," Gali begins. "Obviously."

Then they go on to explain that they have various events with the goal of Palestinian liberation. That they're a Jewish organization and abide by the core Jewish principle of tikkun olam, healing the world. They talk about how antisemitism and anti-Zionism are not the same thing, and equating them is in itself antisemitic.

Some of it goes over my head, but I'm excited to learn. For the first time in a long time, the idea of showing up every week to a room with other Jews and talking about religion and life is more than appealing—it feels necessary. Everyone here is Jewish and almost definitely queer and wants to *help* people, to change the world.

I need to be a part of that mission, too.

The rest of the meeting goes by too quickly, with Gali reminding everyone that there will be a radical interfaith Shabbat on Friday, a protest on the quad on Saturday, and a Rosh Hashanah party on Sunday.

"Fray," Gali calls out once everyone starts dispersing after the meeting. "So, what'd you think?"

She's grinning at me expectantly, and I can't help but smile back. Because what can I say? *My mom would hate this?* That's certainly true, but they don't need to know that. *I feel like I finally found people who understand me?* It's a bit dramatic, sure, but *also* true.

I've never felt fully at home with other Jews before, but for the past hour, I did.

So I settle on, "I'm excited for Shabbat!"

"I'm excited to see you there," Gali says, leaning closer to me. "We haven't had a new person for a while, so you're a welcome surprise."

They smile at me, and, for the first time since transferring, I feel like I'm in the right place.

. . . . .

This has been the best week of my life.

I've strolled into the dining commons every night with my head held high, plopping my tray down next to Gali and Rose and Jonah and the rest of the JVP crew, listening to them debate politics and roast each other in the gentle way that only friends can.

For the most part, I've spent that time staring at Gali. Because they're just . . . so fucking hot. Their hair is short, shaved on the sides and the back and long and curly and floppy up top. When I look at her, it's like she's all there is in the whole world. They know everything there is to know about geopolitics, about Judaism, about life, and I could listen to them talk about the world forever.

Except it's not just Gali; it's Rose and Jonah too. I've been sitting with Jonah in environmental science, and we've been doing lab reports together in the library. They like to doodle in the margins of their notebook, and sometimes I'll doodle something in response. It's nice.

My JVP friends are also the only people who have ever used they/them pronouns for me. To be fair, they're the only ones who know that those are my pronouns, but still, it's incredible. They'll call me handsome and pretty in the same sentence. They'll let me tell them how I want to be seen on any given day. It's so different from the way I've been put into a box in the past, as "good Jewish daughter."

Now I'm just Fray.

Back at home, my mom never moved past the image of me as a bat mitzvah, standing at the bimah in a dress and cardigan and chanting Torah. I did that all for her, and then it felt like I never did anything right after that. My life for the past six years has been one extended disappointment to my mother.

"You're coming to the Rosh Hashanah party later, right?" Gali asks me as she shrugs her backpack on and puts her empty tray away.

"I'm not sure . . ." Even though I feel closer to these people than anyone else at UMB, I still don't want to intrude. It's an old impulse, from a time when I knew people only invited me to parties out of pity.

"Please?" Gali asks, running a hand through their hair. "It wouldn't be the same without you."

It takes almost nothing for me to give in.

"Okay," I say, grinning. "If you insist."

· · · · ·

"IT'S ALMOST 5784," Rose shouts from the corner of the room, and the fifteen or so people who are here throw their hands up and cheer. "WHO'S READY TO FRIGGIN' LOSE THEIR MINDS?!?!"

This is . . . not what I expected.

I grew up going to Rosh Hashanah get-togethers where I would eat apples and honey and try not to spill anything on my new white dress. Then my mom would parade me around the room, telling everyone what I had accomplished in the past year, and they would ooh and aah over my mom's version of my life.

If only I had known that I could've been doing *this* the whole time. That I could live my life with these Jews, who only vaguely care about the rules but want to heal the fucking world and have fun doing it.

"You look incredible," Jonah says as they walk up to me, gesturing at my whole deal. "Please bring this outfit energy to environmental science."

I'm wearing a white jumpsuit and my tallest don't-fuck-with-me black boots, so I can't help but roll my eyes at Jonah's comment. "I'm gonna continue wearing joggers and a hoodie to envirosci, but good try."

They stick their tongue out at me, and I flip them off.

They grin. "Spicy."

"Shut up," I tell them, but really, I could talk to Jonah all night. They're so cool, and it's wild to think of the alternate universe where we were in the same class all semester but never spoke. We would be strangers if it wasn't for JVP.

"WHO'S APPLE BOBBING NEXT?" Rose shouts a few minutes later. We're in her dorm, a four-room suite with a stained couch and a peeling fake-tile floor.

Gali's wearing a white suit with a skinny black tie and black Doc loafers. When they walk up to me, my heart almost stops.

"Fray," they say, nodding like a Victorian gentleman.

"Gal," I say back, and they laugh.

"Do you have an apple bobbing partner yet?"

I'm not the kind of person who goes bobbing for apples. I'm the kind of person who watches other people go bobbing for apples and thinks, *Wow, that must be fun for them.*

But maybe that doesn't have to be me anymore.

I shake my head. "Nope."

They reach for my hand. "Well, come on then, no time to waste."

I trail behind her, and a Red Sea of queer Jews parts just for us.

"Gali and Fraaaaaaaaaaay," Rose announces, holding a hairbrush in lieu of a microphone. "The match-up of the century."

Rose is more than a little tipsy, as are half the people here, but I haven't seen Gali drink anything, and I haven't either.

I stare down into the metal bin filled with water and shiny red apples.

"On your marks," Rose says. "Get set . . ." Before she can finish, Gali's head and shoulders are in the bucket, and I shove them to try to make space for myself.

"NOT FAIR," I shout as they emerge from the bucket to breathe. But I can't say it with a straight face.

I dunk my head under the water, and the sounds of the party are muffled around me. Water keeps getting into my mouth because I can't wipe the smile off my face.

I've never had this much fun on a high holiday.

Unfortunately, though, none of the apples feel like staying in my mouth, and after a few seconds, there's a tug on the back of my jumpsuit.

"HNNNNN!" Gali grunts, a red apple hanging successfully from their mouth.

"What was that?" I ask, laughing so hard that I cough up some of the bucket water.

They pull the apple out of their mouth and take a bite. "I said, 'I won.'"

I tip a fake hat to them. "I can see that."

And then it's my turn to grab their arm as the next two people bob for apples, dragging her across the room.

"Do you want a towel or something?"

She raises her eyebrows. "You have one?"

"Well, no," I say. "But I could figure something out."

"How entrepreneurial."

"I don't think you're using that word correctly."

We both slump down on the wall farthest from the apple bobbing station. This is the biggest party I've been to since I transferred, but it still feels intimate. Maybe it's because these people understand every part of me: my Judaism, my queerness, my desire for connection that's outside of what my old synagogue gave me.

"Where'd you come from?" Gali asks after a minute.

"What?"

They turn and tilt their head toward me. "I just mean, you show up one day at the JVP meeting, and now it's like I can't imagine the group without you."

I have no idea how to respond to that, so I don't say anything.

"No, I'm serious," they say earnestly. "It's like you belong here."

I rub the back of my neck, which is slick from a combination of sweat and apple-bobbing water. "I don't know."

"Don't you feel it too?" Gali asks. "That you were meant to be here, with us, at this party?"

"This exact party?" I wave my hands around the room. "No, not really."

They shove my shoulder. "You know what I mean."

I guess I do. Because I feel it, too. And I tell them as much.

"Good, because I'm being serious." They almost lean their head against my neck, then think better of it. But their face stays close. "You belong here."

Maybe it's because no one has ever said anything like that to me, or maybe it's because we just stuck our heads in the same bacteria-filled communal bathwater, but I can't shake the thought: *I need to kiss them right now.*

I don't know if it'll ruin everything I have here, this new world that I want to live in forever, but I lean in.

I keep my eyes closed as I do, because I can't stand the embarrassment of seeing Gali's face when they reject me.

But I don't have to, because a few seconds later, their lips are on mine. They put a hand on my chest and lean into me. Everything about them is warm and soft and perfect, and I don't know how I made it here, with this person who told me I belong.

When I come up for air (a much more pleasant experience than it was with apple bobbing), I can't stop staring at their lips, puffy from the kiss. From where my mouth touched theirs, soft and sweet.

Gali grins at me, but just as I'm about to lean in again, someone blows the shofar, and everyone heads toward the center of the room to sing and pray and talk about our hopes for ourselves and the world for the new year.

"I wasn't trying to get you to make out with me, you know," Gali whispers when everyone is sitting in a circle. "I meant what I said."

"I know," I whisper back. "But making out with you was a fun bonus."

They snort, and I lean into them, thanking the transfer gods for giving me UMB and JVP and Gali.

· · · · ·

"Do you want to learn more about our Return the Birthright campaign?" I ask a random passerby who shakes their head and plows forward, speed-walking through the quad to get away from me.

Gali just laughs. "You'll get used to it," they tell me.

We're countertabling Hillel right now, and I'm trying my best not to look across at the people behind their table. I recognize some of them from the Shabbat I went to, and I don't want them to see me here, even if I'd rather be hanging out with my JVP friends than them. Maybe it's residual shame from feeling like I'm doing something wrong by being part of JVP. Or maybe it's very justified shame because my mom would flip her shit if she found out.

"I need to get a picture for IG," Rose says, motioning for all of us at the JVP table to move closer together. "Smile like you like each other."

I grin at Gali; I can't help it. They've brought me into the fold of JVP and of their life, and through them I've met Rose and Jonah.

Since the party, we've made out at every possible opportunity. We've talked about Judaism and queerness and a million other things that make me feel like I finally belong.

When we're all sweaty and tired from a day of handing out fliers and trying to get other Jews on campus to join our cause, we traipse over to Rose's suite.

Gali and I choose two seats pressed right up against each other around Rose's crowded kitchen table while everyone flops down around us.

"Gali-and-Fray-stop-making-googly-eyes-at-each-other chal-lenge," Jonah says after a few minutes of idle chatter.

My face gets hot, but Gali says, "Absolutely not."

I grin at them, then pull out my phone to avoid looking at everyone else's faces. I didn't think it was *that* obvious.

But what I find on my screen is about a thousand times worse than being teased about my crush on Gali.

MOM: What is this?

The photo attached to the text is the one Rose took an hour or so earlier at the counter-protest. It's part of a screenshot from a UMB Jewish Parents group "warning" about us. About JVP.

42

The moms move *fast*.

Before I can even respond, my mom sends two more texts.

MOM: I'm coming for Parents Weekend
MOM: And we're going to have a Talk.

· · · · ·

"You didn't have to bring me all this," I tell my mom once she releases me from an extended hug.

She's been scowling this whole time, but she's still plying me with food and clothes. But I can tell she's mad at me because she brought me the scratchy underwear.

"It's fine," she says. "I thought you'd need something nice to wear to Shabbat tonight, anyway. At *Hillel*."

I ignore the last part of what she said and sort through the tote bag she handed me. The non-underwear clothes she brought are, to put it nicely, hideous. She seems to have bought out the entirety of Target's junior girls skirt section. There's nothing wrong with a good skirt, but all of these are ankle-length and floral, and about as far away from my personal style as any article of clothing could possibly be.

Instead of telling my mom that, I quietly thank her again, and then get changed so we can go to services. I'm playing the role I need to play right now, because anything else will stop the plan I've set in motion. I need her to think we're going to Hillel, that I've "come to my senses."

I kept trying to get her to stay home, but I don't think she's ever going to let me be now that she's seen the people I hang out with.

She hasn't addressed it, but I know it's coming. Nothing can stop a Jewish mother on a mission.

And then, as we're walking through the quad, we run into Gali. "Hey!" Gali says.

If we'd run into them accidentally, I'd be embarrassed. But this is all part of the mission.

When I told Gali and Jonah and Rose about the text my mom sent, they immediately swung into action. It was wild—and heartwarming—to see.

"Hi," I say back, careful not to stand too close to them. "Mom, this is Gali. Gali, this is my mom."

"Nice to meet you," my mom says in a way that makes it clear it's not.

"I was just about to head to Shabbat at a friend's house. We're having an event for Parents Weekend if you two wanted to come?"

I look tentatively over at my mom. I'm not sure if she recognizes Gali from the photo, but if she does, then she's got a good poker face. Gali is dressed in a button-down and khakis, a respectable Shabbat outfit.

"We're going to services at Hillel, but thank you for the offer," my mom says, and starts to walk away.

"Wait, Mom?" I ask. "Hillel will probably be crowded. Why don't we just go here?"

It's not the truth, but I need her to say yes.

"I already bought Shabbat tickets," my mom says. She's tapping her foot, annoyance written all over her face.

"Mom, *please*?" I ask, desperation seeping into my voice.

She sighs, then stares at her watch. Then sighs again.

She turns back to me. "Fine," she relents, and the three of us walk in silence to Rose's suite.

Rose and Jonah and the others are all dressed in their Shabbat best—part of the plan as well, since we'd normally all just wear a T-shirt and jeans or whatnot—and welcome my mom as she walks in.

"Fray, this is my mom," Rose says, pointing to a woman who looks just like her but older and grayer.

"It's so nice to meet you," Rose's mom says, pulling me in for a hug. "I've heard so much about you from my Rosie."

I don't know if this is true, but I smile gratefully at her. When I turn back to my mom, she seems slightly more at ease. Maybe it's the fellow-Jewish-mom presence.

There are desserts everywhere, and the suite is steamy from freshly baked challah.

We all start by singing Shalom Aleichem, and when I look over, my mom's singing along, her eyes closed. Singing together is one of my favorite parts of Shabbat; the words feel like they're imprinted on my heart.

Shalom aleichem mal'achei hashareit mal'achei elyon . . .

We sing as one, and my mom squeezes my hand.

After we make kiddush, everyone eats and mingles, and my mom pulls me aside.

"Is this what I think it is?" she asks, and I hesitate for a moment before nodding. I know she's asking if this is JVP, the people she's spent years warning me against.

She sighs, not looking at me.

"Mom—" I start to say.

She shakes her head. "Not right now. Not in front of these people." Then she walks away to talk to Rose's mom.

"Is it working?" Gali asks under their breath as we both power through chunk after chunk of challah.

"I don't know," I tell them honestly.

Everyone continues mingling, and I try to ignore my mom for a while as I laugh and chat and eat and sing with Gali and Rose and Jonah.

When the time comes to leave, my mom thanks Rose and we walk quietly out of the dorm. She doesn't say anything for a long, long time.

"What did you think?" I ask finally. I can't wait any longer.

"Rose's mom was nice," she says.

"That's it?"

"What do you want me to say, Fray?" she asks. "This is . . . shocking, to say the least. If I'd have known you were going to join whatever radical group happened to hand you a brochure, I wouldn't have let you come here."

I'm frozen for a moment, and then—maybe to keep my throat from closing and the tears at bay, or maybe because it's fucking time—I snap. "They didn't 'hand me a brochure,'" I tell her. "I found them on my own. I *wanted* to join JVP. And what do I want you to say? Oh, I don't know, that you're happy I found a Jewish community that actually cares about me? That you're glad I'm taking our faith seriously?"

She sighs and sits on a bench nearby, one lining the now empty path along the quad. "This is hard for me too, you know." I wait for her to collect her thoughts. "I *am* happy that you've found a Jewish community, Fray, but does it have to be *this* one?"

I shake my head. "Honestly, Mom? Yes. I've never loved being a Jew as much as when I'm with them. *You* were the one who taught me that Judaism is a religion of questions, of questioning." I take a breath. "So why are you so surprised that I questioned the beliefs we grew up with?" I think for a second about whether I'm going to say the next part, then decide that it's worth it. That I have to get everything out. "It honestly feels so *good* to question the fact that I had to be some perfect Jewish girl, that I had to support Israel even though I've never been there, even though it's nothing close to my homeland."

"Frayda—"

"No, Mom. You know what? No. I'm *not* a good Jewish girl. I'm not a girl at all." It's out of my mouth before I know what I'm saying. I can't look my mom in the eye as I continue. "I'm nonbinary. And I'm in JVP. And that's not going to change just because you came here for Parents Weekend."

She's very, very quiet for a long while after that.

So am I.

Finally: "If that's what you want."

"What?" I ask, unsure if I heard her right.

"Okay," she says, and when I look over at her, there are tears in her eyes. "I want you to be happy, Fray." She sighs. "It's what I always want, even if I don't understand why you're doing this."

"You don't have to understand, Mom." I'm crying now. "But I wasn't happy before. I really, really wasn't."

She pulls a tissue out of her purse. She thinks for a moment before handing it to me. "Are you happy now?"

I nod, because I am. Or something close to it.

"Okay, then," she says. "I'll try to be happy for you."

So, that's that. She pats my shoulder, hands me a twenty-dollar bill, and walks away.

And I'm left there, in the middle of the quad, a bit dazed. It's not how I wanted that conversation to go, but it's how it happened.

I made it happen. Maybe she'll never understand, but at least she knows that I'm not leaving JVP. That I found community, even if it doesn't fit her standards.

After a few minutes, I get a call from Gali, and it takes all I have to pick up the phone.

"Where are you?" they ask, chatter and laughter in the background.

"On the quad," I tell them. "My mom just left."

"What are you doing out there, then?" they ask. "Come back to Rose's. We miss you."

I smile. "Be there in a minute."

Without thinking, my legs carry me back to Rose's suite, back to Jonah and my new friends, back to Gali.

Back to my community.

OCTOBER

Fall Once More
By Aashna Avachat

Deepika Malhotra generally hated how noisy her next-door neighbors were.

"God," she often said to her roommate, Meg. "I thought we decided to get off-campus apartments to be in a quieter part of town."

Meg would always scoff. "It didn't cross your mind that it would be way easier to throw parties off campus than in the dorms?"

It hadn't, not really. Deepika didn't really party. And that meant she forgot that other people did.

Anyway, Deepika mostly hated how her next-door neighbors broke the city noise ordinance every weekend, but this Friday night, she was secretly glad.

It was nine p.m., Meg had already left for fall break, and Deepika had been crying for the past hour and a half, so loudly that only her neighbors' playlist could drown it out.

Ninety-eight minutes ago, Deepika scrolled on Instagram to find that her ex-boyfriend had posted a photo of him . . . and his new girlfriend going to her sorority date party. Deepika took one look at the photo and started sobbing.

Three weeks ago Jai had called Deepika to tell her he didn't think things were working out. And now, just twenty-one days later, he'd upgraded his dating life. Meanwhile, Deepika was sitting on the futon in her cramped living room, totally, completely alone, bawling her eyes out.

She remembered the things he used to say. "I know most long-distance couples don't make it through college, but we will," he told her, before they left for college. "I'll love you forever and always."

Yeah, right.

It was all over now, over because Jai had had enough. And that, *that*, was particularly unfair. Because if it was anyone's right to have had enough, it was Deepika's. *She* was the one who'd trek across state lines to visit Jai at his college, because Jai was "too busy" to visit Milbridge and Deepika's dorm was "too small." It was Deepika who had to miss out on dorm socials on Saturdays because Jai insisted that Saturday nights were the only nights he was free to video call. It was Deepika who had to deal with Jai texting her one-word messages for days at a time because he "had his demons."

It was Deepika who hadn't really gotten to experience freshman year, because she thought the only person she needed to really focus on during college was Jai, so they'd make it beyond graduation. She hadn't gotten to love Milbridge the way every other student here seemed to, the way they all made being in college such big parts of their identities, because she'd made Jai her whole identity. *She* should have been the one who had enough.

But *noooo*. Jai got to be the one who broke up with Deepika. And Jai got to be the one who *won* the break up too, already moving on to someone new.

Deepika let out a sob somewhere between a wail and a scream in frustration. She cradled a pint of melty ice cream in her hands. She'd tried calling Meg, but Meg was on a flight home. Deepika's parents were vacationing for their anniversary this week—they'd taken nicely to being empty nesters—so Deepika was stuck at UMB by herself for break.

There was a knock at Deepika's door, and she practically jumped out of her skin. Oh, god. The only thing that could make tonight worse would be a serial killer showing up at her door. And fate seemed to have it out for her lately. Deepika prayed silently that if she was murdered tonight, she'd at least end up on a true crime podcast.

Her fluffy pink blanket wrapped around her, tears and snot still caked on her face, ice cream still in her hands, Deepika walked up to her door and peered through the keyhole. There was a shadowy figure standing outside. Deepika had watched enough creepy movies to know she definitely, absolutely shouldn't open the door. But she'd also watched enough creepy movies to know that the heroine always did anyway.

"Who is it?" she yelled through the door, because an axe murderer would surely identify themselves as such.

"Uh, Holden Flores, from next door?"

Deepika's obnoxious, noisy neighbor was at her door? What did he want to see if she had an extra speaker he could borrow to make his music even louder?

That's when Deepika realized she couldn't hear her neighbors' music anymore. How long had it been quiet? Had they heard her scream?

Deepika's fears were confirmed when the boy, Holden, called out again. "Are you okay? We just wanted to check if you were all right."

We? Only Holden was outside.

"I volunteered as the messenger," Holden said. "I have to report back that you're doing okay, or they're all going to start planning a rescue."

Deepika wrenched open the door and stood in front of Holden with her blanket wrapped around her like a cape, her sticky, gross face forming a scowl. "I am perfectly okay, thank you," she said, like a liar.

The light from Deepika's apartment illuminated Holden. He was wearing a UMB crewneck with dark sweatpants, and his hair was damp like he'd just showered. He had on glasses, too, and he looked like someone she'd maybe seen around but hadn't really noticed.

Holden took one look at Deepika and tried, unsuccessfully, to hide a smile. "You sure?" he asked, one side of his mouth upturned.

Deepika was definitely noticing him now.

"I just . . . watched a sad movie," Deepika said.

Holden didn't seem convinced. "Okay," he said anyway. "Well, if you ever want to watch a sad movie with a bigger group, we're just next door."

"I know," Deepika said, despite herself. "With the way you blast your music, it's clear you don't want anyone forgetting you live next door."

Holden made a funny noise, like a surprised laugh. "That loud, but we could still hear you over it, huh?"

Deepika frowned and wrapped her blanket tighter around her. "Did you come here just to be rude?"

"No, no, sorry," Holden said, twisting his lips into a smile. "Are you sticking around all week?" Deepika nodded, and Holden seemed pleased. "Same here," he said. "My friends and I live too far away to really justify the travel expenses. Like, different time zone far."

Why was he telling Deepika all this? All she wanted to do was go back to her couch and resume her crying for the evening, and now there was a nosy neighbor trying to make conversation. A nosy *attractive* neighbor.

"My point is," Holden said, like he'd read Deepika's mind. "You should come by sometime. We do movie nights, play games."

"Listen to music?" Deepika cut in.

His smile widened. "Yeah. You're welcome to come. Even tonight. If you want?"

Deepika didn't need her random neighbor's pity. She pressed her lips together. "Thanks, but no. I, uh—I have things to do."

If Holden didn't believe her, he didn't say anything, just raised his eyebrows. "Okay," he said. "Well, good night."

As he turned to leave, something came over Deepika. "Wait," she called, and he paused, turning back to her. "Deepika," she said.

He stared at her, and she realized she probably sounded like she had half a brain cell.

"My name's Deepika," she explained lamely.

Holden smiled. "It's nice to meet you. Maybe we'll see each other in the laundry room, or something."

Deepika managed a smile back. "The mail room even, if I'm feeling adventurous." She held up a hand to wave. "Thanks for checking on me. And for not being an axe murderer."

Holden's eyebrows wrinkled.

Deepika stepped back into her apartment. "Good night!"

· · · · ·

The next morning, Deepika marched over to Holden's apartment, ready to give her neighbors a piece of her mind.

Their music had woken her up instead of her alarm, yet again. Ugh. Couldn't they just let her suffer in peace?

All she wanted to do was cry in front of the television, eat even more ice cream out of the pint, and draft petty subtweets before deleting them. #Thriving and whatever.

She hated that Holden and his friends had so much energy, while she was stuck feeling sorry for herself.

Their door, number 107, was open just slightly, which explained why the music felt especially loud. She peeked through the crack and saw a small group of people in UMB's deep red and dark gold, laughing as they placed some type of colorful cards on their coffee table, taking turns. In the sunlight, she could make out Holden, with his back to her.

It looked like they were having *fun*.

It made Deepika step back. Her chest squeezed with a certain want. They looked like real, actual college students, enjoying their break from classes. Deepika was still the same as her high school self, only now without Jai. And she didn't even know where that left her. Who that left her. She thought of Jai, probably fast asleep after his night out, dancing and socializing.

Didn't she deserve to have some fun, too?

The thought stilled her, and she raised her arm again to knock, this time out of want instead of anger.

Holden opened the door before she could. "Hey," he said. "I thought I heard some rustling out here."

Sunlight flattered Holden. His brown eyes seemed golden, and his dark hair curled around his forehead, dropping close to his eyebrows. His glasses were just a touch crooked, like he'd leaned his head on his elbow, and Deepika had the funny urge to reach out and fix them.

Deepika felt suddenly embarrassed. Holden had said she was welcome any time, but what if he was just being polite? But she was here now. She had to commit. "Hi," she said. "I was . . . wondering if I could join you all for . . . whatever it is you're doing."

Holden's eyes brightened. "We're playing some games before we get ready to go out. It's game day, against CLU?"

Right. Football season. Another thing Deepika had barely paid attention to, in high school or in college. Jai had never been into sports.

"You like sports?" Deepika asked, studying Holden's frame. He didn't seem athletic.

Holden grinned. "I like cheering. Come on in. You should meet everyone."

Holden's apartment was the same size as Deepika and Meg's, but it looked totally different. While Deepika and Meg had opted to decorate their walls with cute neon signs in cursive and Polaroid collages, Holden and his roommate had covered theirs in prints, from movie posters to maps to postcards. The furniture was all mismatched too, and Deepika was sure she'd seen their couch on the UMB Free & For Sale Facebook page.

Holden introduced Deepika to his group of people: "This is Hari, my roommate. Yujin, my best friend from high school—he also goes to UMB—Eliza, she's a junior, even though practically all of us in this building are sophomores, and Jonah—they're in Enviro Club with me and Yujin, and they're also on the board at JVP, the Jewish Voices for Peace club. Eliza used to be in Enviro Club with us too, for like, a second, but she dropped out when she met her Kappa Zeta Epsilon boyfriend."

Deepika tried to follow what Holden was saying. Five smiling faces looked back at her.

"What are you all doing?" Deepika asked, gesturing at the cards on the coffee table.

"It's called Exploding Kittens," Eliza said. "We're leaving for the game in ten, but we can play another round. You wanna join?"

· · · · ·

Deepika had always considered herself a staunch introvert, and one day at UMB's football stadium wasn't going to change that, but what it was going to do was make Deepika realize that she could both be an introvert *and* love cheering.

Cheering at faraway football players was the best way for an introvert to be energetic in public. There was technically no human interaction. Deepika was just there, with other people, in the same place. It wasn't like the football players were cheering back, or asking her what classes she was taking.

Holden didn't ask about that either.

"Do you want a hot dog?" he asked instead, fifteen minutes into the game.

Something happened on the field, a touchdown, maybe, and the UMB side broke out into cheers. Clearly a lot of students had stayed back for the game. UMB didn't have the world's best athletics, but it had some serious fans. Deepika felt the crowd's energy rush through her, and she beamed at Holden. "Yes, please."

Then, at halftime, while his friends cheered for the marching band: "Want to share some cotton candy?"

Holden had already bought it, so Deepika nodded. They picked at the spun sugar until their teeth turned teal.

Deepika looked at Holden during the fourth quarter. His temples were a little sweaty, and his nose was bright red from the sun, and he had the hugest smile on his face as he yelled at the field. "Referee!" he shouted, and his friends did the same.

Holden caught Deepika staring, and he raised an eyebrow.

"I got dumped," Deepika blurted, out of nowhere. She felt, for some reason, that she needed to explain why he'd found her in such a state last night.

Holden's expression softened. "Oh," he said.

"Three weeks ago," Deepika added.

Holden pressed his lips together, eyebrows going up. "Ah."

"I went on a date," she confessed. "After it all happened. Off of Hinge. It went terribly. He talked about his poli sci class the entire time."

Holden's lips quirked like he was amused, and Deepika laughed for a second, before frowning. "I don't know," she said. "The guy who dumped me wasn't right for me, and I should be better off without the relationship, but god, it sucks seeing him happy and growing while I'm still the same me. Yesterday was hard. I just felt so, so horribly alone." She glanced up at Holden, to see that his face had gone serious. He was so expressive, this boy. He could say nothing, and his face gave everything away.

"I'm glad you're here now, with us." The football crowd started doing the wave, and Holden lifted his arms up when it reached him, then turned back to Deepika.

"And look. You're here with everyone."

Deepika looked out at the sea of burgundy and gold, then down at her shirt to notice she was sporting UMB colors, too. Maybe being here could replace the part of her that had defined herself as Jai's girlfriend. She was Deepika, a UMB student. This was more central to who she was. She just hadn't gotten to really experience it yet.

"These are your people," Holden said, smiling. "A whole team, and even more fans."

There was another touchdown, maybe from the other side, but Deepika and Holden started shouting and cheering anyway.

· · · · ·

Two days later, Deepika found herself sitting in her XL twin bed, scrolling through Hinge.

She'd stopped trying after that awful first date, but spending time with Holden and his friends had given her hope for the UMB student population.

But it was the Monday of fall break, and even though a lot of students had stayed back for the game, Milbridge was quiet this evening, outside and online. Deepika replied to a "Hey" message with a "Hi" of her own, then let herself match with someone who'd commented on one of her photos.

She slurped on microwave mac and cheese and scrolled through profiles, texting Meg screenshots of funny bios intermittently.

A new profile popped up, and Deepika almost dropped her phone.

Holden F. stared back at her, smiling in a fuzzy shot at the camera. So this was where she'd seen Holden before—not in the building or on campus, since Deepika rarely left home, unless it was for her math classes, and she'd heard Jonah say Holden was an English major the other day. They'd never have crossed paths at school.

She'd swiped left, she knew, because she remembered scrunching her eyes at the profile. The photos were all blurry. Holden didn't look good in a single one of them, which was ridiculous because he looked *so good* in real life. His question answers were standard, even a little silly, about the books he liked to read (NOT CATCHER IN THE RYE, Please don't ask me about it! My parents are nerds!), where he'd grown up (Mexico for the first few years of my life, before my family immigrated to America), what he wanted out of a first date (something unexpected).

Deepika frowned and swiped left again.

She kept scrolling, for about ten minutes or so. The guy who'd said "hey" replied, asking, How's it going? What year are you?

Soon enough, Deepika realized that since most of the students were home for the week, there was almost nobody in her radius. Hinge refreshed and started her back up again with people she'd already considered and decided against.

And—oh. There was Holden again, smiling at her from the screen.

His location said he was less than one mile away. Yeah, because he was *next door!* This was ridiculous, the prospect of swiping on him.

But this was the third time Deepika had seen him on Hinge. Maybe it was a sign.

She tapped the heart button at the bottom and held her breath. Nothing.

Right. He probably wasn't online. He had better things to do than swipe on a dating app during vacation week.

Deepika put her phone down, and then it buzzed.

You've matched with Holden F!

And he'd messaged her. What flavor ice cream are you eating tonight? he'd asked.

Deepika opened her mouth in shock. Was he making fun of the

carton she'd brought to the door Friday night? She bit her bottom lip to resist smiling.

None, she texted back. All out.

> **Holden F:** ☹
> **Holden F:** My friends are out doing karaoke tonight. I had an essay to finish up, so I missed it.
> **Deepika M:** Did you finish the essay?
> **Holden F:** Turned in seventeen minutes ago.
> **Deepika M:** You might as well start singing to celebrate.
> **Holden F:** Why, are you missing the music we normally play?
> **Deepika M:** Started growing fond of it, actually.

Deepika heard the sharp sound of laughter through her walls. That's when it really set in: Oh my. Holden was *right next door.*

She could sense him in his own room just a few feet away, separated by drywall. Maybe he was lying in bed too, tapping at his phone. She got up and went to the bathroom to pee and think. What should she say? She spent a few minutes staring at herself in the mirror, patting down her hair and rinsing her face. Then she walked back to her bedroom.

> **Deepika M:** Do you want to come over?

There was a knock at her door.

Well, that was fast. Deepika turned slowly and walked toward her living room.

She opened the door to reveal Holden standing outside, a carton of ice cream in one hand, two spoons and his phone in the other.

"Hi," she said, taking him in.

"Hi," he said. "I remembered I had Häagen-Dazs in the freezer." He winced. "Well, it's Hari's. But I'm sure he won't mind."

Deepika couldn't help it. She smiled.

"So, *Catcher in the Rye*, huh?"

Holden groaned. "I hate that book."

"Maybe you should have thought about that before—"

"What, being born?"

They both looked at each other and laughed.

"Yeah. Something like that." Deepika looked Holden up and down. "So," she said.

"So," he said.

Deepika made space for Holden to walk inside. She felt suddenly self-conscious of her apartment—the dishes were dirty, a stack of homework was spread out on the dining table, and her favorite plush from home was sitting on the couch.

But Holden looked around, eyes wide, at the neon sign on the wall, the framed print of Gustav Klimt's *The Kiss*, the sunflowers Meg and Deepika picked out on their last run to Trader Joe's, and smiled. "I feel like the way people decorate their personal spaces says so much about them. What they like, what makes them feel comfortable, what feels to them like home."

"What does my space say about me?"

Holden thought for a moment. "You like being at home, being cozy and around your own space." He caught a photo of Deepika and her parents at her high school graduation on the living room corner table. "You miss your hometown. And"—he squinted at the

Polaroids on the fridge, of nature shots and silly selfies with Meg—
"you're a romantic."

Deepika felt a smile cross her face. "Nice detective work, Sherlock."

Holden mimed tipping a hat.

"So, what were you up to before this?" he asked. "Besides"—he wiggled his phone in his hand—"you know."

Deepika didn't want him to think that was all she had been doing. She *did* have a Hulu tab open on her laptop, if she remembered correctly. "I've been watching *Love Island*," Deepika said. "The UK version. Do you—do you know about it?"

Holden grinned. "Eliza loves it. I've seen a few episodes. Which season are you watching?"

"The one from three years ago?"

"Okay," Holden said. "Let's do it."

Do what? Oh—he wanted to watch with her. Deepika felt something warm rush through her.

She led Holden to her and Meg's bedroom, which for a moment felt so childish, two twin XLs pushed up against the walls, a fluffy pink rug in between. "This is where I live," Deepika announced awkwardly.

She reached for her laptop, then realized: There was nowhere to sit. The only real furniture in the tiny bedroom was the beds. Would they sit side by side? She stared at her blanket. Would they share it?

He'd be the first man to sit in her bed. Jai had never visited.

But Holden didn't make it awkward. "Is it all right if I sit in my outside clothes?" he asked.

He knew about *outside clothes*?

Deepika remembered her first time trying to explain the concept to Meg. "You can't wear all your clothes inside?" she'd asked.

"Don't worry," Holden added. "I only wore these out to get the mail."

Deepika smiled. "You can sit," she said.

Holden and Deepika sat down beside each other on her bed, her laptop between them, ice cream spoons in hand. She turned on the screen, and then the video started.

"Ready?" she asked. Against her better judgment, she scooted closer to him on the bed, so their shoulders were—just barely—touching. He was warm, that's all.

He nodded, and she pressed play.

They did end up sharing the blanket, after all. Holden kept a running commentary on the episode, as if he were a sports analyst and they were watching a football game, which Deepika rolled her eyes at but secretly loved, because she adored talking through television too, dissecting it down to every scene.

"You can do better than him!" Holden would yell at the screen, just like he'd yelled at the refs and players on game day, then look over to catch Deepika's eye and smile. "Oh, you're gonna just forgive him like that? No way!"

Deepika had never laughed so much while watching a reality show.

· · · · ·

After two episodes, Holden got up.

"See you tomorrow?" he said. "We're playing games and watching *The Princess Bride*. It's Eliza's favorite movie, and we watch it basically once a week."

Deepika nodded. "Yeah. See you tomorrow."

When he left, Deepika leaned against her front door. It hadn't felt like a date—a date was supposed to be in a restaurant, or a coffee shop, or at mini golf. At least, that was what she'd always thought. But they'd made plans off of a dating app. And it hadn't *not* felt like a date.

Regardless, it'd been way better than the other Hinge date she'd gone on.

What was she supposed to do now, text him? Say "thanks for a wonderful evening"?

At least he wanted to see her again—tomorrow.

Deepika's phone buzzed.

It was Holden F, on Hinge. And he'd sent her his phone number.

> **Holden F:** In case you ever need it
> **Holden F:** Goodnight, Deepika.

· · · · ·

On Tuesday night, Deepika went over for another couple rounds of Exploding Kittens and a viewing of *The Princess Bride.*

Eliza and Yujin were the loudest, yelling, "My name is Inigo Montoya. You killed my father. Prepare to die!" right along with the actor, every single time. Eliza held a stuffed red panda in her arms while they watched, and Yujin and Hari shared a blanket.

Deepika learned everyone here really, really liked cheering. They didn't party a ton or go out super often, they told her, but they loved to be loud.

"I can tell," Deepika said quietly. "It's growing on me."

· · · · ·

On Wednesday, Deepika texted Holden's number to see if he wanted to go grocery shopping with her.

She had to pick up new produce, since she'd been eating microwave meals all week. Holden convinced her to buy cookie dough, too, and when they got home, they whipped up the most delicious sprinkle sugar cookies Pillsbury could offer.

"So you like to eat treats and yell at things," Deepika observed.

"You forgot share," Holden said, pushing another cookie at her. "I love to share."

· · · · ·

Thursday evening, the whole gang decided to explore their empty campus.

Deepika called her parents beforehand and wished them a happy anniversary.

"How are you holding up, bachcha?" they asked Deepika. She'd told them about Jai's photo.

"I'm . . . okay, I think. I've been hanging out with my neighbors."

"Oh, yes, I remember them from move-in!" Deepika's mom said. "They are boys, are they not? A good distraction from Jai, maybe?"

"Ugh, *Mamma*!"

"I'm just saying." Deepika's mom had always taken an interest in gossiping about Deepika's life.

"You know, I'm running late to meet them now, actually."

"Okay," Mamma said. "Be good."

"We love you," added Deepika's Papa.

"Love you, too," Deepika said.

It was getting chillier outside, so after she hung up, Deepika pulled on a jacket and met the gang next door.

Eliza had made tea and divided it into compostable to-go tumblers, and she handed everyone their own steaming cup. With the cup warm on her fingers, Deepika walked with the group toward campus—past the Greek life houses and her freshman dorm in Desai. The streets were quiet without the usual traffic of honking cars and students walking up and down the border of campus, backpacks hunching their spines.

Holden led everyone past the student union, with its lights dimmed, and the on-campus café you could use your meal points at. They came upon a grove of trees and a few benches by the creek that ran through UMB.

Immediately, Jonah and Hari sprawled out on the benches, gesturing for Deepika to join. Holden, Yujin, and Eliza followed.

"This is our favorite spot on campus," Holden informed Deepika. "Pitfall Lake can get busy, but the creek is always available. Too many memories goofing around here."

It struck Deepika then that she didn't have a favorite spot on campus. She didn't really spend time on campus except when she was in class.

"Remember when we were all drunk and Jonah fell into the creek?" Yujin said.

"I wanted to show you all how well I could swim," Jonah protested.

"The creek is two feet deep, tops," Eliza said. "How could you ever think you could swim in that?"

"That's what I wanted to *show* you!"

The group burst into laughter and more memories then: more

remember when's and *oh my god, that was amazing.* Deepika listened carefully, a small smile on her face. At the punch line of each joke, she caught Holden looking over to gauge her reaction, like he was trying to make sure she was having a good time.

She was. Listening to the memories made Deepika realize how much she wanted experiences like that, proper college shenanigans. Being here, on campus at her university, with her next-door neighbors, giggling at the absurdity of finding an unlocked classroom to watch movies on the projector or bringing a trench coat to meals to steal extra food from the dining commons, made Deepika realize that maybe she *could* have experiences like that. Late nights studying at the Van, group lunches at the dining commons, picnics on the quad, happy memories at football games and tucked-away campus spots. Clubs like the ones Holden and his friends all seemed to be a part of. She wanted to text Meg that they should get out more. Deepika wanted all of this, too, and she could really have it. She just had to give UMB the chance.

A shiver ran through her as a breeze made its way past the creek, and she took a long sip of her green tea. Holden must have noticed, because he stepped over and took his UMB beanie off of his head. "You look cold," he said, and then pulled the beanie over Deepika's ears. His fingers lingered, just barely, at her cheekbones. He flicked the pom-pom on top of the hat. "There," he said. "All better."

Deepika reached up to touch the UMB seal patched onto the front of the beanie, running her fingers over the stitches. Something about the cozy hat, this moment with Holden and his friends, the sense of just-right-ness at adding campus gear to her outfit—made Deepika grow warm.

She smiled up at Holden as the group launched into another hilarious story.

This moment—full of potential—felt exactly like what college was supposed to be.

They all went back to Holden and Hari's place afterward, for games and movies. Over snacks and laughter, Thursday night turned into early Friday morning, and then Deepika went home to sleep the day away.

· · · · ·

Then it was Saturday.

She'd known her neighbors for a whole seven and a half days now. They'd been nice to her all week, since she'd been stranded and, clearly, in need of some support.

But Meg was coming back tomorrow, and school would start up again on Monday, and Milbridge would be back to normal. Maybe Holden and his friends were just doing community service by hanging out with Deepika over break. Maybe once Meg came back, they'd stop inviting her to things, chat about how relieved they were they didn't have to look out for her anymore.

But, she realized as she brushed her hair in her bathroom, she didn't want that. Holden and his friends were playing Mario Kart tonight, a tournament they'd prepared for all week, and she was invited. Deepika hadn't made the best first impression, what with crying so loud her neighbors could hear it over their music. But this was the day that really counted. If they enjoyed her company again today, maybe they'd want to keep her around even after the break ended.

Deepika got a little more dressed up than usual, in a nice sweaterdress, and in the evening, she arrived at Holden and Hari's with more Pillsbury cookies for the group. "Yes!" Hari yelled, grabbing the plate from her hands and holding it up to show everyone. "*Someone* forgot to bake dessert for tonight," he said, glancing meaningfully at Holden. "So you just saved the day."

Deepika beamed, all flattered.

Holden was at the kitchen counter, and he grinned at Deepika. "You're taking my job," he said.

"You're the one that trained me," she shot back, smiling. He looked at her a moment longer, and she felt her cheeks heat up. Butterflies popped up in her stomach.

"Can I get you something to drink?" Holden asked. He peered into the fridge. "We have hard seltzer, Diet Coke, and . . . oat milk."

Deepika smiled. "Diet Coke is fine." She might have a seltzer later, if she felt up for it.

Holden opened the liter bottle and poured her a glass. Eliza and Jonah walked up to greet Deepika with hugs and open up seltzers for themselves. Jonah diluted theirs with soda.

Deepika set her drink on the counter and reached out to tear a paper towel off the kitchen roll. Just then, Holden turned to reach for another cup, and his shoulder collided with Deepika's, sending her pitching backward.

He grabbed her, righting her again, and she flushed from how close they were, from the thought of them tumbling to the floor against one another, landing in a tangle with their noses barely apart. She blinked to get rid of the image.

"Sorry," Holden said, straightening up. "Sorry, sorry."

Deepika smiled. "It was my bad."

"No, you were—you're fine," Holden said, and for the first time since she'd met him, he seemed awkward, shy even.

They stared at each other a moment, Deepika's eyebrows up, Holden's face turning pink.

"Listen," he began, looking down at his feet.

Deepika noticed Eliza and Jonah walk determinedly out of the kitchen, pretending not to eavesdrop.

Holden's face turned even more pink, if that were possible.

Deepika waited.

"I don't know if you matched with me just because you knew me and thought it would be funny, or what," he said, his eyes soft. "But I'm glad you did. It's been really good getting to know you, and you can totally pretend this conversation never happened, but . . ." He bit his bottom lip and looked up at her. "Would you like to get dinner sometime next week?"

Oh.

Dinner. Dinner was a date.

And next week—that meant . . . Holden didn't want this to be just a one-week thing after all. He wanted to see her again. Next week. And maybe after that, again and again and again.

Her butterflies were racing in her gut.

Deepika stared at Holden a moment too long, caught entirely off guard.

"Sorry," Holden said right away. "I shouldn't have asked. I know you're still dealing with things from your last relationship, and—"

Deepika shook her head. That was the thing. She'd hardly thought of Jai this past week. Not just because of Holden, but because she'd remembered how to have fun again, without waiting for someone to promise her a forever.

"No," Deepika said. "I mean, no I'm not."

"Really?" Holden asked, the corners of his lips turning up. "Because the first day we spoke, it—you know—really seemed like you were dealing with things."

Deepika laughed. She rolled her eyes. "No. I mean. It was

related to that relationship, but it wasn't because I missed it. I just felt lost, because I didn't know what I was going to do now that I was alone."

"But you're not," Holden said.

"But I'm not." She looked down at her feet, then back at Holden. "So yes. I would. Like to go to dinner with you, that is. Like, a date?"

Holden nodded. Smiled. "Yeah. Yeah?"

"Yeah."

"Okay," Holden said. "I'll make a reservation."

Deepika's eyebrows went up. "Oooh, a reservation. Fancy."

He grinned. "I'll even walk you home afterward, like a real gentleman."

"So hard to come by these days, really," she said.

They looked at each other. Deepika felt so giddy, in a way she hadn't felt even with Jai.

"Hey, you two," Yujin called from the living room. "We're ready. You're up first, Holden!"

Deepika lifted her drink and smiled at Holden. "After you," she said, and they both walked out.

· · · · ·

Toward the end of the evening, Deepika excused herself to go to the bathroom.

She needed to call Meg. Meg was the one person she had actually had at her side for the past year, and she missed her now, wanted to tell her that things were better, she was better.

Everyone outside was being super loud, as usual, and Deepika listened to their noisiness fondly. It felt familiar now, what had once driven her up the walls. Besides, now she could video call Meg from the bathroom, and nobody else would hear a thing.

Meg picked up on the first ring. "Hey. Wait—where are you? Did you redo our bathroom?"

Deepika laughed. "No, I'm—I'm next door. At 107?"

"Those neighbors you hate?"

"I don't *hate* them." Deepika frowned. "Well, at least not anymore. And I'm finally learning to love UMB, too."

Meg giggled. "Uh-huh."

"Anyway. I just wanted to call you because . . . I miss you. I'm excited you're coming back tomorrow, and . . ."

"And?"

"I think we should hang out with our neighbors more often."

Meg's eyes grew huge. "Oh, my goodness. You're going to have to way fill me in tomorrow."

Deepika grinned and promised she would.

Back in the living room, Deepika made her way to the couches. Holden scooted aside to make room, and she sat down next to him.

"Who's winning?" she asked.

"We stopped playing by the rules thirty minutes ago."

Deepika laughed and leaned in closer to him, watching her noisy new friends cheer and yell as they pointed their controls at the TV.

Holden caught her smiling and nudged her with his shoulder. Then, turning back to the screen, his eyes totally focused ahead of him, he reached out with his hand and gently took hers, his pinky reaching her first and the rest of his fingers following.

His skin on hers felt electric, like a whisper of something new and wonderful and exhilarating.

Deepika held her breath. She kept her eyes forward, too. And then she scooted even closer and wound her fingers around his, squeezing tight to remind herself that she was here.

· · · · ·

Holden walked Deepika the four feet to her apartment.

"You really are a gentleman," she said, leaning against her door instead of opening it. Holden faced her, his feet square with hers. His eyes, behind his glasses, were bright.

"I wouldn't lie about that," Holden said. He took the slightest step closer.

Deepika did the same, acutely aware of the fact that she was now at a crossroads. She could easily turn around, unlock her door, and go inside. Or she could . . .

She stepped forward and looped her arms around Holden's neck, pressing her face into the place where his shoulder met his collarbone. "Thank you," she said, hugging him tight.

Holden froze, but then his arms came around Deepika too, and he dropped his hands to the small of her back. That spot on her body grew warm, dangerously so.

"Deepika," Holden said, his voice both confused and amused. "You live right next door. It really wasn't a grand gesture to walk you home."

"No," Deepika said, her face still buried in Holden's shoulder. She pulled back, so their arms were still around each other, but now they were looking into each other's eyes, noses close to touching. "For saving my fall break. For knocking on my door that day, and for making this week so wonderful. For making sure I wasn't alone."

Holden's eyebrows furrowed. His eyes softened. "Not just for fall break, yeah? I can still do all that, next week? And the next?"

Deepika smiled up at him. "We'll have to see how the first date goes. I make no promises."

Holden smiled too. "Prepare to be impressed."

"I'm counting on it."

They were very close now. Deepika could feel Holden's breath on her face, and she thought about how just a week ago, she'd been complaining and wishing her next-door neighbors would just zap out of existence.

And now it was like the universe had made them both exist in the same place, side by side, just so this one moment could happen.

Her body grew overwhelmed with the magic of this moment. There was only one thing that could make it even more magical.

"I don't usually kiss before the first date," Holden said.

"Neither do I," said Deepika. She let her gaze go soft, linger on Holden's eyelashes, then his nose, then his lips.

He took in a sharp, tiny breath.

"But I can make an exception."

Holden closed his eyes, and Deepika closed her eyes, and then they were kissing. It was nothing like the way Deepika had been kissed before, with too-big promises of a forever and grandiose declarations of a love that wouldn't last. This kiss was soft and tentative and full of uncertainty, like they were starting something and had no idea how it would end.

It felt amazing.

Deepika put her hands in Holden's hair and breathed him in. She didn't want the moment to end. They kissed more. They pressed their foreheads against one another.

Holden brought his mouth to hers and kissed her again, but before Deepika let her instincts get the better of her and pulled him inside so they could watch more *Love Island UK* and kiss even more, until they'd been up all night and were so tired they'd have to crash on her Twin XL comforter together, she stepped back, bumping into her door.

"Thank you," she said again, flushed.

Holden's cheeks were pink. He swallowed. "Yeah. Um. You're welcome. Anytime, really."

Deepika laughed. She leaned forward and kissed Holden's blushing cheek. "Good night, Holden."

Holden looked at her one last time, a long look over all of her, then shook his head, laughing. "Good night, Deepika."

Deepika unlocked her front door, shut it behind her, and then leaned on it inside her dark apartment. She let out a long breath. It was amazing how one week could change the course of her life so much. She had more friends now. A real sense that UMB could be her place, not just somewhere to be until she could run off with her prince. And all the more reason to make the next three years about herself, not any boy, not anybody else. This was *her* college experience to make wonderful. Her extremely cute, amazing kisser of a next-door neighbor was just a bonus.

A really good bonus.

Deepika bit her bottom lip to hold back the smile now growing on her face.

Next door, she heard Holden's door open and close, and then, after a beat, his friends burst into noise, their exuberant voices carrying through the thin walls.

"You *kissed* her?" Jonah yelled.

"Atta boy, Holden," Hari said.

"Oh my god, you guys," Holden said, his voice exasperated. "She's definitely going to hear you."

Eliza laughed. "Congratulations, Deepika!" she yelled, clearly hoping Deepika was listening.

Deepika giggled, hard. "Thank you!" she called back, and they all dissolved into more hoots.

Apartment 107. They really did love to cheer.

Deepika turned the lights on in her apartment and looked around at her home, just a few blocks from UMB. Yeah. She loved it here.

She opened her phone to a Hinge notification. *Did you meet Holden F?* the app asked. *Is Holden the type of person you'd like to see again?*

Deepika blushed, like a Hinge employee was watching her through her screen. *Yes*, she answered, to both questions.

We hope it works out! Hinge said.

Deepika grinned. She did, too.

NOVEMBER

Powder

By Michael Waters

I tell her not to leave me.

I agree to pull myself out of the haze of my *Lost* binge-watch, I agree to get dressed up, I agree to choke down four shots of tequila, I agree to go out with her to the senior apartments. All I ask is that, once we walk into her philosophy-classmate's friend's suite, she not leave me.

"I swear I won't," Ivy tells me, and I should've known, from the way her voice wobbles, that she is too drunk to hear what she's saying. "I barely even know anyone there. I just want to be with you."

She reaches out her hand, clasping the edges of my thumb and index finger. When she bats her eyes, flecks of pink sparkle along her eyelids. "Please. *My love.*"

I really should know better. About 60 percent of the parties we've gone to have ended the same way: Ivy talking to seemingly every person in sight, and me tagging awkwardly behind her, waiting for a Nicki Minaj song to come on so I can rope her into dancing with me. The problem is that Ivy's definition of barely knowing anyone is not a regular person's meaning of that phrase. She can have met a quarter of the attendees through some combination of dates, other pregames, and chemistry classes, and still she would insist that she is a total outsider.

"If you abandon me for any reason other than to get us drinks, I don't know that I can ever forgive you," I say. "And I'm including bathroom breaks in that."

Ivy is dressed in an all-black open suit jacket, which is cut low along her chest. She trimmed it herself, with scissors from the library, at the beginning of this year, just two hours after she declared her econ major. She said the energy she was striving for was "business formal, but slutty." She only wears this out when we go to queer parties—the straighter ones call for a much simpler jean-shorts-and-strapless-top combo. I take that as a positive sign, at least.

She puts up her hands in surrender. "Swear to god, I will hold my bladder all night in your honor."

"Now you're making me sound like a dictator," I say.

As we step out the door, I notice that, plopped on my beanbag chair, is a small purse overflowing with purple eyeliners and bronze eyeshadows—Ivy's makeup bag. For a second, I think about asking her to do my eyes like hers. Objectively, I know she would say yes. But I can't dredge up the words.

Ivy follows my gaze. "That's okay to leave here, right?"

"Yeah. Um. Yeah." *Just ask her*, I think. I might just be tipsy enough to do it. "I don't think my roommate will care."

I push open the door before I can gather the courage to pose the question, and then we are stumbling across campus to the senior apartments near Greathouse Hall.

The party is in one of the new buildings, complete with tall glass walls and a LEED certification. I hear trap drums pulsing from inside the suite before we enter. Splayed along the door are pixelated photos of each person photoshopped onto a Pokémon character, with their names underneath. Bad omen #1: I don't recognize a single face. Bad omen #2: I really hate Pokémon.

Ivy pauses, touches my hand. "I'm so glad you're coming," she says. When she pushes open the door, we are enveloped in a mass of bodies in tank tops and vintage jackets and the sharp smell of tequila chased with orange juice.

Ivy finds a group of friends, and they hand us Solo cups filled with murky liquid that I down without thinking, after saying a meek, "I'm Quinn," to everyone in the group. "Itty Bitty Piggy" comes on, and Ivy and I trade verses, but it's all a blur. Once the song is over, she is hugging me, telling me, "This is so fun. Isn't this so fun?"

At some point, Ivy drifts across the room, talking to a group of guys I've never seen before. And, of course, I end up in the exact place I asked not to be: standing beside a group of her acquaintances, who by this point are all dancing among themselves, pretending not to notice me.

I think, *I can't do this tonight.* I lie and say I'm going to pee, even though I'm pretty sure they don't hear or care.

When I slip past the throng on the dance floor, I walk down to the hall where the bedrooms are. I pull on each of the doors, hoping that one of them is unlocked. I just need five minutes—five minutes to sit by myself, to flick absently through my phone and then gather the courage to tell Ivy I'm going home and to share her location so I know she's okay. It's a routine I'm used to by now.

On my third try, the knob turns. I push it open, thinking, *If I have to walk in on a group of people fumbling through a blow job, I might actually combust.*

79

Inside is, thankfully, nothing of the sort. It's a small room with a neatly made twin bed, a bookshelf crammed half with books whose dust jackets look like they must be at least four decades old, and a pegboard bearing a poster of Selena Gomez and the Scene. In the corner, a diffuser shoots out rose-scented mist.

It takes until I've slipped inside to notice that, next to the door, is a small desk with a computer monitor. And someone is sitting in front of it.

By the time I process this, the person has already turned, pulled off their headphones, said, "Oh, sweetie, this isn't the bathroom."

I make the mistake of staring at them for a few seconds too long. They are, okay, gotta be real, totally beautiful. They're dressed in pink overalls, the straps hugging their bare skin. Their head is shaved, and thick, smoky eyeliner billows above their eyes. "Oh," I say. Leave it to me to choose the room of the one person in this suite who isn't out on the dance floor. "You live here?"

"Very observant of you, detective," the person says, lips pursing.

Thankfully, I'm drunk enough that my body forgets to cycle through its usual reaction to a comment like this: namely, my cheeks getting hot and then me blurting out some incoherent apology before I disappear back into the party. "Right. I recognize you. You were one of the Pokémon out front."

"Guilty. I'm Charizard." They hold out their hand. "Nice to meet you."

Each of their nails is painted a different color, pink giving way to red to purple to blue. They're done almost perfectly—only the paint on the index finger is chipped. "I'm Quinn," I say, and when I take their hand, I'm surprised by how cold it feels. "I'm going to assume your real name isn't actually Charizard."

"Bold of you to assume. No, I'm Cal." Cal unclasps their headphones from around their neck and places them on the desk. I look at their computer screen. It's filled with rows and rows of white text against black background, which I recognize only abstractly as lines of code. "Don't tell me you're, like, a CS major," I say.

"Honey, it's worse than that. I'm not even a CS major. This is for *fun*." They say, "I'm trying to design a video game. It's a whole thing. Let's not talk about it."

"During your suite's Saturday night party? You're right, that's dark."

"If there's one thing college has taught me, it's the art of how to get my friends drunk, and then respectfully bail on them." They point to the bed across the way. "You can sit." When I don't move, they say, "I mean, if you're comfortable. Your call."

"No, no, I—" Fuck, okay, now would be a good time for the alcohol to wear off. I drop, too quickly, onto the edge of Cal's bed. The mattress bounces as I make impact.

"So," they say, "you're at a senior party, but I know you're not a senior."

I can't decide whether it's a question or an accusation. "Yeah, I'm here with my friend Ivy, who knows . . . everyone. We're sophomores. Undercover."

"A sophomore!" They raise an eyebrow. "So quaint. I forget what it's like not to have existential panic about how your graduation date is looming and you still have no clue what to do with your life."

"Oh, trust me, there's plenty of panic to go around here."

"Intriguing." They roll their desk chair over to the edge of the bed. "So remind me what kind of existential panic sophomores go through." I catch the glimmer of something shimmery on their lips—lip gloss, a little rubbed off.

"Just, you know, parent stuff. Don't make me talk about it."

Cal smiles. "Unless you want me to eject you back to that party, you're going to have to give me something."

I look down at the bedspread, which I'm only just now realizing is *Rugrats* themed. I don't want to talk about it, I don't, but then I hear myself say, "Okay. Well. My parents hate that I'm an architecture major, and every week one of them calls to tell me I'm throwing away my life and career. I don't know why, because neither of them has a stable job and I'm paying for school myself." I lie back against the bed so that I'm saying this not to Cal, but to the poster of Selena Gomez looming above. "And my dad is definitely clinically depressed and seeing a therapist, but my mom keeps pretending it isn't happening, and so he, like, performatively lies and says he's going to play tennis with his friend every Thursday, even though we all know his gym membership expired." I turn back to Cal. "Does that earn me admission?"

"Okay, yes, that passes." They lean in closer. "We love a parent who pretends they aren't mentally ill. Such a classic story. My mom was like that for a while when I was a kid, but she sort of came to her senses by middle school and forced not just herself but *all* of us to see a regular therapist. It was actually good, I think. Probably why I'm so, you know"—they gesture at their outfit, which is far too small for them and reveals several inches of their stomach—"well-adjusted."

I laugh. "A well-adjusted queer. Iconic, really."

"So your parents don't know," they say. "About, you know."

"God no. It was a whole fight to get SSRIs. Layer on homosexuality, and I think they might actually drive down here and kidnap me."

"Down here?" they say. "Are you from the city?"

"I wish."

"Ah. A country boy?"

"Hardly a boy." I'm surprised I actually say it out loud.

"Ah," Cal says, "I know about that. You're beautiful, you know."

They reach out a hand and glide their fingers across my cheek, so softly, before letting them dangle on the edge of the bed, just to the side of my eyes. I don't flinch.

"Glad someone thinks so." I'm pretty sure now my cheeks are actually red, because even the alcohol can't bottle up the sense of nervous excitement brewing inside me. They're totally hitting on me, right? On one hand: This—calling a person beautiful and then caressing their cheek—feels like totally unsubtle flirtation. On the other: There's something about the ease with which Cal moves that makes me think this is, somehow, the kind of thing they do with all of their acquaintances.

"Have you ever done your makeup?" they say. "I think you'd look really good in eyeshadow. I'm thinking gold, maybe."

"Ugh, I've tried." I think back to Ivy's makeup bag, currently sitting in my room. Last time she left it there, I messed around with her eyeshadows for about twenty minutes in the bathroom. I turned on the shower so my roommate wouldn't know. "I always look vaguely like I'm auditioning to play a clown."

"We can fix that." They pump their leg and send their chair gliding across the room. I watch, back still flat across the bed, as they rummage through a Ziploc bag on the bottom shelf of their dresser, pulling out and inspecting a series of eyeliners and lipsticks and eyeshadow palettes. There must be at least three dozen items in there, the kind of collection that you really only accumulate after years of visits to Sephora. I wish I was like that—the friend who just has a bunch of makeup, or shimmery clothes or whatever it is, to give out to anyone who visits their room.

Cal seizes on something—I watch their eyes light up as they hold up an eyeliner. Purple, maybe. Then, with another pump, they're leaning over me again. "Okay, eyes closed."

I look up at them, watch their eyes scan my face. I like being looked at that way—studied, I mean. That sensation when someone isn't just staring at one part of you, but sorting through all of it, because they think there's something in your features worth uncovering.

"Closing my eyes in a stranger's room seems like a recipe for disaster," I say. "I don't know that I trust you enough."

"Yes, you do," they say, and of course they're right: Somehow, I know they aren't going to hurt me.

"Fine." I let my eyes close. "Don't tell me you're the prince who kisses me to wake me from my slumber, though."

"I'm not going to kiss you," they say. "Promise." Which, I have to say, makes my stomach sink a bit too sharply.

Cal's fingers are on me again, one hand on either side of my face, holding me in place. They lean in—I can tell because of the way their breathing gets louder, the smell of spearmint gum filtering out—and I am deeply aware that their thighs are pressed against mine.

I jump slightly when the eyeliner hits my skin—it's colder than I expected, gel. Cal drags it across my eyelids, back and forth, brushstroke after brushstroke. They pause, lean away. I open my eyes, only to catch them looking at me—just standing back and taking me in. When I squeeze my eyes shut again, Cal presses the brush along the rim of my other eyelid.

Around us, I hear the beat change to "Señorita" by Justin Timberlake, followed by a series of muffled whoops. I can hear the faint trace of Pharrell's ad-libs and a voice singing a little bit louder and a little more off-key than everyone else—I recognize it as Ivy's.

"When did you start doing your own makeup?" I say to Cal as they switch over to dusting my eyelids with a thicker brush, which I can only assume means eyeshadow.

"Hmm. Halfway through high school, maybe? End of sophomore year."

"That's early," I say.

"Early is relative, I guess. Given the decade that I tried to hide the fact that I was different, I could make a pretty solid case that it was very, very late."

"Well, you beat me by four years. What made you start?"

"I was just watching so many makeup tutorials on YouTube. And I told everyone I didn't actually care about the makeup itself, I was just doing it for the ASMR, but I have . . . *had* . . . this friend who knew me better than that. They bought me an eyeshadow palette for my birthday. And I started using it, like, secretly in my bedroom at first, and then also started buying more femme clothes, and it kind of clicked for me that, *oh* . . . you know, kind of like you said . . . oh, I'm not a boy."

"So it was like that?" I say. "Just a moment where it all came together?"

"I mean, more like a thousand little ones that built up. But yeah, at some point they all kind of collided at once." They pause, lift the brush off my eyelids. They tilt their head from one side of my cheek to the other, checking to make sure the lines are even. Their eyebrows are narrowed, deep in concentration.

"I don't know that I've had that moment yet," I say. "It's more like, most of the time I think the gender options don't make sense on me. But then sometimes I'm like, I think I'm okay just being a more femme boy. You know?"

They nod as they reach over to grab something else from their makeup bag. "I think for some people the answer to, like, *this is my gender* is clearer than for others. People don't really talk about what it's like not knowing. But I think there's a process to all these things." They pause. "Okay, pucker up," they say. I close my lips, and I watch Cal's eyes as they trace a tube of pink lipstick along the outlines of my mouth.

"Okay." Cal pulls back. "Mash your lips a bit to make sure it's even." They do a mashing motion with their own lips, and I follow their lead. "I think you're done," they say. "My masterwork."

"Are you sure I have what it takes to count as a masterwork?" It's my best attempt at a flirty voice.

"Just barely," they say, "but I think you pass."

They usher me over to the body-length mirror across the room. When I stand up, it takes a moment to find my balance—okay, truly, fuck this tequila—but I manage to make it over to the mirror without stumbling and making a fool of myself.

I'm surprised how much I like the person looking back at me through the mirror. I feel, like, actually pretty: Cal layered a thick line of purple eyeliner just below some bronze eyeshadow. It burns a little, but not in a painful way. The lipstick is pink, and there's a dash of highlighter along my cheekbones.

"Not to compliment myself," they say, "but you look good." They're standing just a few inches behind me. They're taller than me, and they lean in slightly when they say it, so that their lips are almost touching the strands of my hair just above my ear.

I let my gaze drift up, up past my own face, and over to the reflection of Cal's tall, lanky body. Our eyes meet in the mirror.

They lean in and kiss my cheek, holding their lips there for one beat, two beats. A chill races through me. I turn around to kiss them back, kiss them on the lips, kiss them for real, because if there's any signal that proves that this was not a platonic makeup session it has to be this, right?

But by the time I turn, Cal has slipped across the room, picking up a bottle of water, handing it to me. For just a moment, as they press the water into my hands, their fingers thread through mine. "Keep it," they say, "and go check on your friend."

I want to tell them no, Ivy is probably fine, that leaving this place—leaving their room—is the last thing I am prepared to do right now. I want to lean in and kiss them. Tell them, *Ask me to stay.*

Then I think of how pathetic I would look if it turned out I'd misread the situation. A stupid kid who thought Cal was offering something they weren't.

Once I take the water bottle, they untangle their fingers from mine. I nod and say, "Yeah, okay, you're right, I will," and then I head to the door. I take one last look at them, at their beautiful, glittering face, and whisper, "Thank you," before slipping back out into the drunken mass.

· · · · ·

I don't see them the next day.

For brunch, I tell Ivy and our friend Ruby that I want to go to the dining commons at the upperclassman dorms. Before we can use a meal swipe, I look around and realize Cal is not there. So I say, "Sorry, I changed my mind," and we go to another commons instead. They aren't there, either.

"Is everything okay?" Ivy says, because she knows I hate eating here. There's this blue-and-green abstract painting that hangs in the entryway, and every time I look at it, I'm convinced that the collection of spheres is supposed to represent a platypus. And platypuses creep me the fuck out.

"I was just hoping to see someone."

Ruby waggles her eyebrows. "A lover?"

"No." Which is technically true. "Just someone I met at the party." I hold open the doors leading into the dining hall and make a point not to look at that horrible painting. It's a cavernous room with dark wooden tables and windows that stretch nearly from the ceiling to the floor.

"I'm sorry for leaving you. Literally I just tell myself, okay, I'm going to get us a drink, and then the next thing I know, I'm talking to every person in sight," Ivy says. "It's a brain disease."

"It's okay." If it weren't for Cal, I probably would be more annoyed.

Ruby, who has dealt with Ivy like this almost as many times as I have, says, "You've had that brain disease for a while."

I follow them into the kitchen, barely glancing at the tubs of flabby eggs and half-thawed frozen berries. The whole time, I watch the door for telltale signs of Cal—a pair of black boots, maybe, or some kind of pink jacket, or that familiar buzz cut peeking out through the entryway. Or even one of the suitemates from those photoshopped Pokémon pictures in front of their door, because at least then that would mean Cal might be nearby.

"Quinn," Ivy says once we've sat down, and I'm absently twirling my spoon through a bowl of berries and Greek yogurt. "Who are you looking for?" She gestures to the entrance to the dining hall. Then she cocks her head to the side. "A crush?" And when my cheeks start to heat—barely a prick, but enough that Ivy, for one, can sense it—she grins at me. "Shiiiit."

"They did my makeup," I say, like it's an answer. "Last night. It was just really nice."

"Okay." I can tell she's watching me, trying to pry apart my words for subtext. I watch the throng of people pushing into the dining hall. I'm afraid if I look at Ivy too closely I'll give myself away. Ivy must know something about my gender, but we've never discussed it outright. I'm not sure I'm ready to now. Even the fact that she saw me last night, in full makeup, still makes me queasy to remember.

"You looked good like that, you know," Ivy says. "I was thinking about it the whole time we walked home, but I was drunk and I'm not sure if I actually said it. All those extra sparkles, you absolutely pull them off. We should go shopping for some makeup. All three of us. I mean, if you want."

"Yeah, I'd like that," I say. "Okay, so that aside. Tell me about your night."

I try my best to listen as she unspools a story about how she made out with her friend's friend's writing tutor, then immediately found out that the tutor has a boyfriend, but in truth, as Ivy talks, I keep looking back at the door, just in case Cal walks through.

• • • • •

Later that week, I am sitting with Ivy and a bunch of her econ friends at Aesop's Café.

I know I'm getting drunk because I'm a little louder than usual, interjecting in places I normally wouldn't.

After a while, as the conversation drifts to the topic of Christine Quinn in *Selling Sunset,* I pull out my phone and type—like I have maybe ten different times this week—Cal's name into Instagram, TikTok, and Facebook. I've tried every spelling variation of their first and last name, even though I'm pretty sure there are only so many ways to spell Cal, just in case they didn't want to use their actual government or it wasn't available as a username. But Cal seems to be totally off the grid. There isn't anyone with that name who has mutual followers and friends with me.

Yesterday I finally gave in, walked back over to the suite, and quickly copied down the names of all of the residents listed out front before someone caught me. Cal's name is there, but since Cal is very much not online, I figured it's time to move on to their friends to see what else I can learn. Yes, fine, it's a creep move, but I did look them all up on Instagram, hoping they might have tagged Cal in something. I found photos of Cal—posing in front of a cup of soft serve or on top of a boulder—but never with a tag.

At some point during this conversation, I stand up and announce I'm going to get pizza for the table. Ivy shoots me a quizzical look— like, *Are you okay? Do you want to get out of here?* I think because she is overcompensating for ditching me last weekend—and I give a quick thumbs-up before walking over to the cash register.

The way Aesop's Café is set up, there's no wall between the front counter and the kitchen, and you can see the cooks flipping burgers or heating pizzas or falafel in the oven. I order pizza for our table, and when I tap my student ID card to pay, I glance over at the kitchen, just to see if I know anyone on shift.

In the back, I see them. Dressed in a white apron, spatula in hand, laughing about something to the person next to them. At first I think I'm hallucinating. But then I watch them shuttle a packet of falafel from the freezer to the fry pan, watch the ease with which they weave between the other employees, and when they turn to talk to someone, I catch a flash of glitter streaked along their cheek.

I don't know what compels me to do it, but I shout their name. And of course—nothing.

So I do it again. "Cal, it's me!"

This time, their ears perk up, and I watch Cal turn. I can sense other people looking at me, but I don't care. When Cal's gaze settles on me, they grin. They wave. *Nice to see you*, I think they say.

For a moment, it feels like vindication: They're happy to see me. So I wasn't imaging the connection. Now they're going to walk over, and I can ask them if they want to go get dinner with me sometime, and then I can actually tell them how I feel.

Instead, they gesture at the falafel, as if say, *I have to work.*

I nod a little too vigorously, because, right, maybe their manager is strict and they can't leave their shift to talk to me even for a few minutes. What a monster I would have to be to interrupt the vital role of the fry cook on a Friday night. So I gesture over to the table where I'm sitting, which I hope says, *Come get me later*, and Cal nods.

Except they don't come get me. I pick up my pizza, I sit down, and I keep talking to Ivy and co., glancing back every few minutes to watch Cal work.

Eventually, I don't see them in the kitchen. I whip my head around the room, suddenly frantic, because they must be looking for me and I didn't even notice. The place is so crowded, groups of drunk kids crowding around bar chairs and spilling onto the pool tables. It takes me a few seconds to locate Cal: standing in the doorway, phone clutched to their ear.

I try to meet their gaze, give a wave. When they don't notice, I look down at my phone to see if maybe they're calling me. Then I remember we don't have each other's number. A second later, I see Cal walking up to a curly haired girl, hugging her and laughing. I watch, nausea sinking in, as the two of them slip through the doorway and disappear into the night. Cal didn't even remember to come say hi to me at all.

I slump into my seat. I'm at the point of intoxication where it's not that fun anymore, where my head hurts and I realize just how dehydrated I am. I mumble something about going to get water and stumble over to the bathroom. My plan is to cry a bit, but before I can lock the bathroom door, Ivy's standing in the doorway.

"You don't look good," she says.

I don't argue. I gesture for her to come inside. I sit on the toilet, and she crouches down next to me. "I just thought they were into me," I say, looking at the white tile floor instead of at her. "The person from Saturday night, I mean. I don't know. I'm being stupid. I just thought we had a connection."

"What's telling you that you didn't?" Ivy places her hand on the back of mine. "Maybe they were busy, or meeting someone. Or, like—I don't know. Even if they don't like you in the way you think, I've never seen you invested in a person like this. Clearly there was some real feeling there."

"I know it's dumb." I say it to Ivy's hand, which has tightened its grip around mine. "But I just felt really safe with them. Like, more in touch with myself."

"I get you," Ivy says. "Really. To me that's one of the special things about this place. Like, living on a campus. I mean, it mostly sucks, as we've discussed ad nauseam. But then you meet someone for a night, and maybe they say or do something that changes the way you think or how you feel about yourself. They have this whole impact on you, and you might only ever see them again in passing. I know it sucks not to have the closure. But isn't there something kind of beautiful about that? The way a stranger can affect you? I don't know." She sidles up to the toilet, so that our bodies are side by side. She leans her head into my lap. "Fuck, okay, I know that's not actually comforting. I'm sorry. But if a stranger can make you feel like that, just think about how many other people can do the same."

· · · · ·

The last time I see Cal, I'm ordering a cold brew at an off-campus coffee shop in Milbridge.

The concept of the store is plant nursery meets coffee: A thicket of flowers and shrubbery, all for sale, stretches across every marble table inside. Ruby bought me a lavender plant from here for my birthday last year.

I grab my coffee, walk over to the bar cart, and proceed to dump an inhumane amount of Splenda into it before I notice Cal. They're sitting in a far corner, a bird of paradise plant looming over their head. They're typing something furiously into their laptop.

Cal looks up before I can say hi. "A morning person, I see," they say to me. "Honestly, that's sexy."

"You were typing fast," I say, nodding to their laptop. I don't know what else to say. I'm nervous, somehow. I'm pressing my arms against my side, so tightly I'm probably sweating. "Don't tell me you're a novelist, too."

"Maybe to the extent that James Patterson is a novelist." Cal glances back down at their laptop. "Sorry, I just have a bunch of little things I have to get done. Hence the frantic writing."

"Oh?" I wonder for a second if this is their subtle way of trying to get rid of me.

"Yeah, um . . . I'm actually leaving school this week," Cal says, and gives an apologetic shrug. "Like, for good." Immediately, I feel the nausea bubbling up in my stomach. Leaving. Oh. *Oh.* "Kind of wild, but I got offered a job at a game-making studio the other week, and I'm going to take it. I'm graduating early. I finished all my other classes, and all I have left is an independent study, which the registrar said I would be okay to do remotely."

"That's amazing," I say, and I hope it sounds like I mean it. The words feel distant, though—zoned out. I have to clutch my cold brew to remember where I am.

Cal's leaving.

Cal's leaving.

Of course Cal's leaving.

"I'm really happy for you. It makes the fact that you were coding at your own party slightly less embarrassing."

"Thank god," Cal says. "If there's any through line of my life, it's my desperate attempts to be less embarrassing."

They smile at me, eyes wide and sparkling, and it occurs to me then that they really don't realize they've been blowing me off. They thought of that night as purely a one-off—a stranger to fill a void, maybe. Or maybe the connection was real, like Ivy said, but it wasn't what I thought. They may never have even contemplated the ridiculous future that I mapped out for us the morning after.

"So that night," I say, and I hate how much I sound like a child. "It wasn't romantic? I mean, for a second while you were doing my makeup, I thought . . ." I trail off. "Clearly I'm stupid."

I expect Cal to look confused, to frown and ask me to repeat the question. To laugh me off once I do. Instead, they say, "I mean, I would have *loved* it to be. But I'm with someone, and we're exclusive, and I care about her very much." I nod. I guess I should have expected this. How could someone like that not be dating someone? "But I meant it when I said you're beautiful. Anyone, any person, would be lucky to spend the drunken night with you that I got to."

All I can do is mumble, "Oh, uh, I don't know about that."

Cal stands up. "Listen, I'm really sorry, I have to go see my new manager now. But let's meet up before I leave, okay? Oh—" They pick up their tote bag, which is emblazoned with some sketch of a bookstore I don't recognize, and dig around for a second. "Before I forget." They hand me the purple eyeliner from the other week. "This is yours. I want you to have it." They lean in and kiss me on the cheek, a quick peck. Before they pull away, they whisper, "You wear this better than I ever could."

I stand there for a second after they walk away. Watch the door clang closed, watch their tote bag disappear into a car.

I turn over the eyeliner in my hand. It glitters in the overhead lights, just the way it did in Cal's room. After a moment, I unscrew it, and hold out the brush tip, which is sharp and coated in thin purple gel.

I pull out my phone and text Ivy. Let's go dancing tonight, I write. I want to debut a new look.

DECEMBER

Sophomore Slump
By Racquel Marie

There are a lot of things I wish someone had warned me about before I started college.

Your sleep schedule, if you even have one, will get wrecked. People in the dorms will wash their dishes in the communal bathroom sinks, leaving bits of food that stink up the space, and you will have no power to stop them. RAs will absolutely show favoritism.

But by the end of freshman year, I'd had it all figured out. My friends, my major, my place in the world of adulthood. I would've set music and credits to the end of first year if I could've, wrapping up the start of the rest of my perfect, picturesque life.

But the thing no one warns you about in college, more than anything else, is what happens after your movie-like first year: At the ripe age of nineteen, following the most miserably lonely sophomore fall semester imaginable, you start regularly daydreaming in Spanish 2A about "the good old days."

Profesora Uriarte reaches the end of her slide show recapping pretérito conjugation and flicks on the lights. "Okey, eso es todo por hoy y este semestre." A few people politely clap, but by the time I convince myself it wouldn't be weird to join them, they stop. "Voy a hablar en inglés porque es necesario que todos entiendan." Her voice deepens as she switches to English. "If you want feedback on the first draft of your final partner project, you have to send it to me by this Saturday. Feel free to email me with any questions. Other than that, have a great rest of the week, and I'll see you all on presentation day!"

Everyone starts packing up and heading out. I see my assigned partner, Rin, turn to me out of the corner of my eye, but don't look back until she speaks. I don't want to seem too eager to confirm our plans.

"Salomé, we're still on for tonight at the library, right?" she asks as she gets up, swinging her bag onto her shoulder, where it traps her shaggy black hair.

"Yup," I reply, shoving everything into my backpack so I'm not the last one left in the room.

"Could we actually meet a little earlier than planned? Maybe, like, six instead of seven?" She leans lightly on her desk and waits patiently for me, which only exacerbates my need to finish packing quickly. "I don't wanna crowd your dead week, but if we work for a bit longer tonight, we'll have a solid first draft to send to Profesora Uriarte." Her Spanish accent is flawless, and I try not to feel a sting of jealousy when I notice. My pronunciation is fine, but as a Latina, I can't help but feel like it should be better.

"Fine by me." At last, I get everything in my backpack and stand. I'm used to towering over people, and Rin is no exception.

"Great, see you then!"

I wait until she's out the door before I follow, so she doesn't think I'm trying to walk with her. Not that it would be such a bad thing if we did walk together, but I don't want to weird her out by just going for it. Plus, I don't know what I'd say if we weren't talking about conjugations or irregular verbs. *Hey, Rin, it's honestly no trouble to spend more time at the library tonight, considering that us working together is the closest thing I've had to a social life all term. In fact, I wish you would've asked to meet even earlier so I wouldn't be stuck eating dinner by myself in my depressing apartment. Can't wait to ace this final!*

The worst part is, if I wanted more of a social life, specifically one with Rin, I could've had one. A month into the term, she admitted she could hear the music I was listening to every day when I walked into class, and that we had super similar tastes. Phoebe Bridgers, Jensen McRae, MUNA, etc. Then she asked if I wanted to get coffee sometime and swap playlists.

But I, a uselessly anxious queer, was so preoccupied thinking, *Am I being asked on a date? Wait, she can hear my music every time I come into class? God, can everyone hear it? I didn't think it was that loud, I was just hoping people wouldn't try to talk to me before class started, and now I'm the weird girl who blasts music in a silent classroom, and sure, she likes my music, but what if everyone around us thinks it's annoying? I should have been paying closer attention to—* before I realized she was staring, I was staring, and neither of us was saying a thing. Until my mouth opened and pushed out the single, eloquent word: "Cool." Before swiftly moving on out of embarrassment.

Suffice to say, we have not traded playlists, and I've prayed every day for Profesora Uriarte to swap our pairings so I can stop facing the near-daily shame of wrecking the one opportunity I had to make a friend this term. Every other class on my schedule is MWF or TuTh, but noooo, Spanish simply had to be every day of the week.

The other worst part is that anyone else would've just reminded Rin of the offer. I mean, anyone else probably wouldn't have botched the initial offer in the first place, but the point remains. Unfortunately, my brain doesn't work in a way that lets me believe that bringing up the offer again would end in anything but catastrophe. Even the logical side of me that underlies the perpetual anxiety is fairly certain Rin wants nothing to do with me outside the confines of the Spanish language after I rejected her so rudely, likely thinking I'm either a bitch or a weirdo. Or both. She's still friendly, yeah, but I'm sure she's just biding her time until the term is over.

At least I get to spend hours pondering these things during all the free time I have sitting by myself in the bleak, fluorescent lighting of my depressing apartment.

Said apartment—that I share with two random third years who I've spoken a collective seven words to since moving in—is technically "on-campus housing" because it's run through UMB and only students can apply to live there, but it's still a fifteen-minute walk from campus. Which is an especially lonely fifteen minutes in this bitter winter air. So I open up Insta to browse on the way home, hoping to distract myself from the cold and knock the Rin thoughts away.

But the first photo I see, is, of course, Rebecca, Irma, Priya, and Ellie. The four of them are spread out on their living room floor, surrounded by blankets, pillows, and books. The caption: *laughter is the only cure for finals doom* <3

It's the exact type of photo we would've taken together last year in the dorms. Everything about it is meant to look candid: the camera angle, their slight blurriness from laughing, the miracu-lously aesthetically pleasing sloppiness of the room. Rebecca taught us all how to take photos like this; how to make every day of your life look like a Pinterest board come true. And for a while, every day did.

I could like the photo. Maybe it would remind them of how long it has been since we've all hung out. Maybe they'd ask me to join them right now.

Or maybe they'd see the notification and giggle over how pathetic it is that I'm still trying to cling to our friendship when the rest of them seem happy to have left it behind in first year, like one of their many rookie mistakes. Overpacking, thinking an eight a.m. won't be too bad, being too embarrassed to go to office hours, and being friends with Sal Lafferty-Peña.

It was only a matter of time before they'd realize how poorly I fit into the image of us. I was always the one struggling to look relaxed and carefree in the photos, making us take twice as many as they would've needed to without me. They'd been patient, but I swore I could feel it in my chest that one day they'd get tired of dealing with me.

I bet it only took them one try to get a shot this perfect.

I click off my phone and play music for the rest of the walk home, distracting myself by deciding which microwave meal I'll eat for dinner tonight before meeting with Rin.

· · · · ·

Hours later, while my stomach churns around a mostly defrosted chicken pot pie, I sit outside of the Van on a concrete bench that may as well be an ice block.

Crowds of students pass, everyone rumbling complaints about impending finals, packaged in their puffy winter coats. Minus the outerwear, it reminds me of my first trip to the Van during orientation, when I imagined myself there one day—older, wiser, my hair dyed a new color and my style branched out past all black jeans and graphic tees—surrounded by the friends I'd have for the rest of my life. It stings to think I had some of that—the friends at least—and lost it already. Not to mention, my hair is the same light green I've bleached and dyed it for years, my clothes are identical to the ones I wore at seventeen, and I think I've become even less wise somehow.

Well, at least I'm older.

Six o'clock comes and goes without any sign of Rin. *Shit*, maybe I misremembered our conversation earlier. Or maybe we didn't even decide on a solid time. Ugh, I should've double checked before I risked the hypothermia waiting here. What if she doesn't even want to meet here, but at Godfrey Library instead? Do I text her? Is that weird? We've only ever texted about assignments, but this *is* about an assignment, so it shouldn't be too forwar—

"Hey!"

I spin around and see Rin jogging over, two coffee cups in her mittened hands. In the yellowish glow of the outdoor lighting, I notice the mittens look like raccoon faces.

"I hope you like lukewarm hot chocolate," she says, offering me one. "Sorry I'm late, the line at The Last Drop was never-ending."

"It's cool. I only got here a minute ago," I lie, then look down at the drink hesitantly before taking a sip. I'm surprised by the taste. "You got oat milk."

She brightens. "Yeah! I remembered you said you were lactose intolerant during the food unit a few weeks ago."

My chest hurts a little from how much it means to me that she remembered. And there's the dual ache of knowing I'd never admit to remembering something like that about her for fear of freaking her out. Case in point: I don't want to freak her out by getting emotional over milk, so I give a simple "thanks" before we head into the library.

We walk in just as someone packs up their books, leaving open two seats at a long table otherwise occupied by quietly chatting students. I'm worried we'll disturb them while discussing our project, but Rin throws her bag down before I can suggest we move elsewhere. I don't want to be difficult, so I join her.

The library is drastically warmer than outside, a combination of good insulation and the crowd of students generating body heat. I tug off my thick black jacket and hang it on the chair behind me while Rin does the same with her burgundy peacoat. My mouth opens to compliment her on it, or on her mittens and slouchy black beanie that she yanks off as well. But the words just won't come out.

She pulls her laptop out, which I've never seen before since Spanish is the one college course that still insists on forcing students to exclusively use pen and paper worksheets like we're living in the '90s or something. It's covered in stickers—Phoebe Bridgers's album artwork, a lesbian flag, the school's radio station logo, those smiling and frowning theater masks, something written in Japanese. Luckily she's so focused on opening up whatever file she needs, she doesn't notice me staring and cataloging this information.

But when I pull out my laptop, her eyes dart to it and she smiles. "Oh my god, cute." She points at the collection of funky-looking frog stickers I have decorating my case.

"Thanks," I say and fight the urge to put my laptop away again regardless of what sounds like sincerity.

"Okay, so I had some free time this week and typed up a bunch of notes from my family tree and recipe books and . . . *Shit*."

"What's wrong?" I lean over as her screen goes black. "Oh, here, you can borrow my charger."

Both our eyes go to the plugs on our laptops, which are entirely different shapes.

"Can you open the file on your phone?" I suggest.

Rin shakes her head. "It was a Word doc. I can't access it anywhere else."

"You didn't back it up? Or save it to drive?" I ask, more incredulously than I should. Rin shrinks away, and panic jolts me. I was just surprised that she wasn't as anxious as I am about losing important files, causing me to triple save and back up everything in case of emergency. But I replay my words and know that I sounded more judgmental than shocked.

"Sorry, my fuckup," she says, smudging her thick eyeliner as she rubs her eye. "I could run home to get my charger, but at this time it'll probably take me, like, an hour and a half to get there and back."

"Wait, do you not live on campus?"

She slides her now useless laptop back into her bag. "Nope, I commute. Which I've never hated more than in this moment. And that's really saying something."

This seems like the perfect time to ask her to elaborate, to learn more about her outside of Spanish class. But would she think I'm being nosy? What if I come across as judgy again somehow?

"Anyways," she interrupts my thoughts. "We can at least use this time to talk about you and your culture. We can figure out the half of the project focused on me later."

"Right," I say, brushing aside any thought of rekindling

friendship efforts between us. She's here for a project, nothing else. "You can take notes on my laptop if you want." I slide it over to her, a Google Doc already loaded with the prompt questions.

"Perfect, thanks." She scans the screen. "So, good place to start is just where your family is from."

"Oh, uh, my dad is Irish American, but, like, fourth generation."

"Irlanda, nice." She types away. "Luck of the Irish."

I'd laugh if it weren't for what I need to say next. "And my mom was Colombian."

Her fingers stop moving. "Was?"

I clear my throat. "Yeah, she, uh, she passed away when I was a baby. Breast cancer."

"Oh my gosh, I'm so sorry, Salomé."

"It's fine." I wave away the pity. It's why I don't like talking about my mom. People get weird about it sometimes, either asking too many personal questions about the trauma of losing her so young or moving awkwardly past it as quickly as possible so they don't accidentally catch my grief. My discomfort comes out in the harshness of my voice as I ask, "Next question? And shouldn't we be talking in Spanish for this?"

Rin blinks at me, lost for a second. "Uh, yeah, sure. I mean, sí. ¿Cuál es tu comida favorita de tus dos culturas?"

"De Irlanda, las papas en general," I say, my brain rushing to keep up with my mouth. Reading and writing in Spanish is fairly easy for me. But speaking in English is hard enough with anxiety, so speaking Spanish is twice as difficult with the added pressure of translating correctly to not embarrass myself as a Latina and disgrace my late mom. "Y de Colombia, pienso que las empanadas de papa y carne."

"Qué ricas," Rin says, quickly and easily. "Did you grow up eating a lot of food from both sides of your family?"

I scan the screen. "I didn't see any questions about that."

"Oh," Rin says. "No, I was just asking. Sorry, you're right, I should focus."

Shit. I am well and truly incapable of navigating a friendship with this girl. Whatever, it's fine. I'll save myself the trouble of inevitably losing more friends if I just give up once and for all. "Sounds good."

We run through more questions, all of them relatively basic and simple in concept. But they're still hard for me to answer, poking at my tenuous relationship with my heritage and talking about myself.

"¿Y qué idiomas se hablan en tus dos culturas?" she asks. "Oh, well, English and Spanish, obviously." She stops typing, looks up at me and opens her mouth, then closes it.

"You can ask," I say in a moment of bravery. "Whatever it is. Even if it's not a prompt."

She smiles in understanding, and I feel immediate relief. "I was just curious whether or not your family spoke Spanish growing up, since you're taking this class and all."

"Not really." I toe the ground with my boot. "My mom was born in Colombia but mostly grew up here, so she was bilingual and fluent in English. My dad was the one who raised me, though, and I think he just figured I didn't need to learn it any more than the next person. Which sucks, to be honest."

"I bet."

"Honestly, I was sort of relieved when I saw that two years of a foreign language was required for all humanities majors. But it was embarrassing to only make it to Spanish 2A on the placement test."

"That's pretty good for someone who didn't grow up speaking it fluently," Rin offers.

"I guess."

She clears her throat. "You know, we don't have to, but we can talk about this in the project." The panic must show on my face, because she adds, "It's just that this seems to play a part in how you connect with your heritage, so it might be interesting to expand on that."

"I don't know," I say. "It's complicated. Spanish is so significant in contemporary Latine culture, but it's also a language that was imposed onto my ancestors. It's like, it feels so important that I learn and be perfect at it, but also feels like a lazy attempt to grasp at what I feel like I've missed out on my whole life."

"I don't think it's lazy." She shrugs. "Sounds like you're trying to explore a part of your mom's identity for yourself. I get the fixation, though. I mean, it's not the same thing, but it always makes me sad that I'll never know how my last name, Takagi, was written in kanji. I tried researching it after my grandpa passed away, but we lost a lot of family records over the years. It hurts to know a part of my family history may be lost forever."

"You're so good at Spanish, I guess I didn't really think about whether or not you also were at Japanese."

"See? No soy perfecta," she says, her smile matching the joyful lilt of her words. "I've been thinking of minoring in Asian American studies, or at the very least reaching out to some of the professors in the field to ask for nonfiction recommendations about Japanese history and culture in the United States. You could do something similar with the Latin American studies department. Language isn't the end-all-be-all."

I did take a class on colonial empires my first year, and learning more about the Inca Empire specifically was fascinating, albeit incredibly frustrating. Confronting just how Eurocentric my education has always been, even in the framing of colonization as an ultimate elimination of all Indigenous communities when so many still persevere to this day, horrified me. I want to learn more, especially about Colombia, but it almost feels like it isn't mine to look into. Whether that's the mixed heritage, the reality that my closest connection to Colombia—my mom—is long gone, or the anxiety talking, I don't know. But it feels like Rin has just given me permission to do something I didn't realize I've always been allowed to do.

"Yeah, I think I'll look into that," I tell her, and we share a smile.

Of course it's this moment that I look around, taking in the scenery for my new snapshot of what sophomore year could be instead of what it's been, when my eyes freeze on them.

Rebecca, Irma, Priya, and Ellie are simultaneously giggling and shushing each other at a table in the far corner. Though I saw the photo of them all earlier, it's different in person; seeing Irma's sparkling smile as the light hits her braces, Priya's new tattoo curling around her exposed shoulder where her cardigan is slipping off, Rebecca's new blond highlights, and Ellie's freshly dyed purple hair. They all look so much older, so changed. Meanwhile I'm only having my first moment of development right now, still looking exactly the same.

"Who are they?" Rin asks. She's following my line of vision, nodding to my old friends.

"Freshman year hallmates," I answer plainly.

"Oh, you should go say hi!"

"Probably a bad idea."

"One of them an ex?" she tries, smirking.

I laugh, then realize how misleading that could be. "No,

definitely not. But they could be . . . like, hypothetically, I could have dated them." Rin squints at me. "I'm a lesbian, so, you know, not out of the ballpark."

She laughs gently. "Good to know." I look away, flustered. "So why would it be a bad idea to say hi?"

I pick at my nail polish. Rin doesn't want to hear about my loneliness, about the months I spent wishing my old friends would invite me over or swing by my place for a surprise, even though I couldn't get myself to reach out to them either. Boring her to death with my woes of anxiety is the last thing either of us needs.

But I look up at her, watching me politely, and remember the conversation we literally just had. I'll forever be astounded by how easily my brain can forget progress the second it becomes inconvenient for my anxiety's chokehold on my happiness. Not only did I share something personal and private with Rin, she reciprocated. And proved to me that I'm not the only one who has something to be insecure about when it comes to my heritage. Maybe I'm not the only one with insecurities about friendship either.

"We were all really close first year," I start, and she nods me along. "But I worried that if we lived together in an even more confined space this year, they might get sick of me." It was easy to hide away in my own dorm when my anxiety was acting up or I needed time alone to recharge, but in an apartment with multiple people sharing each bedroom, it felt inevitable I'd fuck up somehow or they'd be weirded out by how bad my anxiety can get. "I thought living separately would give us some balance, but instead I isolated myself."

Rin tilts her head in sympathy. "Y'all don't hang out at all anymore?"

"Not since the beginning of the semester. It started with

conflicting schedules, but we'd still at least send texts or try to make plans." I sigh. "But it felt like me joining in on anything they suggested would just inconvenience them." Going to a party hours late because I had a night class, extra Uber charges to drop me off at my place first, making them stay up to be sure I got home safe because I thought I'd be in the way if I slept over. "So I said no to almost everything, and eventually they stopped asking." I thought I was doing the right thing for all of us, but nothing about this has felt right. "I've been pretty lonely this year."

The following moment of silence tells me everything I already knew. I shouldn't have said this much or been so open so quickly. Rin thinks I'm some loner freak now who pushes all her friends away, and it's going to be awkward for the rest of the night trying to get this project done in spite of me making a fool of myself. I open my mouth to apologize, but Rin interrupts me.

"You know, commuting here has isolated me a lot too," Rin says, fiddling with her hands. "My first year, I still hung out with friends from high school who stayed local. But then they made their own college friends, and it felt like I was constantly intervening or inviting myself to their stuff. They said it was cool, but I couldn't shake the feeling that I was the problem."

It's so precisely what I've been dealing with, that all I can say is "Sucks, huh?"

We both start laughing, a little too loudly for the library, but no one shushes us.

"Yeah, it really sucks," she agrees. "I've been making friends at the radio station and through the theater department this year, which has been great for me, but it's still so hard to keep up friendships when they're not as convenient as they were growing up."

"Exactly," I say, almost breathless. I'm practically vibrating with the excitement of being understood. "In high school, I just hung out with people from my classes because I saw them every day all year. I didn't have great friends, but at least I had people to spend time with. Classes change so quickly here and then people go home to their own apartments with their own roommates." Roommates that could've been mine too. "Doesn't help that everyone talks about college like it's the best time of everyone's lives when you're arguably having the worst time."

"Literally!" Rin whisper-yells. "And people always want to grab dinner or hang late, but traffic can get so bad at that time for me. Plus I have to wake up super early every morning to make it in time for my eight a.m. classes, so I'm basically a glorified high schooler again, but with almost no friends this time around."

"Okay, well, taking eight a.m. classes is simply asking for your life to be terrible," I tease.

She laughs. "I didn't have many options if I wanted to take Spanish 2A. And if I hadn't, we wouldn't be sitting here."

For the first time since I met Rin months ago, I get butterflies. "I suppose I can concede that you made the right choice. All things considered."

Her smile grows. "However will you survive vocabulary unit tests without me if we don't end up in the same Spanish 2B class together next semester?"

I sigh dramatically. "No sé."

"Guess we'll just have to meet up to study. I can't be known as the girl whose ex-Spanish partner suddenly starts failing. What would people think?"

"I suppose that could be arranged, for the sake of your reputation of course."

She rolls her eyes. "How kind of you. If only I could repay the favor with a functioning laptop."

I have a lightbulb moment and look across the room at my old friends. Miraculously, I catch Rebecca's eye from over her laptop screen. The same exact type of laptop as Rin's.

"Actually, seeing as I owe you a playlist or two, I think I need to repay *you* with a functioning laptop," I tell Rin as I stand up. "I'll be right back."

My body doesn't feel like my own as I walk toward my old friends. It's one of those rare moments when I seem to detach from it, my brain shutting off so I can do what needs to be done without my anxiety interfering.

Rebecca nudges Irma, who nudges Priya, who nudges Ellie, until they're all watching me approach them. Suddenly, I want to turn around and run. But I just had an honest conversation about things I've hardly ever spoken to anyone about, and I had it with Rin, who is both the closest thing I have to a friend at school right now and essentially a stranger. So I can handle this. I can.

"Do you have your laptop charger?" are the first words out of my mouth, regrettably.

"Sorry?" Rebecca's face twists in confusion.

"Sorry," I repeat back to her. "Sorry, I'm here with my classmate, I mean friend, and her laptop died and she needs a charger, but I don't have the same charger. But you do, if you still have the same laptop, and if you have your charger. So, I was gonna ask if I could borrow it. Well, if she can borrow it. Sorry."

Slowly, Rebecca's confusion slides into a tentative smile. "You still do the rambly thing when you're nervous," she says, but there is no hint of callousness in her voice.

"And you're letting your dark roots grow out," Ellie adds, leaning over Irma to get closer to me as she touches her own hair. "It looks good with the green."

"Really pretty," Irma agrees. She pushes Ellie off her lightly then holds her hand. Oh, well, that's a development. One that it stings to notice, remembering that I was the only one Ellie told about her crush on Irma last year.

But the sting is quickly replaced by the realization that they're being nice to me. And it's not that I expected them to be mean, but after so much silence between us, I'd filled the space with presumed cruelty, rewriting them in my brain as ruthless and unkind. Maybe to justify how much I'd pushed them away first.

"It's been so long," I say out loud, on accident. But they all soften their smiles and nod. And it hits me that just like I didn't consider Rin might also have anxieties and insecurities about her culture and friends and language, I hadn't considered that these friends might've assumed I'd left them behind too.

"Well, what have you been up to?" Rebecca says, nodding toward the seat across from her. I'm tempted to stay, to catch up and let myself fall back into this, the friendships I'd thought I'd lost. But then I look over at Rin, sitting by herself, also having been left behind time and time again.

I'm worried if I walk away now, whatever olive branch is being passed to me will break under the pressure of more time passing. That if I reach out tomorrow or a few days from now instead, the offer to reconnect will be off the table. But I'm tired of worrying about the fragility of things. Of life and friendships and people's care for me. Maybe I need to stop treating everything around me like glass. Maybe living with anxiety and losing my mom so young means my brain will always assume the world is breakable. But maybe, instead of accepting that and bending myself backward to keep everything safe, it's time I let a thing or two slip from my grasp and see what I can make of the shattered pieces, if they even break at all.

"You know, I really want to catch up, but I have a project I have to finish. And my friend is waiting for me."

I brace myself for Rebecca to frown or get mad. Instead, she smiles, and I remind myself that the alternative was likely never even on the table. "Maybe you can come over after winter break? Or we could meet up during finals week to study."

"I could seriously pick your brain for this art history lecture I'm taking," Priya slips in.

I sigh and smile. "I'd love that."

"For now, though . . ." Rebecca reaches into her rainbow tote and pulls out her charger, wrapped in a neat bundle. "For your friend."

"Thanks," I say as I take it from her.

"Now you have to hang out with us again to give it back to Rebecca," Irma says, laughing. "Or we'll have to finally see your place and take it." And I know what she means is, *This is a real offer to hang out. Please accept it.*

"Deal," I say, and walk away from them, for the first time in forever leaving a conversation feeling better than when I entered.

Hours later, having learned all about the Takagi family and Rin herself, we're outside the Van, tossing our long-empty cups into the trash.

"If we don't get the highest grade in class, I'm suing," she says as we walk away, both of us bracing against the fresh chill.

"I'll join in on the lawsuit, but I make no promises about being great in court. Public speaking is not exactly a skill of mine."

"Yeah, I think I get that now," Rin says. I shoot her a look out of the corner of my eye. "I just mean . . . I thought you maybe didn't like me at first. I'm pretty outgoing, so I confuse shyness with disinterest sometimes."

"I'm not the best at making friends, or responding to people trying to be my friend," I admit. "I think I may be getting better at it now, though?"

"Is that right?" Rin smiles.

"Do you want to hang out next term?" I ask suddenly. "Exchange playlists and study together?"

"Sounds like a plan," she says.

We split ways when we reach student parking. She offers to drive me back to my apartment, but I want to walk. The brisk night air refreshes me after hours in the stuffy library. I pull up Instagram and see I've got a new follower request from @rin_tag.

There are a lot of things I wish someone had warned me about before starting college, but I think there's a lot you've got to figure out for yourself.

I accept the request and follow her back, then slip my phone into my pocket. I take a deep breath and hold it for a few seconds before setting it free.

Next semester is going to be okay.

The Final Countdown
By Laila Sabreen

The shrill ring from my alarm fills the room, and I reach for my phone.

Heaps of blankets make it harder to move, but they block out the chill that slips in from the window next to my bed. I glance at my roommate's side of the dorm, and the emptiness startles me before I switch my alarm off. Silence makes the emptiness more eerie, and the stress I tried to sleep off falls back on my shoulders. My calculus final scheduled for six thirty is my last exam for this semester, and it's the only thing standing between me and winter break. But that still doesn't make me want to take it.

Though, even with the countdown to the calc final, it's going to suck to leave UMB for the break. From the people I've met to the sociology class that I loved to having constant access to iced coffee, there's a lot I'm going to miss. Going home will be like going back to an old reality. One that barely feels like it even exists now that I've been at UMB for three months.

I scroll through the notifications on my phone and read the text messages that came in while I was asleep.

Dad: Good luck on the calculus final!
Kaiden: Do u wanna study together at the van?

My heart flips at seeing his name, and I text back absolutely and add a thumbs-up emoji for an extra touch. I swipe out of that chat before going to the one with my friends Aarti, Heather, and Zoya. We haven't come up with a cute name for the group chat yet, but we have seven more semesters to do that.

Me: I'm up + heading to the last drop to grab a bite before cramming!

I sigh as I set down my phone. Realistically, I know if I don't understand the material by now, I'm not going to. But I can't be pre-med and fail this exam. Not when it's worth a quarter of my grade. Plus, my parents will be disappointed if I don't do well in the class, and I don't want them to think I'm wasting my scholarship.

My phone buzzes, pulling me out of my spiraling thoughts.

Zoya: I'm heading over to LD now, so I'll grab us a table
Aarti: Finishing packing! I'll be there in a bit.

There's no response from Heather, and I push down the twinge of annoyance. Even though she's one of the first friends I made at UMB, she's been hanging out with us less and less. The two of us made lunch plans a few days ago, and she didn't show up.

I climb out of my bed and grab the UMB sweatshirt and pair of joggers that I set out last night. I thank the dormitory gods every day that I got a suite bathroom instead of having to use the communal bathrooms. Sharing with my roommate and two suitemates is so much better than having to experience the horror stories that Zoya tells me about. Like that one time where she went to use the communal bathroom in the middle of the night, and she stepped on a used Band-Aid and didn't notice it until she woke up the next morning. She washed her sheets twice, but never fully got over that.

Music from my calm morning playlist fills the space as I brush my teeth and do my morning skin care routine in front of the sink and mirror. I throw my passion twists into a top knot and ignore the slight frizziness at the roots. I've been putting off doing my hair so that I can go see my hairstylist when I get back home. After slipping in my hoops and putting on my crescent moon and star ring, I look like much less of a wreck than I feel. Thank goodness.

My phone buzzes again as I grab my backpack and lock the door behind me. A gust of cold wind greets me as I step outside, and my breaths appear in small puffs. I tap on the message, expecting it to be from Heather, but it's not, and my stomach drops. The notification that there's a new message in "The Squad" makes my hands start to sweat despite the chill.

> Natalie: Hey everyone! I hope finals are going well. I'd love for all of us to get together once we're back in town.

A gust of wind rattles past, and I put my phone away and bury my hands in the pockets of my winter coat.

The Squad. I haven't seen that name show up on my phone in ages. My high school friend group was always using it, so much so I had to mute my messages if I wanted to get anything done. But after graduation, that all changed. No one's texted in The Squad group chat since the falling out. I remember the shock I felt when Natalie said that we were all outgrowing each other and that maybe it was time to go our separate ways. Her tone was so calm, as if she wasn't shredding six years of friendship.

When everyone else suggested that we change the plan from FaceTiming monthly to every other month and I was the only one who objected, I realized I cared too much. Once Natalie said that I was being too sensitive and went on a whole rant about how I shouldn't expect things to stay the same, I shut down. There wasn't much to say after that. The nagging feeling that history is repeating with Heather causes dread to settle on top of the stress that's already on my shoulders, and I try to shake it off as I speed walk through the cold.

UMB looks like a ghost town as I head to The Last Drop, the café that I visit every morning. Usually, it's bustling, but now that it's the last day, only the most unfortunate of us are left. I spot a few people pulling along suitcases as they head to the edge of campus to be picked up or catch a ride to the airport or train station. Longing fills my chest, but that'll be me tomorrow. Though now that I have to figure out how to handle Natalie's text, going home feels like even less of a reward for getting through my last exam. If I don't agree to meet up, then I'll be the one throwing away six years of friendship like I accused Natalie of doing. At least here, at UMB, I have some semblance of a social life. But back at home, with everything going on, my social life will be lackluster at best and a hot mess at worst.

I walk into The Last Drop, and the sound of voices and the sharp smell of coffee set me at ease. The coziness of the space and the little reading nook in the back corner have made the coffee shop one of my favorite spots near campus. Scanning the space, I spot Aarti and Zoya at one of the booths.

"Hey, Arisha," Zoya says, sliding down to make room.

Her box braids are thrown into space buns and her peach glasses and UMB sweatshirt are identical to my own.

I drop my backpack into the empty spot. "Hello, lovelies. Lemme grab something to eat real quick."

Aarti nods. "We'll be here."

Even though she's dressed casually in a T-shirt and jeans, her eyeliner and kajal are impeccable. Whenever we're going out, Aarti's the one I go to for makeup help.

It hits me again that Heather isn't here, but I push the thought away. She isn't here, but Aarti and Zoya are. Besides, she's shown that I can't always count on her.

At the beginning of the semester, one of my biggest fears was standing by myself in the middle of the dining commons, having people looking at me and pitying me until I just ate in some corner alone. Granted, maybe it's a weird fear, but I ended up telling Heather about it and she didn't clown me for it. Which made me feel even worse when she stood me up at lunch a couple days ago. I kept looking for her until I realized she wasn't coming. Things come up, especially at UMB, where everyone's so busy, but a text with a heads-up would've at least been nice. As much as I love my friendship with Heather, I can't keep chasing people who show they don't value me. I did it with Natalie, and I'm not going to do it again.

"Y'all want anything?" I ask as I grab my wallet from my

backpack. "I've got a couple of meal points to spare." Even though whatever I don't spend will roll over to the spring, it's the last day of the semester, so it doesn't hurt to live a little.

Zoya sighs. "I probably shouldn't have any more coffee, but I'll take a pastry."

"What about you, Aarti?" I ask. "Anything for the road?"

"A matcha latte would be great. Thanks, Ri!"

Unlike the rest of us, Aarti isn't taking calc this semester, and she took her last exam yesterday evening. If I could trade places with her to get out of taking this final, I would. Academics have usually come easy to me, but college classes are harder. Even though my sociology class was a lot of reading, at least the articles were interesting. With calc, it's hard *and* boring. The rest of my STEM classes haven't been much different, and since most of them are pre-med requirements, it's hard not to wonder if pre-med is even right for me. Which is terrifying, because if it's not, then what is?

"Of course," I say, ignoring the existential dread about my future.

I make my way to the display counter and barista, weaving through the tables that fill the center of the space. People chat with their friends or are hunched over their textbooks and notes, and my heart squeezes. I'm going to miss this while I'm away. The same indie pop playlist that plays on loop, and the comforting scent of freshly baked pastries, and the feeling of being around so many people but not feeling lost. UMB feels like home, and I know part of that is because of Aarti, Heather, and Zoya. They make me feel as though I've found my place on campus. After what went down with Natalie and the rest of our old friend group, I was so scared that I wouldn't.

I order everything and swipe my school ID before heading back to the booth with my arms full.

"Here we are," I say, passing everything out before sliding into the booth next to Zoya.

Aarti glances up from her phone. "Give me one sec, I'm finishing up this text to Rohan."

Zoya and I exchange knowing smiles. Like Aarti, I also met Rohan on the first day of orientation, and the two of them have been joined at the hip ever since. Aarti says they aren't dating because it's too early in the year to risk messing things up, but who knows what the future will hold.

She sets her phone down and takes a sip of her latte. "I can't believe we're really done with our first semester."

"I know, right? Time really flew by," Zoya says.

"So, what's everyone doing over winter break?" I ask.

Zoya sighs dramatically. "Not thinking about bio or chem until the new year. I'll be in Europe with the fam."

"I'm going to be at a beach resort with my sister for a few weeks! I'm really excited to see her," Aarti says. "This semester was kind of brutal, so I just want to recharge and be away from anything math-related."

My stomach sinks. Both of them are going to be off living their best lives during break, as they should. But I'm going to be stuck in my hometown trying to deal with Natalie. Just like I'm stuck in this neuro major. The beginning of winter break feels like a dead end, and I'm scrambling to find a new route for basically everything.

I nod. "Trust me, I get it. After tonight, I'm burning all my calc notes, and I never want to hear the word *calculus* again. No more math please."

"I think most STEM majors have to take Intro to Stats," Zoya adds.

My coffee suddenly tastes bitter, despite the amount of sugar and cream I dumped in, and warning bells ring in my mind. This constant question that runs like an undercurrent rises up to the surface: Shouldn't I be excited about the classes that I have to take for my major and pre-professional track? I know it's unrealistic to like every single class needed for the neuroscience major, but still. If I'm barely making it through the weed-out classes, and not even enjoying them, then is the path I always dreamed for myself the one that I'm really meant to follow?

I shake my head, clearing away my thoughts. I'll have time to figure this all out over break. The background chatter in The Last Drop centers me, and I lean forward, resting my elbows on the table.

"So," I say, drawing the word out. "I actually need you all's advice."

"About what?" Aarti asks.

"One of my friends from back home reached out to our old friend group asking if we could all meet up once we're back. We had different ideas of where our friendship would go after we graduated, which led to us falling out. I haven't really talked to her, or the rest of our friend group, since then. I'm not sure if I should say yes to meeting up with them."

Zoya drums her fingers against the table. "Hmm."

"I think—" Aarti starts, before she breaks into a grin and waves at someone behind us.

I turn to follow her gaze, and my face pinches when I spot Heather making her way over to us. Heather's roommate, Rani, walks next to her, her thick black hair thrown into a bun and her colorful wardrobe rivaling Alex's best friend in *Wizards of Waverly Place*.

Rani says something that stops Heather, and I can hear Heather respond, "Yeah, this'll only take a few minutes and then I'll be right there." Something twinges in my chest, and I try not to feel it deep enough to determine if it's just annoyance or something heavier, like jealousy.

Rani waves at Aarti, who waves back, and I remember that the two of them know each other from being a part of UMB's South Asian student group.

"Hey," Heather says, sliding into the booth next to Aarti. "I was hoping that I'd run into you all here."

Heather flashes her megawatt smile, and her wash 'n' go looks flawless. Her sweater hangs off one shoulder, and along with her jeans and wedge boots, it's clear that if she's going out taking the calc exam, she's going out in style.

Zoya nudges me, and I paste on a tight smile, knowing whatever I'm feeling is written on my face.

"Great to see you," Aarti says, filling in the silence. "We were just talking about how much things have changed since the semester started."

I send Aarti a grateful smile for not bringing up my stuff about back home.

Heather nods. "Yeah, it's weird feeling like we're at this ending when really we're still at the beginning of our college experience. But change isn't necessarily a bad thing."

I shrug, making sure to keep my expression neutral. "True, like with majors and friendships and stuff."

"Exactly!" Heather says. "It's totally unrealistic to expect someone to come into college knowing exactly what they want to do. I mean, that's a lot of pressure. And most people don't really expect friendships formed during the beginning of the semester to last anyways."

I fight not to grimace or show my underlying confusion. It's hard to tell where we stand with comments like those. Her words cut, even though she isn't wrong.

"I'm going to go cram with some other friends, but it was great catching up with you all," Heather says, standing up. "Aarti, have a safe flight home, and, Arisha and Zoya, I'll catch up with you both around dinner before the calc final."

"Have a wonderful break," Aarti says.

Zoya wishes her good luck with studying, and I manage a forced bye. Heather leaves, making her way over to where her friends sit on the other side of the shop, and relief replaces the tension in my chest.

Aarti turns to me. "You know, you should just talk to Heather."

"There's nothing to talk about," I say. "She's allowed to make other friends."

Even though Aarti and Zoya think too that Heather is pulling away, they aren't as concerned about it as I am. Which I guess makes sense, since I'm the one who's closest to her. Or was. Maybe Aarti and Zoya are just better at dealing with change.

"All right, you all, I've got to head out," Aarti says, sliding out her side of the booth. "My Uber is supposed to be here in five minutes." She holds out her arms. "Hugs before I go?"

"Of course," I say.

Zoya and I both get up, and Aarti squeezes me lightly when I hug her.

"I'll see you in the new year, Ri," she says, letting go.

Aarti and Zoya share their goodbyes, and Aarti grabs her backpack and suitcase.

I glance at my phone and see that it's almost noon. "Wait, we'll walk you out, Aarti. Zoya and I should probably head to the Van anyways so we can study."

I send a quick text to Kaiden letting him know that I'll be heading to the library soon and slip my phone back in my pocket, so I don't worry about getting a response. "There's my ride," Aarti says. "I know you're both going to crush that calc final, and make sure to have fun tonight afterwards. But don't do anything that I wouldn't do."

I laugh, but tears prick my eyes, and I blink them back in surprise. She waves at us from her Uber, and Zoya and I both blow her a kiss back. We watch until her ride disappears around the corner.

"And then there were two," Zoya says, linking her arm through mine.

I nod, my sadness increasing. Seeing Aarti leave is a shift moving me from this reality to the one that I left behind. The one that I'm getting closer to returning to. My phone burns in my pocket, reminding me of that.

Zoya and I walk past the Main Gate, and I stop at the moose statue. The bronze is ice-cold, but I tap the statue twice for good luck. One of my orientation leaders explained the tradition, and even though I forgot a lot from o-week, that's one thing that stayed with me. Zoya does the same, and we continue toward the Van. As we get closer, more people appear, and we fall into the sparse flow of students heading to the library.

I tap my school ID against the sensor to get through the revolving security gate. Zoya and I head down to the basement floor, and the silence that greets us is eerie. Usually, this floor is bustling, since it's known as the louder part of the library. Most days it's so hard to find a table, especially on the weekends, but today only a few of them are taken. We head over to one of the longer tables that's right next to a whiteboard with outlets, and I freeze when I see the person sitting at the table next to us. It's hard to miss him with his height, but it's his familiar coils, black-rimmed glasses, and Poké-mon hoodie that catch my attention.

"You gonna go talk to Kaiden, or just keep staring at him?" Zoya asks.

"Um—"

But before I can make a decision, Kaiden looks up from his notebook and his eyes lock on mine. He breaks into a grin, and its warmth is so infectious I can't help but do the same.

"Hey," I say. "Care to join us?"

"Sure, if you have room! I don't want to be cramping y'all's style," Kaiden says.

Before I can respond, Zoya says flatly, "It's only the two of us. Of course we do."

Kaiden laughs, his eyes never leaving mine, and the eye contact makes my cheeks warm. I feel my hands start to sweat, and I grip my notebook tighter so I don't embarrassingly drop it. The last thing I need is for all the papers that I should've filed in my binder eons ago to go spilling out all over the floor.

I give a small shrug. "Well, you're always welcome."

Kaiden gathers his stuff and comes over and sits in the seat next to me. His arm brushes mine, and even though I'm wearing a sweatshirt, goose bumps rise and my heart flips. It's difficult to resist Kaiden's steady calmness and his nerdy cute charm. Getting to know him, not only in calc but also through our Black Student Union and Muslim Students Association, has been a highlight of my semester.

My face warms as the memory of what happened between us at the BSU Winter Gala pops into my mind. We were dancing together, and I thought for sure he was going to ask to kiss me. But the slow song changed to a more upbeat one and whatever bubble was around us popped. His arms dropped from around my waist, and he dipped to use the bathroom, and I was left wondering if I'd misread the entire situation. I know I could just tell him how I feel, but in some ways that feels scarier than potentially letting go of being pre-med. But if neither of us does anything, I'll just be stuck wondering *what if.*

"All right, let's get down to business," Zoya says, opening her binder. "Let's start with derivatives and then we'll go to integrals. Lemme throw a problem on the board."

Kaiden and Zoya walk through the problem, and just when I think I understand what's going on, they move on to the next step, and it hits me that I definitely don't. My stomach sinks with the realization that I'm going to barely scrape by in this class, and that's only if I don't tank this exam. The urge to rest my head on the table and cry rises, but I push it aside. I've almost made it through the entire semester without having a meltdown in the Van.

"You good, Ri?" Zoya asks.

Tears prick my eyes, and I blink them away. The overwhelming feeling of regret suffocates me, as I choke on my own expectations.

"I'm just thinking that sociology is looking better by the day."

I should've switched calc from being graded to pass/no pass when I had the chance. But a mix of stubbornness and fear of disappointing my parents talked me out of it, and now I'm just hoping for a C.

"Well, you could definitely be pre-med and major in soc," Kaiden says.

He's right, but I'm not even sure I want that. My parents have always wanted me to go into medicine, and I never really questioned that dream. I just carried it. But now I'm realizing how heavy that dream really is.

I shrug. "I know it's silly, but I'm not sure pre-med is for me either. I think I want to switch out my spring math class for a core sociology class."

"Why would that be silly?" Zoya asks. "You should do it."

"I mean, we all met through that STEM pre-orientation program," I say. "And I don't want to have taken calc for nothing."

Kaiden bumps his shoulder against mine. "It won't be for nothing. You'll have gotten the math general ed requirement out of the way."

I open up a new tab on my laptop and go to the sociology class in my cart about the relationship between individual and society. The tiny voice in my head gets louder, and I take that as a sign to switch out Calc II for the soc class. A circular icon pops up as the request is processed and when the screen refreshes to show my updated list of my spring classes, my shoulders drop with relief.

"I did it," I say.

Switching classes isn't the biggest deal, but it's a small step toward going after what I want. Zoya squeezes my shoulder. "I'm proud of you, and you know I support you no matter what. And don't forget, you don't have to figure out everything today, Ri."

Her words lift some more of the weight off my shoulders. Sometimes it feels like everyone around me has all their shit together, and I have to do the same. But it's okay if I'm still figuring things out, or I don't know what direction I'm moving in. I'm moving forward, and that on its own counts for something.

"You're right." I take a deep breath, feeling my nerves ease. "All I have to do right now is get through this final. So let's do this."

•••••

"If I study any more, my brain is going to fry," Zoya says.

I glance at my phone to see that it's around three, which means that there's only three more hours until the calc final. Kaiden nods. "Agree. And worse comes to worse, there's always partial credit."

"Truthfully, that's the only thing that's gotten me through so far," I say.

We all pack up and head out of the Van. More people are out and about, but with the bare trees and cloudy gray skies, campus still feels ominous. My nerves aren't as frazzled as they were this morning, but maybe that's because I'm slowly starting to accept my fate.

"I'm actually going to go take a power nap before the exam and also hopefully finish packing," Zoya says. "I'll catch you both at the dining commons for dinner."

"Sounds good," I say.

She waves before heading toward Desai Hall. I glance at Kaiden, and he bumps his shoulder against mine when he catches me looking. If it wasn't so cold, I'd ask if he wanted to go sit by Pitfall Lake.

"Want to grab something to eat?" I ask.

Kaiden nods. "After all that studying, definitely."

We head to the Student Center, and I grab a sandwich from the cart. Like the Van, the Student Center is usually packed, but today, only a few students are taking up the furniture that's scattered across the open space. I slide my backpack off and sit down on the curved couch next to him.

"So, what are you going to be up to over winter break?" Kaiden asks.

I hesitate, not sure if I should bring up all of my friendship drama. But then again, Kaiden has seen me cry over calculus, so maybe we are close enough. "Mostly relaxing." I shrug. "I may catch up with my friends back home, but I'm not sure yet. We all kinda left on bad terms."

"I'm sure you'll all be able to work things out," Kaiden says. "But if not, that's also fine too."

My brows furrow. "Yeah, I guess."

"It's just that sometimes friends grow with you, and sometimes they don't. And if they don't, it's not always because there's beef, but just that you've grown apart."

I sit with his words, processing. I've always been so wary of change that sometimes I forget that it isn't always a bad thing. Change leads to growth, and as I look back on this semester, it hits me how much that's true. I've changed and grown, and so have Heather, Natalie, and the rest of my friends back home. None of us are stagnant. If I keep viewing my friendships as fixed, of course I'm going to get hurt when they inevitably change.

"I actually really needed to hear that." I give him a shy smile. "Thanks."

He grins. "Anytime."

Kaiden tells me about the trip he's taking with his family as we finish our food, and I feel at ease.

"Even though we don't have a class together next semester, I hope we stay in touch," Kaiden says.

My chest warms. "After what we went through in calc, you're kinda stuck with me."

I don't know how our friendship will change, but I'm excited to find out.

"I want to try to relax before this exam, so I'm going to head back to Desai and watch some Netflix." He stands up and extends a hand. "Need me to throw away your trash?"

"Sure, thanks."

I hand him my empty sandwich wrapper, and sparks shoot up my arm when his fingers brush against mine. I tear my hand away, unsure if he felt the same thing, and the plastic wrapper falls on the floor sadly between us. Kaiden bends down to pick it up, and he winks at me as he stands. Throwing away trash should not be cute.

"Uh, sorry about that," I say.

He laughs. "Not a problem."

He goes to throw it away, and I gather my belongings as he comes back.

"I need to get some packing done, so I'll head over with you," I say.

We leave, passing the empty quad to get to Desai Hall. The tables in front of the dorm are covered in a thin layer of frost that's starting to drip as it melts. Kaiden pulls out his student ID and scans us in. "See you later, Kaiden," I say, with a wave.

He gives me a little salute before he heads upstairs. I scan my student ID to get to the ground floor. The sign pinned on my RA's door says HAVE A GREAT BREAK with a doodle of a snowman, and it cheers me up as I unlock the door to my room. I take a deep breath and glance at my phone.

Two more hours.

My phone buzzes as I sit down at my desk, and I glance at it to see that one of my friends has responded to Natalie's text.

Tiffany: Sounds great Natalie! I can't wait to see everyone!

My fingers hover over the screen, but I can't get myself to type out a response. I sigh and set my phone down. Not knowing whether Natalie was right that we've outgrown each other is hard. Maybe meeting up will help me see if what she said is true, but I don't want to be hurt if that ends up being the case.

I shift my attention back to my desk, trying to see if there's anything I need to pack. Figuring out whether I want to respond to Natalie's text can wait. I grab my journal from the drawer and flip through it. The words blur together, a recollection of the highs and lows of my first semester. I scan through some of the entries and chuckle at the things that past me was worried about. Almost everything has worked out one way or another. Two lines that I wrote on the first day of classes stand out now: *By the end of the semester, I want to know that I stayed true to myself, stepped out of my comfort zone, and found people that feel like home. I want to look back and see how far I've come and be excited for how much further I have yet to go.*

The pages show how much has changed, how much I've changed. And instead of looking back and trying to figure out if there's anything that I need to hold on to, I close my journal knowing what I have to do to move forward. I go to the wall beside my bed that's filled with Polaroids clipped to fairy lights with lavender wooden clothespins. There's one of all four of us that's dated from fall break. My head is thrown back mid-laugh, and I look happy. We all do. I shift down, moving toward where the Polaroids begin.

Together, the photos form a visual scrapbook, but I think there are some memories that I'm ready to let go of for now. I unclip a Polaroid of Heather and me, both of us wearing our Desai Hall T-shirts and matching face paint. Though it's a cute photo for sure, something in my chest loosens as I slip it inside the drawer beside my desk. Heather will always be a part of my journey at UMB, but I'm not going to try to make her be a part of all of it anymore.

The next couple of hours pass with reruns of my favorite comfort show playing in the background, as I finish packing. My phone buzzes with a text from Zoya saying that she's heading to the dining commons. Even though nerves twist my stomach into knots, I know I need to eat something before the exam. I text back that I'll meet her there, and I make sure that my lucky pencil is in my backpack before heading out.

The sun hangs low as it begins to set, and I join the flow of people walking to the dining commons. A cacophony of voices greets me as I search for Zoya. The dining commons is packed with a palpable communal energy. It's hard not to sense everyone else's nerves, but it's a bit comforting knowing that I'm not alone. There's a table with a variety of different to-go dinner selections, and I grab the vegetarian option before making my way through the crowd of people.

"Hey, lovely, did you get some rest?" I ask, sitting down across from Zoya.

She nods. "I feel ready."

"That's great! One of us has to."

The alarm that I set for five thirty rings, and I turn it off. Anxiety ties my stomach into knots and erases my appetite, but I force down a couple of bites of my veggie wrap. The last thing I need is to be distracted by a growling stomach during a two-hour final. I'm so nervous that I barely notice the fact that Heather didn't find us like she said she would when we were at The Last Drop.

"We should go to Aesop's Café after we're done," I say. "To celebrate."

Zoya nods. "Sounds like a plan."

The noise in the dining commons picks up, and I glance at my phone to see that it's five forty-five. Chairs scrape against the floor as people throw out their trash and compost and start to leave. This is it.

"Looks like it's time to get this show on the road," Zoya says, gathering her stuff.

We both pack up and join the tide of students walking to the lecture hall. The lamps that line the path and the lights from the buildings cast a glow across the dark night sky. The scene feels almost serene, but the sharp scent of lemon cleaner and frantic conversations break up the moment as Zoya and I enter the building.

"I'll see you on the other side," I say.

Zoya squeezes my hand. "We've got this."

We part ways, and I head down the hall to the room that my class was assigned to. My hands start to shake a little as I tighten my grip around the handles of my backpack and try to take a couple of deep breaths.

"Arisha, wait up!"

I turn to see Kaiden jogging over. He falls into step next to me, and I look up at him and grin. My nerves ease a little, and I try not to focus on the effect that Kaiden has on me. I can dissect that after this exam.

"How are you feeling?" he asks.

"You know, sometimes all you can do is say it is what it is and keep it pushing."

He laughs. "That's true."

Before she lets us into the room, the proctor tells us to leave our bags and phones at the front of the class where she can see them and to sit at least a chair apart from anyone.

I hold out my fist to Kaiden. "For old times' sake."

Before we took the first calc test of the semester, he gave me a fist bump for good luck. The gesture stuck, and today I definitely need all the luck I can get.

Kaiden taps his fist against mine, and we take our seats. Once the proctor hands me the exam, everything passes in a blur. There are problems that I have no idea how to do, but I scribble something, hope for partial credit, and move on to the next one. Even though I have until eight thirty to turn in the exam, once the clock strikes eight, I'm exhausted. I take one more look over everything before calling it a wrap. I've done the best I can, and that's enough. Kaiden looks up from his exam as I scoot past him, and he flashes me an encouraging smile. My steps feel lighter as I turn in my exam and grab my stuff.

The chaotic energy in the main area of the lecture hall is heavy. Some people are crying, some are comparing answers to the questions they remember, and others are just heading right out. I find an empty chair in the sitting area and send a quick text to Zoya letting her know that I'm done. Tiredness replaces the adrenaline that's been powering me through. I'm glad it's over. I made it through the hardest class of the semester, and now I'm ready to enjoy the rest of my last night on campus.

I look up from scrolling on TikTok, spotting Kaiden and Zoya before waving them over.

"We're done with our first semester!" Zoya yells, and I cheer in response.

Kaiden looks at both of us, amused.

I elbow him gently. "What? You're too cool to celebrate?"

He laughs. "No, it's just great to see you happy."

Zoya looks between the two of us. "Kaiden, Arisha and I are heading to Aesop's Café, and you're welcome to join us."

"Sure, let's go be festive."

We leave the lecture hall, and exhilaration bubbles in my chest as we head over. Zoya walks a bit ahead of me and Kaiden because of the narrow sidewalks, and the adrenaline from before rises again as Kaiden's hand brushes mine. The overwhelming urge to tell him how I feel makes my thoughts spiral, and I start to talk myself out of it, but my thoughts come to a screeching halt when it hits me that this is really the last day. If there was a perfect time to say fuck it, now would definitely be one.

"Hey, Kaiden?"

He turns to face me. "Yeah?"

My heart beats so loudly I can hear the blood rushing through my ears, but here goes nothing.

"Um, I like you, and I was wondering if maybe you'd want to go on a date like when we get back? Of course, if you don't want to, that's totally fine. You know, no pressure or anything. It's just that—"

"Arisha," Kaiden says softly, and I press my lips together to keep from rambling further.

"Yes?"

He smiles. "I'd love to. And for the record, I like you too. I like your energy, and how your forehead crinkles when you're concentrating really hard, and how much you care, and your boldness."

I laugh, taking in him, and his words, and this moment.

"I'm not that bold."

He nudges his shoulder with mine. "I mean, you asked me out. And I think you being bold is going after what you want."

"Yeah, actually, I guess you're right."

This whole semester has been about figuring out what I want in terms of my academics, friendships, and love life and then finding the courage to pursue that. I'm still working on things, but I think maybe being bold is also just being more honest with myself.

"Are you two coming or what?" Zoya asks from over her shoulder.

"We're coming!" I say, as Kaiden and I jog a bit to catch up with her.

The bell on the door to Aesop's Café chimes as we walk inside, but I can barely hear it over all the noise. The diner is packed, and I spot a ton of people who were at the lecture hall for the calc exam. Someone toward the back of the restaurant is getting their photo taken by a waiter to go on the challenge wall.

A different waiter leads us over to an empty booth, and my stomach flips when Kaiden slides in next to me. I pick up the miles-long, book-length menu, even though I already know what I'm going to order.

"Next semester, we have to do the challenge," Kaiden says.

The Fabled Feast, a pie filled with meats or vegan replacements, is the specialty at Aesop's Café. Anyone who can eat it in under ninety minutes gets a free meal and a Polaroid on the wall.

"Next semester," I say, savoring the words. "Definitely."

I push my menu to the edge of the table with the others.

"The usual, right?" Zoya asks.

I nod. "Is that even a question?"

Every time Zoya and I come, we always order the baklava. It's sweet and nutty and delicious. That, along with their vegetarian gyros, always hits the spot.

My phone buzzes, and I look down to see another response to Natalie's message. I could ignore it . . . or I could take another leap of faith. Asking Kaiden out could've gone a completely different way, but it worked out well. So maybe reconnecting with my friends will be the same?

I won't know unless I put myself out there. And isn't that the point of the first semester of college anyways?

I bite my lip, and before I can overthink, I start texting.

Me: Looking forward to seeing you all!

There's no way for me to tell if those friendships will end, but if they do, I'll know that it's just a product of growth and that some things change. But Natalie reached out, and Heather stopped doing that, and it's that difference that makes me press send.

I flip my phone over on the table and turn toward Kaiden and Zoya.

"How different do y'all think next semester is going to be?" I ask. "Besides completing the challenge and getting our photos on the wall."

"Well, for starters, maybe you two will finally go on a date," Zoya says sweetly.

I kick her under the table. "Zoya!"

Kaiden laughs, looking at me. "Yeah, maybe."

"If you're lucky," I say, trying not to laugh.

He holds out his hand, and I go to fist-bump him, but he catches my hand and slowly loosens my fingers so that my palm rests against his. I slowly weave my fingers around his and he squeezes.

"Well, well, well, just call me fairy godmother," Zoya says. I snicker, and she narrows her eyes. "Wait, did I miss something?"

"Not much. Only Arisha telling me she likes me and asking me out," Kaiden says, his voice deadpan.

"Oh my gosh, oh my gosh," Zoya says. "Yesssss."

Kaiden and I laugh. I don't know where any of this will lead, but I'm okay with that. There's still so much for me to figure out, with my major and my friendships, but I have time. Right now, being here in this moment is enough.

"That calc final definitely finished our first semester with a bang," Zoya says. "What an ending."

"And what a beginning," I say.

SPRING SEMESTER

Catch You on the Quad

By Oyin

From: UMB

To: Students

II.

Imagine   for a moment   clouds   frozen   with bated breath
hear   the answers in the dead   leaves underfoot   the newness
in the (y)ear   the questions   in groved trees   the whispers
of a campus mo(u)rning   in fragile   wonder   if Greathouse feels   the quiet
in abandoned apartments   the hope in airy lecture halls   if Godfrey
books long for caress   for fingers tapping   dancing with ink
to muted music;
a campus longing   for the song of voices: professors
breaking down   into digestible little tidbits big ideas about
derivatives   space   language,   students   pondering questions of
internships and scholarships,   discussing duality of self   and Dua Lipa
in the same breath,   finding truths in being fearless (Taylor's Version);
a campus hearing
the hum of turnover   of change in the air   like trees once bare,
clothed   once more
like majors shifting   in sophomore year and junior year and
(sometimes)   once more   and telling (disappointed) family   like trainees
who went   from days spent in exam-ed battle to home
back once more   like those   whose worlds are falling   apart,
no longer hometown heroes   or first-year victors once more
like the ones who can't recognize the face in the mirror, can't even see
the smile once more   like friends   stuffed with secrets and sadness
and confessions and   cotton   reunited once more   like two
bees buzzing past each other three four five   times   (almost) never
meeting;   imagine   for a moment   the redoing renewing and reinventing
of intros of faces whose lines and shapes   are   to be memorized
again   the joy   in the return   of names whose letters are old
friends;   knowing   the legs   the torsos that fill the excited
quad;   seeing a flower bud springing   begging for   sunlight.

JANUARY

Rani's Resolutions
By Arushi Avachat

There is nothing new to New Year's Day in the Desphande household.

Every year, Ajoba reads poetry on the porch swing to avoid being roped into housekeeping tasks. My twin brothers sleep through the morning, still knocked out from their New Year's Eve sugar crash, while Baba wakes early to clip pansies from the garden for a dining table centerpiece. Aai peels potatoes as she watches him through the kitchen window.

There is something comforting to the routine, a promise of family and constancy even as the calendar changes. Today will be no different.

This is the lie I tell myself as I fumble through my morning skin-care routine.

My fingers are shaky even as I brush back my hair, and I have to pause on the steps to do some breathing exercises before heading down to help Aai. It wasn't my goal to create chaos on my very first trip home from college, but here we are.

I land beside my mother just as she's turning on the stove. "Happy New Year, Aai." I kiss her cheek.

She gives my shoulder a squeeze with one hand, using the other to drizzle oil into the pot. "Happy New Year, Rani."

I take in the spices and ingredients laid out on the marble counter and make my guess. "Sabudana khichdi?"

"Only the best for our guests," she sings, and I have to smile at the rhyme, even though the words are true.

Aai's sabudana khichdi is beloved by all, and it is my favorite dish of our annual brunch. Each New Year's, a handful of Desi families from our corner of Seattle suburbia gather in the backyard for food and drink. We always invite guests to come at eleven, so naturally we don't expect anyone until well past noon. After a semester away, a part of me is truly looking forward to the festivities.

"What can I do?" I ask.

Aai looks pleased at the inquiry, as I'd intended. Keeping my mother glad and on my side is essential to making the rest of today go smoothly.

"You may make the seating arrangements," she says. Her lips pinch at the corners. "Just this morning, the Mehras informed me they will be coming. So it is very important seating is done right."

My mouth drops. "But the Pujaris RSVP'd yes weeks ago."

Aai gives a helpless shrug. "You know Shilpa," she says as she scrapes chopped green chilies into the pot. The chilies hiss and sizzle. "She has always had a flair for drama."

I purse my lips as I absorb the information. Analyzing then maneuvering around aunty social politics is one thing I have most definitely not missed while I've been away at Milbridge.

Shilpa Mehra has been at war with Sonal Pujari for the last two years. When Shilpa's son got engaged, the Mehras planned a lavish ceremony at a dreamy lakeside resort, one of the most coveted wedding venues in the Pacific Northwest. But then the engagement broke off—and a date opened up at the venue. Within hours of hearing the news, Sonal Pujari swooped in to book the location for her daughter, who had just gotten engaged herself.

Though Shilpa swore there were no hard feelings, and the Mehras even attended the Pujari wedding, tension between the women has only intensified with time. The rest of us respectfully pretend away the feud, and sometimes we get lucky and don't need to worry about it at all, when only one family is available for an event. Clearly, today won't be one of those times.

"I'll be sure to seat them as far apart as possible," I say finally. I grab a pen and paper from the kitchen island and sit down on the stool facing Aai. "What's the total head count?"

"Mehras are two, Satoors and Pujaris are three each, Khannas are four," Aai says. "Plus us six." She pauses to do some mental math. "Eighteen total," she concludes.

I barely register her last words; my mind has gone numb. "Did you say the Khannas are four?"

"Yes," she says, giving me a side glance. "Suresh's mother is visiting for the holidays."

But this I know already. Noori Aunty, Suresh Uncle, and Suresh Uncle's mother. That makes three. Dread sinks in my stomach because I can guess the fourth.

"So," I say. "I take it Kush is back home."

I thought his absence from brunch was a guarantee—his Instagram stories and tagged photos had been full of ski trip content, not that I'd been checking or anything. Kush with a snowman, Kush and friends beside a cabin fireplace, Kush somehow still managing to look attractive in ridiculously puffy navy snow gear.

Kush Khanna is always a bother, but his attendance today is the worst complication. I can't bear to have our community's beloved model son witness me sink in everyone's regard.

"Yes," Aai says with another side glance. Her gaze is assessing. "He cut his vacation short."

"Got it," I say. I take a deep breath to steady my nerves. I remind myself I'm nothing if not adaptive. "Okay. That's totally cool."

I steel myself for a meal's worth of parents praising Kush and his list of accomplishments in his school's prestigious pre-med program. I should be used to it; by virtue of us being so close in age (he's only a year older than me), I've been compared to Kush my entire life. I could take it when I was younger and the plan was always for me to be similarly remarkable. But things are very different now.

"Rani," my mother says, turning to face me. There's a trace of amusement and exasperation in her tone. "Tula ajunahi tyachavar prem ahai?"

"Aai!" I exclaim. I scramble to my feet. My cheeks are aflame. "Of course not! And what do you mean 'ajunahi'?"

Implying I am mooning after Kush Khanna is one thing. Implying I have long *been* mooning after Kush Khanna is an invitation to mutiny.

"Rani, please," Aai says. "You may not hide these things from me. I remember how you would behave around him during primary school years."

"*Aai,*" I say again, but some of the embarrassment is fading. "It doesn't count if I hadn't hit puberty yet."

It's true that I had a mild crush on Kush in fifth grade. It wasn't very discreet, either, though I never thought Aai would call me on it. But it ended as quickly as it began, and today's Kush Khanna is far likelier to provoke a headache than butterflies.

"Whatever you say, Rani," Aai says, and she turns back to the stove, a smile still playing on her lips.

I roll my eyes. I suppose it's better that Aai mistook my anxiety over Kush's attendance as the effects of a girlhood crush instead of guessing the truth. Still, I'm suddenly eager to leave the kitchen.

"Has Ajoba taken his medication yet?" I ask, certain he hasn't. "I can see to it now," I offer.

Aai frowns. "Please do," she says, as I knew she would. "I have not seen him all morning. I had wanted his advice on table setting up."

Evading that, of course, is the very reason for Ajoba's disappearance. I bite back a smile before excusing myself.

· · · · ·

I find my grandfather sitting cross-legged on our porch swing, a shawl spread across his lap and a book of Marathi poetry open in his hands.

He scoots to make room for me, and I sit down next to him. "Good morning, Ajoba."

Ajoba tugs the shawl so it covers my legs too. "Good morning, my Maharani."

I smile at the nickname. My name is Marathi for *queen*, and *maharani* is Marathi for "great queen." When I was younger, Ajoba liked to tell me stories about ancient Indian queens and claim they were written about me.

"Here," I say, handing Ajoba a glass of water and a bowl

containing his morning medications. "You should have taken these an hour ago."

He offers no explanation for his tardiness but wordlessly swallows the pills down. Then Ajoba tilts his head to face me. "You will tell them today?" His green eyes are stern and fixed on mine.

I look at the ground, hands twisting in my lap. My stomach feels queasy. "Maybe," I say.

Ajoba shakes his head. "You will tell them," he says again, and this time, it's not a question. "Aai Baba will come to support you, but you must first be honest. And there is no time for honesty like the New Year."

I meet Ajoba's gaze and find myself nodding. My grandfather's encouragement could make me agree to just about anything.

Ajoba was the first person I told about Milbridge's opportunity for aspiring educators: a paid assistant position for college students in the local elementary's summer school. I was most excited to hear about the program's guarantee of a job offer following graduation. It felt like a dream—my entire future secure with one application. I asked my department advisor for a reference the day after seeing the posting.

But now the deadline is tomorrow, and anxious nerves have replaced the excitement. I know my application materials are strong, but there are only two spots available, and I'm just a first-year, so the selection process will be highly competitive. More than that, Aai Baba have no idea I plan to apply. They have no idea I want to teach elementary school at all.

It's not like I haven't tried to tell them. I discovered I was meant to be a teacher in eighth grade, when I began babysitting Sanju and Nabhi, who had then just entered kindergarten. Sanju was bored during silent reading but loved puzzle time—so I found him a series of mystery graphic novels that made him look forward to library visits. Nabhi was struggling with his numbers but excelled in athletics—so I made up playground games with mathematical elements. He was counting by threes in no time.

Helping my brothers grow excited about formerly challenging subjects was thrilling. I knew I could do this forever. But when I mentioned what I was thinking to my parents, I was met with lectures and WhatsApp links to salary comparison charts. I never brought it up again.

Ultimately, I know my parents only want joy and success for me. But they still have fears and expectations, and they are very easily influenced by our community's opinions.

"Remember, when it is your turn to speak at the table today," Ajoba says now. "You may announce."

We have a tradition at our brunches to go around the dining table and say one thing we are grateful for in the New Year. Days ago, Ajoba suggested I use the opportunity to tell everyone about Milbridge's teaching program and my dream of pursuing education. I was resolved to the task—but now Kush is coming, and that makes my announcement impossibly harder.

After a moment, I manage a nod. I can't allow one boy to rewrite my plan for the day. "Okay."

"Good," Ajoba says, satisfied. "Besides," he adds, leaning in like he has a secret. His crow's-feet deepen in mirth. "If anything goes wrong, I will fake another stroke. It will be the perfect diversion."

I draw back, aghast. "Ajoba!" I exclaim, and he laughs loudly. "Don't ever joke like that again."

His laughter grows. After a moment, in spite of myself, I allow a laugh too.

Just then, Sanju and Nabhi (also known as our resident human menaces) come dashing out the front door. Nabhi is first, Sanju closely behind. Sanju looks positively furious.

Nabhi catches his breath first. "AJOBA! RANI!"

"Rani *Tai*," Ajoba corrects, reminding Nabhi of the required honorific.

Nabhi waves his hand. "Whatever, Rani *Tai*—"

Sanju elbows his brother. "Nabhi, don't you DARE!"

Nabhi dares. "Did you KNOW," he says. He pauses dramatically, eyes alight with fresh gossip. "That Sanju has been talking to a GIRL?"

"I have not, I have NOT!"

Sanju elbows Nabhi again. Nabhi hits back. I step forward, pushing my squirming brothers apart. In the middle of the mayhem, I find Ajoba's eyes, and we both bite back a giggle.

"Didja hear?" Nabhi says eagerly, even as Sanju tries to maneuver around my waist to land a punch. "A girl, Rani!"

"Rani *Tai*," Ajoba interjects again.

"How many TIMES," Sanju exclaims. He's finally stopped shoving me, and now his eyes are screwed shut in anger. "Do I have to tell you that Anjali isn't a GIRL, she's my FRIEND!"

There's silence. Ajoba does the dignified thing and turns his head to laugh.

I need a moment to collect myself too. Anjali Satoor is the twins' age, and she'll be arriving for brunch with her parents in just over an hour. "Is it possible," I start, "that she might be both?"

"Yeah, it's possible," Nabhi snickers. "It's possible she's his GIRLFRIEND."

"I'm gonna kill you, Nabhi!"

This fierce declaration forces me to insert myself between the twins as a human blockade once again. As if this day could get more chaotic. I can only hope Nabhi doesn't embarrass Sanju in front of Anjali, but . . . it's hard to have high hopes with my brothers.

"I must remark," Ajoba says drily, "this spectacle is rather like watching a boy fight his own reflection."

And then he picks up his poetry book and resumes reading.

I muster my most commanding teacher voice. "Sanju, Nabhi, that's ENOUGH!" I push both boys apart for what I hope is the final time.

They huff and sulk and cross their arms, but they are no longer violent, so I count it as a win.

"Now," I say, taking a deep breath. I am going to be covered in bruises tomorrow. "I need you boys to be on your best behavior for the guests. Speaking of, they'll be here soon, and neither of you are even dressed."

Nabhi groans and rolls his eyes to the ceiling. "Whatever," he says.

"Yeah," Sanju agrees, unified with his brother now that I've established myself as an authority, and by extension, the enemy. "What*ever*," he says, and the twins dash inside.

Sighing, I sink back down beside my grandfather. "Parenting is hard," I say.

Ajoba nods. "Good for you to learn now."

I give him a look. "I'm going to need you to be on your best behavior too, you know."

"When am I not?" he asks innocently.

"Ajoba!"

My grandfather's singular entertainment in events like New Year's brunch is poking fun at our family friends and blaming old age for his poor manners. To be fair, it is very easy to poke fun at our family friends.

Ajoba gives a theatrical sigh. "My own granddaughter does not trust me," he laments, and then he returns to his book.

· · · · ·

An hour later, I've done my makeup and slipped into the brunch outfit I laid out in the morning: a rose-patterned turtleneck tucked into my favorite black jeans.

My roommate, Heather, a STEM major with effortless style, approved the ensemble back in December, when we went shopping to celebrate the end of our first college exam season. I snap a fit check picture to send off to her, and she responds in seconds with a string of exclamation marks and heart-eye emojis.

I smile at the text. When we first met, Heather described my fashion sense as "Harper from *Wizards of Waverly Place* minus the props," so validation from her is always appreciated.

In our backyard, I finish setting up the dining area. We've pushed two tables together so that there will be six guests on the long ends, three guests on the short ends. I place name plates by each chair according to the seating chart I had Aai approve earlier, and then I lay out dishes and napkins.

Our home garden is Baba's greatest joy. As a boy, Baba had marveled at an affluent friend's backyard garden, filled with blooming buds and winding vines and swollen fruit. He had sworn one day he'd grow his own, and now he has.

Baba wasn't raised in wealth like Aai and Ajoba, who belong to one of Mumbai's new money families. He worked throughout his adolescence to afford his education and excelled enough to land a job practicing medicine at one of Seattle's premier research hospitals.

It's Baba's personal history that makes me most tight and

anxious about revealing my career plans. My father's primary professional objective has always been financial success. I don't know if he will understand my more fanciful ideas about what constitutes a successful career.

I take a deep breath and pluck at the sleeve of my sweater. I've resolved to go inside and try to push the worry from my mind before guests arrive, but then I catch sight of something shiny glinting under a chair leg.

On closer inspection, I see that it's leftover metallic paper from last night's confetti poppers. Given our brunch tradition, we never do much for New Year's Eve, but the twins begged me to buy them poppers for midnight. I agreed under the condition that they clean up after themselves, a task on which they've clearly fallen short.

There's nothing to do but crawl under the table to pick up the confetti. I've collected most of the scraps when I hear a familiar voice from behind me.

"Rani?"

I straighten on instinct. A mistake; my head collides with the underside of the table, and pain shoots up my spine. Head throbbing, cheeks flushing, I crawl back out as gracefully as I can and find myself facing Kush Khanna.

He's dressed in an olive green sweater and black slacks. and his dark hair is overgrown but in a purposeful way. There's a gift bag in his hand, and even though his forehead is creased in concern, amusement glitters in his eyes. Like he would laugh at me if doing so wouldn't jeopardize his status as Perfect Son Who Is Everything Rani Is Not. Unofficial status, anyway.

"You all right?"

Irrational annoyance flares in me at the question. I ignore it and attempt pleasantries. "Kush, hi. I'm great. Thanks. And you?"

"Good, yeah."

We fall silent. I massage my head, hating that he caught me in such an embarrassing position. From inside the house, I hear Aai and Noori Aunty greeting each other.

"Your family's a bit early," I say after another beat.

He cocks his head. "An hour late, actually."

"Oh," I say. I clear my throat. "Right."

He finally remembers the gift bag in his hands and holds it out to me. "Holiday present," he says. "For the whole family," he rushes to clarify.

"You didn't need to," I say, even as I gesture for him to put it on the table.

"It was no problem," he says pleasantly. "It's organic maple syrup. A special kind. Exclusive to the Canadian village where I was skiing last week."

"Wow," I say. "Aai is going to love that."

The gift really is certain to raise Kush even higher in Aai's esteem. My mother loves exploring specialties in local cuisine. I remember a little grumpily that my holiday gift to her was fuzzy socks.

We are silent again. He adjusts his stance and runs a lazy hand through his hair. I glance back at the house and wonder when the others will join us. There's something about being near Kush that always makes me nervous.

I haven't seen him in months, probably not since last Diwali, when he spent the entire time we weren't in prayer or in front of parents texting his girlfriend. He doesn't have his phone out right now. I wonder how his girlfriend is.

Kush opens his mouth to say something—more small talk,

probably—but I'm starting to feel restless, and my hands are still full of the twins' confetti, so I speak before he can.

"I should probably go toss this," I say, glancing at the scraps. He nods, and I give a small smile before retreating to the house. "See you."

• • • • •

By the time I return outside, more guests have arrived. I see the twins by the plum tree chattering away with Anjali, who is dressed in a pink frock.

Sanju's cheeks are bright red, but he doesn't seem to be at risk of running at Nabhi with his fists, so maybe we're safe on that front. A few feet away, Aai and Neena Aunty are practically pinching Kush's cheeks.

Predictably, Ajoba is isolated from all the guests, alone on a chair in the corner. I head in his direction, but I haven't made it a few feet before I'm stopped abruptly by Shilpa Aunty.

"Rani," she says. "My sweet girl." She embraces me, and I hug her back, albeit a bit belatedly. "Happiest New Year to you."

"To you as well," I say after she pulls away, and she beams.

She leans in now, her voice dropping to a conspiratorial whisper. "I have heard the sad news that Kumar might not be attending with Pritika today. Is that so?"

Pritika is Sonal Pujari's daughter, the one whose wedding sparked the ongoing Mehra-Pujari conflict. Kumar is Pritika's husband, and I can guess from Shilpa Aunty's tone exactly where she's headed.

"Yes," I confirm. "Unfortunately."

Shilpa Aunty's smile deepens. "That is distressing indeed," she says. "My heart pains to think the newlyweds may be going through marital strife."

"I'm pretty sure Kumar is just on a business trip," I say, recalling the reason on his RSVP.

"I pray that is all," Shilpa Aunty says. "But young couples choosing to part during holidays is a very dark sign for the health of a union."

I'm saved from the displeasure of responding when Ajoba appears next to me.

"Shilpa," Ajoba says. He's changed into dress clothes since the morning and his white hair is parted neatly at the center. I wonder how much Aai had to plead with him to make him get ready. "I wanted to wish you a Happy New Year."

"So good of you," Shilpa Aunty gushes. "Same to you, Uncle, same to you."

"And," Ajoba continues, "to tell you how lovely I find your dress of the day. It is splendid."

I give Ajoba a bemused look. My grandfather has never been one to care about fashion, and to be totally honest, Shilpa Aunty's floral frock is forgettable at best.

Shilpa Aunty looks silly with gratification. "Thank you so much," she says. "My Mukesh had it custom made. Very much a favorite—"

She trails off when she notices Ajoba glance at something behind her. She frowns and turns. I do too, and I almost gasp audibly at the sight. Sonal Pujari has entered the backyard, and by a twist of fate, she is wearing the exact same flowery dress as Shilpa Aunty.

I watch as Shilpa Aunty's expression tightens, then sours.

Beside me, Ajoba chuckles under his breath at a joke well done. I fight a smile too, knowing as I do that this is going to be a very long meal.

· · · · ·

We sit down to eat once all the guests have arrived. The dining table is set with delectable Marathi and Punjabi foods, everything from spicy aloo tikki to sweet mango barfi.

It's the kind of feast I have been craving for four months. The Desai Hall dining commons, where Milbridge freshmen have most of our meals, is not exactly known for quality Indian food.

I serve both myself and the twins, who I've had sit near me to prevent too much misbehaving. Sanju and Nabhi campaigned hard for the abolition of the kids' table, and I finally gave in, but this is a necessary precaution. I don't need the boys to start a fight in the middle of brunch.

Every once in a while, I catch Kush looking over at me. I very intentionally seated him about as far from me as Sonal Aunty is from Shilpa Aunty, but somehow his dark eyes find mine even still. I am always the first to look away.

About ten minutes into the meal, Sonal Pujari taps a fork against her raised glass of rose chai. A hush quickly falls over the table.

"Please excuse me," she says, her pink-painted lips stretching into a wide smile. "But I have just had a thought."

Ajoba tilts his glass toward her. "Congratulations," he murmurs.

Sonal Aunty doesn't seem to hear. "Why don't we begin our activity now? We may begin with our hosts." She smiles at Baba, who is seated right next to her. "Gopal, do you want to start us off with your blessings for the coming year?"

My stomach knots because the suggestion means I will be one of the earliest to go. I gulp down a sip of chai.

Baba laughs, and the sound is loud and gravelly. Aai likes to tease that though it's hard to tell when Baba smiles (my father has a rather thick and glorious mustache), his laughter is unmistakable.

"Why not," Baba says. He glances around the table, eyes crinkling when they find mine. "I am of course grateful for the health of my family," he starts. "And so grateful that dear Rani is home for break," he adds. "It has been hard to do without her."

My cheeks go warm, and my heart squeezes inside my chest. "Oh, Baba."

"So sweet, Gopal," Shilpa Aunty says. She's donned a coat to cover her dress despite the rare gift of sunny weather in a Seattle winter. "It is always hard when kids leave, though I am sure Rani has been learning so much in college." She beams at me. "Our future lawyer."

I smile, but the knot in my stomach tightens even more. While applying to Milbridge, I made the mistake of telling our family friends I wanted to pursue law. Shilpa Aunty had asked me what on earth I planned to do with an English degree, and "attorney" was the first answer to my lips. The label has stuck ever since, and it's another complication to finally being honest.

"It has been very hard," Aai confirms. "Especially as the boys need all the supervision they can get. The three of us have been struggling all on our own."

Everyone laughs but Sanju and Nabhi. "*Aai!*" they say in unison, and I see Sanju check discreetly if Anjali is poking fun too. Luckily, she isn't, but everyone else only laughs harder.

I join in too, but the sound feels false in my throat.

· · · · ·

I excuse myself to use the bathroom just before it's my turn to give thanks.

Nabhi is waxing on about his gratitude for extended lunchtime, and no one interrupts to question me.

I enter the downstairs bathroom, lean against the closed door, and bury my face in my hands. Our annual icebreaker is the perfect avenue for me to reveal my love for teaching to Aai Baba and our community. In company, reactions will be tempered, and maybe by the time Aai Baba have a chance to speak to me alone, they'll have gotten fully on board.

Or maybe not. Maybe the disappointment will just be delayed. Maybe anger at my publicizing what should have been a private matter will now accompany the disappointment. Maybe when break ends and I return to school, Baba will no longer find it so hard to do without me.

A tear slips down my cheek. I wipe it away, careful not to smudge my makeup.

I realize with some anger that this announcement is all the harder to make because Kush is here. Perfect Kush with his perfect grades and his perfectly respectable career choices. Last I heard, he was at the top of his class in the pre-med program.

The recollection makes me furious. Is it that much to ask for him to have *one* obvious flaw? Just one thing that makes parents cluck their tongues and turn their cheeks? It is so much worse to be the disappointment when the success story is presented right in front of me.

I sniffle again, tired of feeling sorry for myself. I know I have to go back out to brunch. I'm not sure how much time has passed since I left the table, but if I'm gone much longer, they're bound to send someone in to search for me.

I roll back my shoulders, practice my best smile in the mirror, and open the door. And almost walk right into Kush Khanna.

I blink, startled by the sight of him. Plus deeply aware of the fact that mere seconds ago, I was quite literally praying on his downfall.

"Hey," he says. He blinks too. Indoors, his dark eyes look even darker, almost approaching the color of asphalt. "Everyone's wondering where you are."

"I had to use the restroom," I lie. I frown, not wanting him to infer something unsavory from the length of my absence. "Um, number one."

I wish I could sew my lips shut. Kush makes that face again, like he wants to laugh at me but is refraining from propriety.

His phone buzzes now, and he pulls it from his pocket. The screen is alight with an incoming call. He purses his lips before sliding the call to voicemail.

"Meera," he explains, when he sees my inquisitive glance, and I vaguely recognize the name from some Instagram couple pictures Kush posted over the last few months. "She's a little upset that I left our ski trip early."

Involuntarily, I remember Shilpa Aunty's assertion that choosing to spend the holidays apart from your significant other indicates relationship issues. I shove the thought away.

"I'll call her later," he says. He slips his phone into his pocket and nods at me. "So what's got you hiding back here?"

My voice comes out defensive. "I haven't been hiding."

He raises his eyebrows. "It was almost your turn to go," he says.

There's a draft in the room. I cross my arms against it. "I know."

"They had to skip you," he tells me. His lips push into a small smile. "Though I guess that just means I'm up sooner."

"And that's a good thing?"

"Sure."

My eyes narrow. "What does that mean?"

He gives an infuriating shrug. "It means I have some good news."

An awful feeling enters my stomach. I ask anyways. "Kush, what are you planning to say?"

Something about my tone must strike him because he pulls back. "I learned I'm receiving my department's annual Student of the Year award, that's all."

My eyes slide shut. "Of course you are." I feel certain that my resentment earlier willed this into being. "Is there anything else?"

"Um, it comes with a summer research opportunity?"

I will never doubt the existence of bad karma again. "Right." Anxiety is climbing up my throat, and I try to swallow it back. "That's wonderful." I push my hair behind my ears and find my fingers are shaky. "Though maybe you could hold off on your news? Save it for another time."

His brow creases. "Pardon?"

"Just a slight delay," I say. "So temporary. You could announce tomorrow, even."

It's pathetic and it's bitter, but I know that I will not be able to take it if Kush unveils his big accomplishment at the brunch table today. Not when I'm about to out myself as a letdown.

He looks baffled at the suggestion. "I think I'm good," he says. He shifts in his stance, uneasy. "And we should probably get back out there, as it is," he adds, making like he's going to leave.

Even as I know I shouldn't, I reach out to grab his arm. *"Kush."*

He jolts at the contact, muscles tightening beneath my hand. I watch as his cheeks flush the faintest pink, and his dark eyes narrow at my fingers closed around his wrist.

I release him. My throat feels sticky. "I'm asking you," I say. I know how desperate I must sound, but I can't bring myself to care right now. "Don't tell them today. Please."

He blinks. "Rani—?"

I realize with horror that my eyes are hot. Like I'm about to cry. In front of Kush. I take in a long breath and speak on the exhale, words tumbling out in a rush. "Just not today. You can't be so obviously better than me today."

The plea is over-honest and vulnerable; panic has taken away my filter. But before Kush Khanna became the bane of my existence, he was just a boy who was nice to me. A boy ten-year-old Rani liked a little too much. I'm hoping that somewhere beneath it all, that boy is still there.

He blinks again. After a beat, he opens his mouth, but the back door swings open just as he's about to speak.

It's Nabhi, running inside for a very real bathroom break. "I need to *go,*" he sings, as he pushes past me and Kush. "And you both are wanted outside," he adds before closing the restroom door.

I swallow hard. I smooth down a crinkle in my sweater. Then I walk back out to brunch, Kush not far behind me.

· · · · ·

When we return to our seats, Shilpa Aunty is preparing to speak.

She holds her husband's hand on the table.

"This year," she says, smiling broadly. Some of her lipstick scraped off during the meal, and now only the edges of her mouth bear the fuchsia stain. "Mukesh and I have the same blessing to share. We are delighted to announce that our son Shekar is newly engaged."

Cheers and congratulations resound around the table at the happy news. I wonder if the well wishes are premature. Shekar doesn't exactly have the best record at maintaining engagements, as we all know. Still, Shilpa Aunty's last-minute decision to attend today's brunch is now crystal clear.

"If you need guidance in selecting a venue," Ajoba says after the chatter has died down a bit. "I know of a lovely resort."

He takes a sip of rose chai. Shilpa Aunty pretends not to understand his meaning.

"The most wonderful news," Sonal Pujari says. "May I ask whether a date for the occasion has been set yet?"

Shilpa Aunty's smile sharpens at being directly addressed by her rival. "July end," she says. "Shekar is too in love to stand for a long engagement."

"How sweet," Sonal Aunty says. "But I must tell you, Shilpa," she adds, with a glance toward her daughter Pritika. "If the date is for July, you must give us Pujaris an additional invitation."

Shilpa Aunty frowns as she considers Sonal Aunty's words. Sonal Aunty rushes to explain herself.

"My dear Pritika is to have a baby," she says. Exclamations of shock and delight ring out, and Sonal Aunty glows. "This is the blessing I have been wanting to share. We are deeply grateful."

Noori Aunty and Neena Aunty leave their seats to hug and kiss a beaming Sonal Aunty and a weary-looking Pritika. On the other side of the table, Shilpa Aunty sips her chai and tries her best to look equally pleased.

When the questions and congratulations die down, we raise our glasses in a toast: to Shilpa Aunty gaining a daughter and to Sonal Aunty gaining a granddaughter. I drink to both causes, but also to a third: another year of the utterly meaningless but deeply entertaining Mehra-Pujari feud.

"One minute, please," Noori Aunty says as we are getting ready to dig into dessert. She smiles at her son and then at me. "Between all the lovely news, we have forgotten that Kush and Rani have yet to share their blessings."

"Quite right, Noori," Aai says. She turns to Kush. "Guests may go first this time," she says, and I can practically feel my heart drop to my stomach. I take a deep breath to steady my nerves.

Kush clears his throat. He looks at his empty plate. He runs a rough hand over his neck. "I guess I'm grateful for my family and my friends," he says at last. He clears his throat again. "Those would be my blessings. For the New Year." He nods once to show he's done.

I blink, taken aback. I fully expected Kush to move forward with his planned announcement. Instead, he gave what may have been the blandest answer to the prompt all day. I feel my body relax the slightest bit.

"So lovely," Aai says, and the others murmur their assent. I twist my pinky in compulsion because I know what's coming next. My mother turns to face me. "Rani?"

My hands knot in my lap. I can't predict the responses of Aai Baba or the other families, but I know this is something I have to do for myself, regardless. I look up at Kush, who gazes curiously back at me, at Ajoba, who gives a gentle nod, and finally at the twins, who are my reasons why.

I take a deep breath. "So, there's this program that I'm considering . . ."

Heavy Rotation
By Joelle Wellington

Trina doesn't know it's all ending, when it does, in fact end.

She's lost between the bass rattling through the sticky floor-boards and the half-snarled argument and a haze of cigarette smoke and the wash of cheap liquor—she can still taste the burn. This is one of her favorite songs, one of those hypno-trance beats that she heard the first time that she listened to Percy's radio show as they signed off and she'd been setting up for her own thing.

Isra's narrow face is cast purple in the cheap LED lights taped to the ceiling, her teeth gleaming neon as she tries to shout over the music. Liz is more than three inches shorter but gives as good as she takes, rocking back and forth in her sticky Converses, bouncing on her toes as she snaps back. And there in the middle of them all is Malik, both hands filled with crunchy red Solo cups, jungle juice spilling over the brim.

"It's not *about* your stupid boyfriend," Isra growls out. "It's about the fact that you blew us off last weekend and you're trying to blow us off again—"

"Hop off my *dick*, Isra," Liz grits.

Trina jumps up and down, twisting and looking through the thick of co-eds, searching for someone—anyone—to dance with. Liz and Malik and Isra don't want to dance. They don't care about the music. They're too busy . . . talking? Arguing? They're always arguing. About Liz's boyfriend. About Isra's bossiness. A cheap shot at Malik for being too compromising.

It doesn't matter. She thinks she shouts that—*It doesn't matter, it's not that serious.* But, they don't seem to hear her either.

It all sounds the same underneath the pulse of the music.

Trina Whitaker is maybe a little drunk, maybe on jungle juice or maybe on the vibes, and she doesn't know this yet, but this moment—the one that sounds the same under the music—this is the moment her life falls apart.

· · · · ·

Trina comes awake violently, mouth tasting like cotton and the dining commons' dry day-old bagels that they set out every Monday morning after Sunday brunch.

She coughs, twisting onto her side, groaning under her breath as she buries her face in her flat pillow and reaches for her head. She sighs in relief; she at least had the sense to put her bonnet on last night. Trina lifts herself onto her elbows, squinting at her roommate.

The other girl is buried underneath her oversized duvet, motionless. She'll stay that way, presumably for the rest of the day. It's like that every time Trina looks at her; once Trina thought she was dead and poked her, and the girl didn't even rise, just lightly batted Trina away. Trina wonders how she'll pass any of her classes if she's always asleep.

Slowly, Trina sits up, groaning as the sudden rush turns her stomach.

Fucking hangover. Being on air is going to be—*fuck. Being on air.*

Trina launches herself from her bed, banging her knee against her bedside table and responding with a hearty "Mother*fucker.*"

It's a race against the clock after that.

Trina prides herself as someone who's *always* on time. Whether that's her military grandfather's generational impact or her own deathly fear of walking into a quiet, but *filled* room, Trina can never tell, and she doesn't have the time to unpack it. She shoves her feet through a pair of sweatpants and does something that she always thought she was too cool to do—rep her own college. UMB's moose mascot scowls out to the world, and Trina thinks it might be the perfect representation of her mood.

She only narrowly remembers her keys and laptop, stuffing them into her bag before she darts out the door, stomach aching with hunger. Trina takes the stairs instead of the elevator, going down the one flight and shimmying down the narrow hallway to the third door on the right.

Isra's RA doesn't really care, so instead of the cute cloud nameplate that Trina and her roommate have, Isra's name is scrawled out on a clumsily decorated index card.

"Isra! Isra, are you awake? You said you wanted to get breakfast and then sit in on my show last night. Are you there?" Trina calls, banging on the door.

"Shut up!" comes a call from the next room over.

Trina winces and then tries not to feel bad—it's ten in the morning, a perfectly reasonable time to be going about one's day. Even still, Trina's knock is softer this time.

"Isra, it's me. I'm not getting any younger, and I'm only nineteen," Trina says more insistently. She softens. "I've gotta eat, or I'm gonna miss my show."

She thinks she hears movement for just a moment—Isra has a single—and then nothing. There's nothing. As if Isra just shifted in her sleep. Trina sighs and reaches for her phone to text her and then stops. She forgot to charge her phone. There's only 9 percent, and she needs the time to make sure she gets to her show on time.

Hastily she sends out a text: Isra, Malik, Liz, brunch in the Caf after my show?

She stuffs her phone in her back pocket and then keeps it moving. Making her way out of the door, she dodges a group of sophomores just heading in. Probably on their way back from the city. There's no way any party around UMB went that long.

Outside, she debates whether or not she has the time to get something really quick to eat as her stomach snarls, but decides to book it to the WMBS studio instead. As she runs across the straw-colored lawn of the quad, she can just see the beginnings of town, the jutting buildings only just starting to feel like home. It's been a year and a half, and only now does Trina start to *not* feel like an imposter, like she might actually fit in at this place. It helps that she has friends, a group that she can rely on.

Trina was lucky to meet Isra, Liz, and Malik on the first day of orientation. They'd all been in the same group, gravitating toward each other through the power of freshman awkwardness. Their bond had been sealed in blood: The Hydra Race, a terribly weird tradition involving being bound by rope around the middle and hobbling together toward a finish line, had ended in scraped knees and laughter.

Sometimes they argue. Well, sometimes Isra and Liz argue,

because they're both hard-headed and high-strung, but Trina and Malik balance them out. It's perfect. Most of the time. Sometimes.

Trina shakes her head hard, like a wet dog. As she passes a lecture hall, she looks at her reflection in the window and sighs. Her hair is only a little messed up, the short curls atop just a little frizzy. Hopefully, *Percy* won't be in the studio to see her look less than her best.

The WMBS studio is in a tiny room tucked at the top of the Student Center. The actual studio part of the room, with glass and everything, is stuffed to the brim with wires and old cleaning supplies and back issues of *NME* and *Kerrang!* so the radio setup is actually against the wall on a big old table full of monitors and a soundboard. Foam is carefully plastered to the walls to absorb sound.

And the chair—the chair that gives access to the radio waves of Milbridge and the next town over, and sometimes the outskirts of the city—is occupied.

"And that's all, folks. I'm Percy Mason, and I'll be back next week for another episode of *Stone Cold*. Hint for next week's topic: If you don't love me now, you'll never love me again. Laters."

They don't turn in the chair right away even as Trina gently closes the studio door with a click, wincing and only relaxing when the heavy rotation playlist starts to grow louder. They push back on their heels, flicking the ON AIR sign off, the red glow dimming and then, finally, they twist in their seat.

"Morning, Trina," Percy Mason says with their *perfect* snaggle-toothed smile.

Trina's mouth goes dry. It always goes dry when Percy Mason speaks to her.

They're tall. Taller than her, at least, with a thicket of dark curly hair hanging around their face in layered curtains—a wolf cut. Their nose is a little pointy, jaw a little too crooked, but they look perfect to Trina. Trina's always thought they looked perfect, since last year when she saw them at the WMBS table for the activity fair, before they were VP of the college radio board, when they were just Percy Mason, host of *Stone Cold*, UMB's premier rock and roll show.

"Morning . . . morning, Percy," Trina stammers. "Ah . . . what did you talk about today?"

"What, you didn't listen?" Percy asks.

"No, I—" Trina only stops because Percy is smiling, which means they're teasing, which of course they are, because Percy is nice. Percy is the nicest person that Trina has ever met in her entire *life*, and she's got a high school friend who literally builds houses for the homeless instead of going to college. "Not today, sorry."

"I'm fucking with you, Trina, you're good. Talked about the David Bowie to Harry Styles pipeline today," Percy says. "It was a good mix of songs to play during my breaks. Next week, I'm—"

"Doing Fleetwood Mac," Trina interrupts. Percy raises an eyebrow. "You mentioned *Rumors* to me, remember? The album. I gave it a listen. It's really good."

"Right?" Percy asks, nodding their appreciation. They're wearing the coolest baggy shorts, revealing scabby knees, and a floral crop top. God, they're so cool. Percy leans over to grab their messenger bag and their penny board.

A fucking penny board. Trina is a cliché. Everyone has a crush on Percy. She's no different.

"Trina," Percy starts when they're by the door, looking back at her with a discerning expression. "There's a club lunch after your show. Around twelve thirty. You should come."

Trina never hangs out with the college radio board outside of meetings. She fulfills her duties as radio treasurer and nothing more. She's always with Isra or Liz or Malik.

"I can't. I told my friends we'd get brunch," Trina says. She lets herself believe that Percy might even look a little disappointed.

"Oh . . . that's cool. But, if you change your mind, come through, yeah?" Percy asks.

Trina regretted saying no the minute she did, but Percy doesn't linger anymore, eyes flickering to the clock. It's nearly time for Trina to be on air.

Trina checks her phone just in time for the screen to flicker black. She sighs and sets it to the side of the board. She plugs her laptop into the aux and pulls the headphones over her ears as the sound of the heavy rotation plays her onto the air. Trina pushes the volume of the mic on, leaning back in the rolling chair to flick on the ON AIR sign before scooting forward just as the playlist slowly fades away. Trina presses the cool techno sound effect that opens her up, and then:

"The world is turning, out there and in here. The Navy eagerly awaits a new album from their captain—they'll be waiting a long time for that one, since she's moved on from making makeup and panties to being a home goods *conqueror*. Will Beyoncé finally win her well-deserved AOTY this month at the Grammys, or will it once again go to an undeserving Justin Bieber wannabe? And will we ever get a Starbucks here at UMB—here's to hoping we don't, because who could ever replace The Last Drop? This is Trina Whitaker, and we're here for *State of the Uni on Saturday Mid-mornings*."

· · · · ·

It's only been a week, but to Trina, it all feels like a century. Every look at the dark mode of her phone makes it feel even longer. Her last text, an invitation to Malik and Liz, looks lonely there and startlingly pathetic. Trina sighs as she turns it over again, attempting to pay attention to her stupid anthro homework. She isn't even sure why she's taking Anthro 101, when she kinda hates the professor and knew she would from Rate My Professors. He's the kind of neo-lib that looks at everything through a Western lens, which pisses Trina off, but she's never been brave enough to say it out loud in lecture; she'll save that for the midterm paper that the TA will read.

The chapter on FGM is dragging, and each word blurs together into a mess of black ink until all it resembles is her text inviting her friends to brunch, the one that she's memorized by now: *Isra, Malik, Liz, brunch in the dining commons after my show?*

She's spent all week analyzing each word, debating word choice and syntax as she moves along, alone. She knocks on Isra's door when she knows she's home, and thinks about the text—Isra never opens the door. She goes to class and thinks about it. Goes to work and thinks about it. Her weekly radio show board meeting. The Van, her library of choice, where she usually spends every Thursday morning brainstorming her playlist and scripting the pop culture agenda of *State of the Uni on Saturday Midmornings*. Every day she thinks about it in between the growing list of items on her to-do list. She even thinks about it when she's doing her fucking hair, which sucks because her gel-to-curling-cream ratio is off that first time and it leaves a white cast that she has to *wash out* and redo.

The only time she stops thinking about it is when she finally sees Isra again as she passes her on the quad. Trina knows that she's on her way to French 302. She also knows that Isra sees her, because she hesitates just a moment.

For a minute, it's like they're the only pair on the quad. Isra tugs on her turtleneck. The bright purple one that Liz picked out. Trina remembers that trip into the city, when they bought Isra a whole new wardrobe, camisoles over turtlenecks and wide-legged pants and long skirts that she could feel comfortable and cute in. They'd gotten dinner and then finished the night at Cinema City, bags of clothes stuffed into sticky movie theater chairs.

Isra's face crumples, and Trina thinks it might be regret in the lines of her expression.

And then the minute ends, and Isra doesn't say anything as she walks past Trina, too quickly for Trina to find the right words. Or any words. She moves as if she's seeing right through her, and Trina's whole stomach twists violently with the urge to vomit as she starts to walk faster toward the dining commons. She tries to convince herself that she's just hungry, but she knows that's not it.

It's worse than when she'd seen Malik earlier in the week, sitting with his bio friends. He'd smiled at her, invited her over with a wave, but he'd always been the more social one of the group, always knowing everyone from everywhere. He'd texted her, separately from the group chat, mentioning that he had group projects, that he'd love to hang out, but Trina doesn't know what to say. She's never hung out with him outside of the context of the group.

And worse, he didn't need them. He had other people when he was feeling lonely. Trina doesn't know how to carve out a space for herself, doesn't know how to ask for a space to be made either.

And then it gets worse. Because Trina should remember this is real life and it can always get worse.

Liz and her boyfriend are cuddled together on the bench right outside of the double doors leading into the cafeteria. Their heads are bent over Liz's phone, and Liz is grinning widely, looking at her boyfriend like he's hung every moon, every star in the entire universe.

"Fuck, not you too," Trina mumbles. Her luck has never been the greatest, but it's also never been *this* shitty.

Liz looks up and her mouth twitches with a smile. Muscle memory. Liz checks herself swiftly and scowls.

"Hello to you too, Trina," Liz says sarcastically.

She doesn't look like her world's been shattered. She doesn't look lonely. Instead, she looks perfectly fine, nestled into her stupid boyfriend's side. Her stupid boyfriend who started all of this, that upperclassman boy that gives blonds a bad fucking name, thanks so much.

Trina draws herself up. She's never been one for confrontation, but suddenly it all hits her. All week, she's been alone. All week, she's been in limbo, wondering what she's done wrong, what went wrong, were the foundations always so weak, were they so easy to crack. All week, she's gone ignored, as if their friendships hadn't mattered, as if she didn't *matter*.

"Why didn't you ever answer my text?" Trina demands.

"Got busy," Liz says sharply. "Midterms coming up."

Trina scoffs. It's *February*.

"Don't give me that. You left me hanging all week," Trina retorts. "Friends show up, Liz."

"Oh, is that what we are? Friends?" Liz asks, the volume of her voice rising just enough to catch the attention of others. Trina bears the brunt of that attention with as much dignity as she can.

Her boyfriend's arm is around her shoulders, a big hand rubbing up and down her arm. "Babe . . ." he warns.

"Yeah, that's what we are. Or were," Trina mutters, and finally, she looks away from the piercing stare Liz centers on her.

"It didn't feel like it. You always taking Isra's side—"

"I didn't take sides. I didn't care at all," Trina says firmly. Then she looks at Liz's boyfriend. "No offense."

He shrugs. "None taken."

"Maybe that was the problem. You think Isra and I didn't notice? We know you didn't *care*. I get Malik. Malik is a people-pleaser. Confrontation makes him anxious, but you're not like that," Liz says. "It's like you can't manage to care. Like it's *beneath* you. Isra is always pushing, and you just watch like it's fucking entertainment, like it doesn't bother you. Like it doesn't involve you. That night, you could've said something. You could've said, *Hey, maybe you should lay off Liz*—but no, you would've had to do something."

"But you *were* ditching us for him. You tried to ditch us that night, just like you always do, without warning, leaving us high and dry, like you did to me all week—" Trina says, her voice rising with panic, with frustration, with the feeling of *why don't you get it?*

And then, it all ends as Liz sneers, "It's not my fault that you don't have anything else going on, Trina."

It's not true.

Trina has *everything* else going on. She has work and radio and too many classes as she tries to figure out her major. Trina's one refuge besides her radio show was her friends. They were the only part that wasn't part of the "everything else," because they made her float, they made her feel real.

But maybe it wasn't real at all.

• • • • •

It's not my fault that you don't have anything else going on.

Trina can't stop thinking about it. She doesn't think she'll ever stop thinking about it. It's probably why she's fucking late to her own radio show. She only realizes how late she's running when she happens to check her phone out of habit, despite knowing that there won't be any more texts, that she will remain unmoored. And then she sees that it's 11:27. Trina *hates* being late, so she runs.

When she slams into the studio, the ON AIR sign is already off, and Percy is packing up their laptop, the heavy rotation playlist playing.

"I added this," Trina says instead of saying hello like a normal person.

Percy is too cool to startle. They look up and smile at her. "House music? Nice."

"My mom is really into it." Trina pulls out her laptop, throwing it open to her script, her eyes glazing over the screen. *It's not my fault—*

"You're *never* late. Are you okay?" Percy asks. They sound genuinely worried for her, like they actually care, and Trina isn't sure if that's because they're the VP of the board or because they're just that nice or maybe—Trina hopes—something more.

But it makes Trina feel safe.

"I think . . . I'm friendless," Trina admits.

And then she realizes how completely humiliating that sounds. She looks up at Percy, wild-eyed, scrambling for a follow-up, but suddenly everything is blank and only the throbbing croons of that neo-disco singer fill the space between Trina's ears. Lyrics about the singer dancing with somebody else while their ex-lover just watched.

"Oh, shit, did . . . did something happen with you and your friends?" Percy asks. "Is it your first fight?"

"Ah . . . well, I didn't . . . It's complicated?" Trina says. And then she looks away, cheeks burning as she rubs the shaved side of her head, trying to ground herself. "It's whatever. It's no . . . no big . . ." She can't even say it. It'd be a lie. Trina looks up at the clock. "I'm running late."

"Oh, right. Right," Percy says. They still look worried for her. Percy opens their mouth, closes it again and then claps Trina on the shoulder. It makes Trina feel like a bro, and that . . . that's not it. Percy seems to realize too, their cheeks flushing pink beneath their freckles. "Um, sorry."

Percy's hand slides over Trina's shoulder, fingers dragging over the flesh of her biceps and Trina balls her hands into a fist to keep from shivering underneath the warmth of their hand. Percy smiles and then takes a step back, grabbing their bag before going off into the ether.

Except, this time, they stop. "There's . . . our—meaning the board's—monthly dine out coming up. If your social calendar is feeling a little . . . empty, you should come, yeah?"

"I've got a lot of work," Trina says. "And I also work. I mean, like, I have schoolwork and then I, also, have a job. I work for Professor Beckings in the German department."

"I didn't know you spoke German," Percy says, sounding impressed.

"I don't," Trina says bluntly, probably too bluntly. "But, I do know, like, very limited Latin."

"*Et tu, Brute?*" Percy asks with a grin as they back up toward the door. "Well, the offer still stands—"

God, they're such a nerd. God, *Trina likes them so much.*

"When is it?" Trina blurts out.

Percy stops, eyes wide. Trina tries not to think anything sappy, like how their eyes are amber in the cheap fluorescent lighting. It's hard when Percy smiles like that, as if actually *pleased* that she wants to go to their dumb bonding event.

"Friday night. At my place. Check the GroupMe for the address. BYOF. Bring your own food . . . so we can share," Percy says.

"Got it," Trina squeaks.

Percy leans in, grin never relaxing. "Looking forward to seeing you then, Trina."

For a moment, Trina *believes* it and hopes it to be true—that they want to see her as badly as she wants to see them. And then she realizes it's 11:35, and who, if not her, will tell campus that the star of HBO's latest dramedy was caught with his pants down in the middle of Houston and that the school *purposely* buys one-ply toilet paper that hurts everyone's asses when they wipe?

• • • • •

Aesop's Café is crowded for a Friday evening.

It's not even after prime party hours, and the diner is packed, the dull roar of students giving Trina just the slightest of headaches. She shimmies her way past the waitstaff toward the counter, the bar already packed to the brim with students sipping Shirley Temples and eating off heaping plastic platters. It's an old place and cheap, but Trina is too well acquainted with Aesop's Café. She knows how good the food is.

Unfortunately, she also knows that the menu is massive, always too large to make a decision for at least twenty minutes, and Trina does not have twenty minutes. She flips through the sticky menu, squinting to make out the blurry pictures next to some of the meals and huffs to herself.

"Oh shit, Trina!"

Trina jerks at her name. She passively recognizes the voice and when she turns, she hopes that it's Isra or, maybe, Liz. And it's not. It's Rin Takagi, assistant head of tech and sophomore radio show host of *Eat Up, Meese*—a show in which Rin talks about Aesop's Café's *extensive* menu that she's attempting to take on over the year.

"Ah, hey . . ." Trina says, singing out the word awkwardly.

Rin grins. "It's Rin."

"I *know*," Trina insists, and Rin smirks like she doesn't believe her.

"Late-night run to the diner?" Rin asks, leaning against the tile walls, tapping her foot against the crooked linoleum in a classic 4/4 beat. "Homework?"

"Ah . . . no, the dine out," Trina admits. "But you're here . . ."

"Oh, wow, you're going?" Rin demands, pushing off from the wall, taking a step closer with a wide smile. She nods, her head bobbling on her skinny neck. "Amazing, I'll finally not be the only underclassman. I was thinking about the Fabled Feast."

Trina's eyes widen. "Oh, really?" The Fabled Feast is an Aesop's Café specialty, a ninety-minute challenge food stuffed to the brim with meat or vegetables. She hadn't even known that they let you take it out of the restaurant.

"Oh yeah, I'm tight with the manager on account of the show. But, then I thought I'd make that a specialty show, you know? So I'm bringing disco fries. It's the last item on the appetizers list that I haven't tried yet. And I think I'll bring the lobster bisque. You know, finish the appetizers, start the soups. A twofer, for Wednesday night."

Trina doesn't really know the numbers for the shows, but she knows that Rin is *unfairly* popular, right after Percy and before the club's actual president, Maxine. Trina is lucky that she's top five with *State of the Uni*. Percy is an anomaly, being so popular on a Saturday morning. Trina rides that wave right on to success.

"I have no idea what to bring," Trina blurts out when she realizes she's been silent for too long. She rubs the shaved side of her head and then regrets it when she feels the cast of gel breaking.

Rin hums, tapping her chin like she's seriously considering it. And then, "You could bring corned beef hash. And fries."

"*What?*"

"Who hates corned beef hash and fries?" Rin asks, flashing her a smile.

It's infectious, to Trina's annoyance. She tries to pull away from Rin's good humor, but Rin doesn't allow her to. Rin is chatty about everything—from Sal, the girl she's talking to, to plan of attack on the next part of Aesop's menu—all throughout Trina's order and their wait time until their food is finally delivered to them in aluminum foil pans and plastic bags.

"Percy's house isn't far. It's a little before the apartment buildings by Milbridge Mall," Rin says.

Trina's stomach begins to sink. She's deeply familiar with the few blocks of suburbans where some of the students live off campus, mixed amongst the townies of Milbridge and some of the professors. As they get closer, Trina's dread begins to grow, sitting low in her belly like lead as they walk up the pavement toward the pale green suburban on the corner. Because Trina knows that house, unfortunately, through the memory of hazy smoke and LED lights.

It's where everything fell apart.

Rin, of course, doesn't share her trepidation, swinging her bag in her hand, unmindful of the lobster bisque inside of the plastic container as she rings the doorbell. Trina wonders if she can turn back now, maybe hide behind a bush before anyone else from the board can see her.

The door swings open.

"You made it!" Percy says, and then they're hugging her.

Oh, they're *hugging* her. Trina just hugs them back before Percy pulls away and stares awkwardly at her before jerking forward to hug Rin. Rin snorts.

"Oh, we hug now?" Rin asks sarcastically.

Percy groans, shoving at Rin. "Shut up and come inside." They pull Rin into a headlock, laughing as Rin fake struggles out of it, and releasing as soon as Rin taps their arm. "You guys just met up?"

"No, I saw Trina in Aesop's. Couldn't *believe* my ears when she said that she was coming to dine out. It's like she hates us or something," Rin says with a shit-eating grin.

"I do not," Trina protests. She has very little feeling about the college radio board in general aside from Percy, though that's starting to change. Rin seems to realize it too, smirking over at her, as if she *knows* that she's just that likable.

"What are we feasting on tonight?" Percy asks. "I made a cake. It's really ugly, but it'll suffice."

"From scratch?" Trina squawks, because if Percy is talented

enough to know how to make a cake from scratch, she might scream—

"No, boxed cake, because boxed cake rules," Percy declares.

"Oh thank god," Trina mumbles and then ducks her head at Percy's bemused stare.

The pair are led into the living room, and it's a stark relief for Trina that it looks so different. The LED lights are no longer the bisexual hues of an A24 film, the coffee table is in the center of the room, the couches aren't pressed up against the wall, and there's a smattering of people, none of them in too-tight clothing as lofi plays over the Bluetooth speaker stacked on top of the console table.

"I literally didn't believe you, Percy, I'm so sorry. I can't believe you got Trina to show. Our mighty treasurer comes home," Maxine declares, shaking her head as she stares at Trina in disbelief.

Trina feels weirdly exposed.

"Sick, right?" Percy asks as they hop over the arm of the couch and slouch down in their seat next to Maxine.

Maxine sinks into the back of the chair, her box braids slipping from the bun over her forehead. She pats the seat on the other side of her. "Come through, Trina. God, you're so funny, I'm glad you came, I wanna know your sources about the one-ply toilet paper situation," Maxine declares and then instantly switches gears. "You're new here, so I'll give you a rundown."

Trina sits next to the other Black girl, and it almost instantly puts her at ease as the upperclassman gives her wrist a reassuring squeeze.

"I brought disco fries and corned beef hash," Trina blurts out.

Maxine blinks slowly and her smile, genuine, is just a few seconds too slow. She's so high, it's admirable that she's not on the floor in a coma for the next twelve hours. "Right on. I love disco fries."

"Told you!" Rin shouts from across the coffee table where she's sitting cross-legged between the PR chair and the editor of the radio zine. The head of tech is sitting at the end of the coffee table on the floor, legs stretched out, their feet meeting the programming director's knees.

"Plate. Food," Maxine directs, juggling her own plate in her lap before she turns to Trina. "We're sharing stories."

"What kind of stories?"

"Music stories. Like, where is your love of music from?" Maxine asks. "I just told this story about my grandma's vinyl collection that I found in her basement in middle school and the day I discovered Rick James and—"

Percy leans over her and grins.

"She tells this story every single month, and it's always slightly different," Percy says. "This time it's Rick James, last time it was Betty Davis, and the time before, it was Otis Redding."

"Shut up, Perce, I'm telling a story," Maxine snaps, shoving Percy away even as Percy laughs—*cackles*.

It's probably the ugliest sound Trina has ever heard.

It's amazing.

"You got a story, Trina?" Rin asks. Trina hesitates, and Rin leans forward and volunteers, "I can tell the beginning of my love affair with adult contemporary. It all starts with my discovery of Enya."

The programming director groans and pelts a chip at Rin, loudly declaring that he's tired of Enya, and it devolves into a playful argument on the merits of Enya's mezzo soprano and diction.

Trina's friends never asked her about music. They knew about her radio show, but they'd only vaguely been interested in the most forefront part of it—the tongue-in-cheek gossip, the pop culture roundups, Trina's sarcastic attempts at humor. They never asked about the music that she carefully curates each week. Trina doesn't even think that they listened to her show after the first month or so.

Maxine listens. Maxine is the president and listens. Trina thinks Percy listens too.

These people listen, and she thinks they might care. About the things she likes and the things she says and maybe her, too?

So, very quietly, Trina interrupts and says, "My mom listened to house music when I was growing up. She played it around the house because she said that it reminded her of being young and dumb and pissing off my military grandfather, until he was just pretending that it pissed him off, because he liked it too. We used to play it on Saturday mornings, when we had to get up to clean. My parents would put it on to get me and my older brother out of bed, and we'd start cleaning the house from top to bottom, but it always devolved into this . . . dance party in the living room."

By the end, the entire room is silent, and they're staring at her. Percy is staring at her with a soft look in their eyes that Trina ducks her head away from.

"That's really fucking rad," the tech chair declares. "House and electronica are super tied, right?"

And then, they're all talking about house music and asking questions and want to know who she listens to. They want play-lists and derivatives and everything in between. Trina loses herself in every thread of conversation and grows looser with each passing moment. The conversation shifts to instrumental work and who was better—Prince or David Bowie—and Trina realizes that she actually has an opinion and she joins the fray.

Briefly, she slips out of the conversation as Maxine turns to her and says, "I really like your hair. Did you shave it just before school? Growing out your natural curls?"

"Yeah," Trina says with a grin, because her friends never asked her, they don't really know what it's like. They're all Black and brown, but being a Black girl is different on its own. "It was totally fried from high school."

"It looks mad healthy. If you ever need someone to braid it, I've got you," Maxine promises. "Lemme get your number."

And Trina gives it to her, and Maxine actually *saves* it.

Trina learns that Percy is an applied mathematics major, which is a little less hot, because Trina hates math, but it makes Percy more real, which makes them more hot—it's confusing. Rin already knows she's going to be a philosopher one day, and Trina feels something like relief and a little bit of interest when Maxine says that she had no idea what she wanted to be so she just made her own major.

"What about you?" Maxine asks. "What's your major?"

"I don't know. Undecided. Super undecided," Trina says. And then she scrambles to add more context: "Not like you, though. I'm not good at planning out something like a major."

"Well, what do you like to do?" Percy asks.

"What does that have to do with anything?" Trina asks bluntly.

Percy looks so taken aback, their eyebrows nearly disappear into their bangs. Maxine barks out a laugh.

"I know parentals always tell you to be practical—be a doctor, be a lawyer, be a *whatever-the-fuck*—but it helps to like what you're studying," Maxine teases lightly. "So, what do you like to do?"

Trina hasn't really had time for hobbies at all. She works. She studies. She—

"Radio. God, I love doing radio," Trina blurts out, and it sounds like a line. Like she wants to really impress upon these people that she loves radio even though she's been weirdly antisocial. But she thinks it comes through—how much she's not lying at all.

"Comms major, then. Think about it," Percy declares.

And Trina nods. She's grateful when the focus moves off her. Liz likes to say that she's above it all, that she likes to pretend that she's too cool for it, but really, she likes to listen.

Trina smiles through everything, the knots in her stomach slowly coming undone with each nugget of information. Each one feels like a shared puzzle piece, a fragment of what makes someone whole. It's a puzzle piece that Trina is allowed to keep, and she finds that she has none of those from Isra or Liz or even Malik. She doesn't know what kind of music Isra listens to. She doesn't know why Liz likes her boyfriend or how Malik feels about his new stepfather.

But Trina does know that Maxine is the third of six. That Rin used to be a vegetarian. That Percy isn't so perfect, because they have a terrible opinion on the current state of rap.

It's nearly one thirty in the morning when Trina yawns, and immediately, Rin hops up and says, "Do you wanna walk back to campus together? That's where I parked. I gotta drive back home before it gets too late."

Trina nods excessively. "Yeah, for sure."

They start the great exodus. The PR chair and tech head move closer, their conversation not yet over, but the programming director heads toward his room, dragging his blanket behind him. Percy immediately starts clearing up with Maxine, talking in hushed tones.

"We're heading out," Rin calls, and Percy immediately drops trash into Maxine's hands and rounds after them, walking them out.

Rin hops down from the porch and backs away.

"What are you doing?" Trina calls.

Rin waggles her eyebrows and swiftly turns her back on Trina, not saying a word.

"Thanks for coming tonight," Percy says.

Trina nods. "Thanks for inviting me," she says, and then, there's an awkward silence where they just stare at one another. Suddenly, she feels a little brave. She wants to tell them that she likes them, that she thinks they're the cutest person on campus, kind and funny and perfect. But. She doesn't. Instead, she says, "I think you are really cool and intimidating, and I'm really excited to be your friend."

Percy's mouth parts, and they tilt their head. Trina doesn't know them well enough to read their expression just yet, but she wants to. She wants to know them properly, so badly.

"I think you're really cool and intimidating too," Percy confesses. "You always saying no before . . . really bruised my ego, gotta admit."

"I'm sorry." Trina laughs quietly.

"Well . . . forgiven, as long as you keep coming, and . . . Will you actually text in the GroupMe instead of being a lurker?" Percy asks.

Trina snorts. "Gotta admit, I didn't even lurk, I muted it."

"Yikes, that hurts, I'm the admin of that GroupMe," Percy teases.

"It wasn't personal," Trina says, backing away and nearly tripping off the porch. She smiles one more time. "Bye." And then she runs off to join Rin, falling into step with her halfway down the block. She pretends not to see the look on Rin's face.

"So—"

"We're not close enough for this yet," Trina declares.

Rin leans in, nudging her shoulder against Trina's. "But we will be?"

Trina can't stop smiling.

Maybe.

Ruby
By Camryn Garrett

Ruby Gardner had one presentation, three papers, and a test to study for.

But all she'd managed to do this morning was get out of bed, put on her fluffy red robe, and sit at her desk. She stared at the blinking cursor on her screen. Quite frankly, she felt like she was going to cry.

It wasn't her fault; it seemed like everything was falling apart. School had always come easily to her. She was the type to sit quietly and absorb everything a teacher was saying. The type to take endless notes, to highlight everything in textbooks, the one people came to when they needed help. Somehow, between her freshman and junior years of college, that had changed. Now it felt like she was barely treading water.

The cursor blinked at her again. What was she supposed to be writing about? The relationship between Black women and labor during the nineteenth century? What kind of idea was that?

Her eye caught on the stacks of books piled up near her desk.

Right.

It had been her idea. A final paper for her capstone class. Although she wasn't a senior, Professor Higgins had taken a liking to her, and she was doing senior coursework.

Several months ago, at the start of the semester, Ruby had been excited. It was a dream to be in an advanced class. But now it seemed like a burden. Had she even retained any of the information from the books and articles and journal entries she'd spent weeks reading? How many notes had she taken that she couldn't remember?

Ruby tried to take a deep breath, but it seemed a little harder to let it in all the way. What was she going to do if she wrote this paper and it was bad? Would Professor Higgins hate her? Would juniors be barred from taking senior classes again?

She glanced down at her phone, but didn't see any messages from her friends. The only other history major she knew was a senior named Gali who she sometimes asked for notes but mostly complained with. Gali, though, wasn't answering. She was probably busy studying for midterms instead of staring at a blank screen.

God. Ruby might as well drop out of college. There was no way that she would get to all of this homework, that all of it would be good enough to keep her spot on the Dean's List, that her professors would continue to be proud of her.

She pushed herself away from the desk and sucked in a deep breath. Suddenly, her dorm room seemed too small. When the scholarship office had let her know that she'd be receiving a single in Greathouse, the upperclassman dorm, Ruby had been thrilled. But now she just felt lonely. Knotting the tie around her robe, she forced herself out into the hall, not even bothering to close the door behind her.

Unlike the dorm she'd lived in freshman year, Greathouse was actually like a gigantic house. Since most upperclassmen moved off campus, the space was separated into apartments. Instead of a tiny dorm hall, one where she could hear and smell everything, it was like stepping into a hallway in a house. Sure, she could hear the TV playing downstairs in the common room, smell the popcorn someone had burnt again. But it felt more private than Desai, the dorm she'd lived in her first year. Safer, almost. Almost like being home.

She rushed down the hall, her flip-flops flapping noisily, loud enough to embarrass her. Her friend Emma lived on the same floor. Her door was decorated with a whiteboard with her name in big purple letters and the name of her roommate, Lily, underneath. Ruby knocked on the door. She wasn't sure, but it seemed like her hand was shaking.

The door opened—yes! Emma was here. Emma would know what to do and how to fix things. She usually did.

Lily appeared in the doorway. Her eyebrows bunched in together as she took in Ruby's appearance. No doubt she was judging the hell out of Ruby's robe and flip-flops and generally disheveled appearance.

"Emma isn't here," Lily said, leaning against the doorframe. "Is everything . . . okay?"

Ruby felt herself nodding, even as she took a step back.

"Okay? Of course everything's okay." She cleared her throat. "Totally fine. Uh, when Emma comes back, tell her I was here?"

She didn't give her the chance to reply before heading toward the stairs. Lily was nice enough, but the fewer people who saw Ruby like this, the better.

The only problem was that she felt like she couldn't breathe. Ruby knew there technically wasn't anything wrong with her, but she barely made it three steps before feeling like her chest was going to explode.

She sat down on the staircase and tried to exhale. It was okay. It was all right. Somehow, she'd figure out a way to get everything done. She always did, didn't she? It didn't matter that she no longer felt the excitement she did when she'd first come to college. God, she'd been so excited to come here when she got the acceptance letter. Back then, history seemed interesting. It seemed almost like magic. It seemed unbelievable that there were so many stories and people and fights and funerals that people didn't know about. She wanted to know everything. When she was still taking AP history classes, it felt like maybe she could.

What had happened?

Ruby had no idea. The act of having to actually find things out herself, to track them down in archives and artifacts, didn't seem as magical as reading them from books. But admitting that felt . . . sad. More than embarrassing. Like she was turned off by hard work. And she, Ruby Gardner, was most definitely *not* afraid of work.

She just didn't like this kind.

"Do you need help there?"

Ruby shrieked, banging her head on the wall in the process. She winced, and someone made a hissing sound next to her. Then there was a hand on her shoulder. She blinked to see Violet, her supermodel-tall RA, looming above her. This close, Violet's messenger bag was almost touching Ruby's shoulder.

"Damn," Violet said. "That looks like it hurt."

Oh. This was embarrassing.

It was odd that the upperclassmen still had RAs, in Ruby's opinion. Sure, it made sense to have someone to guide you, help you adjust to dorm living when you were a freshman. But when you were a junior, like her? She didn't need someone to make rules for the common areas or plan events every Friday night. But here Violet was.

Anyway, it wasn't that Violet was annoying. She seemed to understand that the other occupants of Greathouse were older and didn't constantly want a babysitter checking on them. Instead of weird events like parties in her room, Violet had spa nights, and there was no pressure to stay if you didn't want to. Ruby had been to one. She'd barely said a word, leaning back with a mask on, listening to everyone chatter about their favorite shows and who was dating who on campus.

It was . . . nice.

"No," Ruby said, rubbing her forehead. "I'm fine, I think."

"Are you?"

"Yeah," Ruby said. "Of course I am. Why wouldn't I be?"

Instead of answering, Violet just raised a brow. It was bad enough that Ruby had run into an actual person while having her freak-out, but Violet also happened to be Black. Meaning that she, unlike the non-Black people in the dorm, could probably tell that Ruby's cornrows were in desperate need of rebraiding. As if that wasn't bad enough, Violet's twists looked fresh, as if she'd just walked out of a salon. Ruby wanted to sink into the floor.

"You don't have to lie, you know," Violet said. She smiled kindly. "Do you want me to get you some ice from the kitchen?"

Ruby meant to shake her head, to make an awkward goodbye and disappear back to her room. What she *didn't* mean to do was burst into tears. But that's exactly what she did.

"Oh," Violet said. "Oh shit."

"I'm sorry," Ruby said, rubbing at her face. "It's just . . ."

What was it? That studying history was nothing like she thought it would be, and she'd been ignoring that realization for more than a year? That *college* itself was nothing like she thought it would be?

She settled on "I don't know. My entire life is falling apart."

Violet blinked rapidly, eyelashes almost waving. Then something like recognition settled over her features.

"Oh," she said. "Midterms are next week."

"Well, yeah." Ruby swiped at her nose. "But everything else is fucked, too."

Violet put an arm around her shoulders and settled next to her. For a moment, all Ruby could hear was the sound of rummaging in the kitchen below, someone washing dishes. She'd been in the kitchen enough times to know they probably couldn't hear her. Still, she found herself praying that no one would decide to climb the stairs anytime soon.

"Okay," Violet said. "Everything, like what?"

"Just everything," Ruby said. "I'm probably gonna get kicked off the Dean's List, and I think I hate history but I decided to major in it, and now I'm going to graduate soon, and I don't even think that I'm going to get a job or be able to finish any of my work, probably?"

"Whoa," Violet said, eyes wide behind her glasses. "Let's take a deep breath, okay?"

She rubbed a hand on Ruby's back. The touch almost shocked her, but after a moment, it felt normal. Like Violet always rubbed her back. Ruby sucked in a breath.

"If you don't like history," Violet said, "why don't you change your major?"

Ruby laughed. "I can't."

"Why not?"

"I mean . . ." Ruby shook her head. "No one changes their major junior year."

"I'm sure lots of people do," Violet said. "I didn't choose my major until junior year."

Ruby swallowed. What if she *could* change her major? She'd disappoint her professors, maybe, but if it made her happier . . . Were things moving too fast? Or had she waited too long?

"I don't know what I like." Ruby sniffed. "That's the problem."

Violet made a humming noise.

"Well," she said after a moment. "That's what college is for, right? Finding out what you like? Maybe take some gen-eds that you're interested in. I didn't know I wanted to major in psychology until I became an RA last year."

"But what does one have to do with the other?"

"When I became an RA, I got to help people," Violet said, gently bumping her shoulder against Ruby's. "I get frustrated a lot. It seems like there are always horrible things happening all over the world and there's nothing I can do to stop it. But when I'm on duty for the night and someone needs a first aid kit or even just to talk, I feel like I'm helping. When a transfer doesn't know anyone and I help them find their group of friends, I feel like I'm having an impact. Even if it's small. Does that make sense?"

This close, Ruby could smell Violet's orange blossom perfume. She bit her lip. Violet sounded so passionate; an hour ago, Ruby wouldn't have believed that anyone actually *liked* being an RA. When was the last time Ruby had felt that way about something? She wasn't sure if she ever had.

"I can't change my major now," she said instead. "I'll be behind."

"There are summer classes," Violet said. "And, if you need, you can take another year."

Ruby rubbed her face again. She wasn't sure if her scholarship would extend more than four years. But it was worth asking, wasn't it? She could take another political science class, or maybe a class in communications.

"I wouldn't worry about the job part," Violet said. "Not to freak you out more, but it seems like we're all going to have a hard time finding work, no matter what the major."

Ruby giggled, surprising herself. "Yeah," she said. "I guess you're right."

Her throat felt less hoarse. She sniffled again, but she didn't feel any more tears coming.

"It's just weird," Ruby said. She slowly stood, wrapping her arms around her middle. "When I was a senior in high school, I had a whole plan. I was so completely sure about the future. And now that I'm here . . . I don't think I know anything."

"Yeah," Violet said. "I mean, I didn't know anything about anything in high school. But that's how it works, right? We always think we know more when we're younger."

Ruby glanced at her. Violet smiled. Her eyes crinkled when she smiled. She was beautiful. And kind. They were close. So close. If Ruby leaned in a little more, maybe, they could—

"Don't worry," Violet said, patting her on the back. "Everything will work out."

Ruby blinked as if snapping out of a dream.

"Yeah," she said, stepping away. "Um, thanks."

She'd been thinking about kissing Violet. Violet, her RA. Violet, who was a *girl*. Ruby couldn't rush back to her room fast enough.

What the hell was going on?

• • • • •

Ruby had gone to prom with a group of friends instead of a date.

She'd dated once she'd gotten to college, but not very much. She'd always been busy with her schoolwork. But she'd never dated a girl before. She hadn't thought about it. So why was she thinking about it now?

God, she hated that all of her friends were probably in class right now. Nevertheless, Ruby tossed herself on her bed, kicking her slippers off of her feet. She knew Emma would never pick up the phone. So, at risk of embarrassing herself, she called Gali.

Who didn't answer.

Ruby threw her head back and groaned loudly. When the phone finally beeped, letting her know that it was time to leave a message, she considered hanging up. But she needed to talk. If not *to* someone, then *at* someone.

"Gali," she said. "I know this is weird, really weird, but I think I might be gay? Maybe. Or not completely gay. Not fully gay. Just a little? Or maybe half? I have no idea. And I'm waiting for Quinn to get back so I can ask him, but . . . like. I don't even like my final paper idea anymore. It feels almost like I was tricking myself into liking it because I was scared. And now . . . what if I don't know anything about myself? You know?"

The words surprised her. She hadn't thought about them before they came out of her mouth, but she knew everything she'd said was true. And that was terrifying. What *if* Ruby didn't know anything about herself? She reached for her pillow and gripped it tightly in her arms.

Violet hadn't seemed to be scared of anything. To her, the idea of not knowing what you wanted to do or be wasn't a big deal at all. It must've been easier for her, though, since she had settled on a major she actually enjoyed. Ruby wasn't sure if she'd even be able to do that in her last year of college.

What would happen if she didn't? Well, she reminded herself, lots of people had degrees that had nothing to do with their jobs. Even if she picked the wrong major again . . . her future didn't have to be completely horrible. Maybe she'd find a job she liked doing, something that made her feel like she could make an impact, like being an RA did for Violet.

Ruby bit her lip. What if . . . what if she didn't have to know what job she wanted right at this moment? What if she did what Violet said? Thinking about it now, in her bed, it didn't seem so horrible. It seemed . . . hopeful. Like there were more possibilities than she'd first imagined.

She glanced back at her blinking laptop. Part of the reason why she'd settled on history was because she'd done so well on the AP exams. It was silly, but maybe the College Board website still had those quizzes that told you what job you should get.

Ruby entered the link into her browser.

The website was still familiar, almost comforting, until she started taking quizzes and the results came back.

Social work? Ruby couldn't be a social worker. She wasn't sure why she'd scored so high for psychology. She had absolutely no interest in studying why people acted the way they did. There was English, but her dad had ranted about English majors so many times during her high school years that just the word made her shiver a bit. And anyway, what job could an English major get?

Oddly enough, though, history didn't come up.

Ruby knew objectively that a bunch of quizzes on the College Board website didn't mean anything. But still.

In a rush, she opened up her email account and started typing almost manically, entering her advisor's address into the recipient line.

Her email to her academic advisor seemed frenzied, almost panicked, but didn't they always? The only difference was that now, instead of asking about classes or schedules, she was asking about changing her major entirely.

Ruby gulped. Was she really going to do this?

She flipped back to the empty tab that held her final paper. The final paper she hadn't even started working on. If she wasn't going to work on this, she had to do *something*.

What had Violet said? *Everything will work out.*

Ruby forced herself to take a deep breath, to ignore the sweatiness of her hands, and turned back to the email.

Everything will work out.

She closed her eyes and pressed send.

· · · · ·

When Gali finally called back, they didn't comfort Ruby like she thought they would.

They didn't tell Ruby that everything would be all right or that she just needed to get through finals. They didn't give Ruby a pep talk, at all, actually. Instead, they said one thing: "Damn, Ruby. You need to get laid."

"But that's it," Ruby said. "I don't feel horny."

Gali was quiet for a long moment.

"What actually happened today?"

Ruby took a deep breath and started from the beginning.

Instead of interrupting to give an opinion or laughing at Ruby's pitifulness, Gali was silent until Ruby finished. So silent that Ruby almost thought they'd hung up.

"Is this about Violet specifically?" she asked. "Or your major? Or about girls in general?"

"I don't *know*," Ruby whined. "That's the whole problem. It's everything."

"Okay," Gali said. Ruby could practically hear her scheming through the phone. "If you don't like what you're studying right now, you don't have to change your major. You could apply to grad school."

"More school?" The words burst out of Ruby before she could stop them. "Are you serious?"

"Come on," Gali said. "Don't act like you hate school."

If Ruby thought about it, she knew she didn't *hate* college. She loved the small group of quirky friends she'd managed to create, Gali included. She loved being alone, having a room to herself, getting to decide what she'd eat for dinner or how late she could stay out—but also loved that she didn't have to worry about health insurance or retirement, like a real adult. She loved UMB, with its grassy hills and nicknames for buildings and its weird history. Even if she was stressed about not knowing who she was, she knew she loved school.

"Plus," Gali said, "one thing at a time, right?"

• • • • •

At first, Ruby thought about asking Violet out for a date. But it only took a few quick swipes through her Instagram feed to see that she already had a boyfriend. So now, a day later, she was sitting in a corner of The Last Drop instead of studying for midterms, waiting for a new girl Gali had set her up with.

Ruby couldn't stop tapping her foot against the floor. The Last Drop was a cozy coffee shop Ruby normally loved to spend time in, but today it seemed to be packed with students with open laptops and textbooks in every available seat or reading nook.

Just another reminder that Ruby basically had no idea where her future was. But, you know, no pressure at all.

She glanced down at her phone again. The date was for noon, but it was fifteen minutes past already, and there was still no sign of the girl. Not that Ruby actually knew what she looked like. All she knew was that Gali had a few classes with her and that they were supposed to meet by the comfy beanbag chairs in the corner.

Ruby sighed. This was probably a sign that she needed to get up and go do some actual work. Did it matter that she didn't feel passionate about history anymore? It wasn't like most adults felt passionate about their work, right? Maybe yesterday had just been a normal breakdown. Not something worth changing her entire life over.

Maybe she didn't even like girls. Violet had been there when no one else would. She'd listened. Ruby had probably just been happy to have someone there.

She'd just gathered her iced tea and bag when the door swung open. In walked a girl with brown skin, a septum piercing, and purple-tinged locs. Ruby had barely begun to stand up when the girl walked over to her.

"Hey," she said, eyes sweeping over Ruby's hands. "I'm not that late, am I?"

Ruby bit her lip. Technically, the other girl was late, but not by an annoying amount. And she was pretty. Very, very pretty. It was just that Ruby couldn't tell if she wanted to *be* her or be *with* her. It was quite confusing.

"No," Ruby said. "You're not too late, at all."

"Awesome." The girl stuck her hand out. It was covered with silver rings. "I'm Fran."

"I'm Ruby," she said, shaking Fran's hand. It was dry, unlike hers.

"Cool," Fran said, actually grinning. "Do you wanna sit?"

The next two hours flew by in a blur. It turned out that Fran was amazing. She was studying biomedical engineering because she wanted to make cool prosthetics. She was from Portland, in Maine, which—Ruby didn't even know there were Black people from Maine, really. She was minoring in Russian "just because."

Ruby couldn't stop making heart eyes, and she wasn't even embarrassed about it.

"Wait, no, Josefina was the best."

"I'm sorry, but you're mistaken." Fran counted on her hands. "Kit Kittredge was not only a badass journalist, but she was an entrepreneur and clearly a lesbian."

"I thought you were anticapitalist?"

"I am," Fran said, trying not to smile. "But it was the Depression, Ruby. She had to help her family survive somehow."

Ruby grinned goofily at her.

"What?" Fran leaned back. "What did I say?"

"Nothing." Ruby shook her head. "Just . . . nothing."

After tea, they walked around the quad, deep in conversation. Normally, Ruby was overwhelmed by how beautiful the quad was. She liked to sit out there and just listen to other people's conversations sometimes. As much as she was confused about her major and her future, she knew she'd made a good choice with this school.

Today, though, she wasn't paying attention to the quad.

"Is it messed up that neither of us are vouching for the only Black American Girl doll?" she asked, mostly joking. "What does that say about us?"

"I mean, Addy is . . . fine . . ." Fran made a face. "And I think there's a new Black girl, anyway."

Ruby laughed. "I think it's too late for us."

"That it is." Fran paused. "Other lesbian American Girls. Go."

"Okay," Ruby said. "Uh, definitely Felicity. Samantha—"

"Samantha?"

"Of course!" Ruby laughed. "Fuck, Fran," she said, the words bubbling up before she could think about them. "You're so fucking cool."

Fran smiled a little, suddenly seeming shy.

"Yeah?" she said. "You think so?"

Suddenly, Fran seemed vulnerable for the first time all afternoon. Ruby didn't think, she just reached her hand out. Fran glanced at it for half of a second, but it seemed to last longer, stretching out in Ruby's mind. Had she made the wrong move? Was she reading this all wrong?

Fran reached out and grabbed Ruby's hand. Fran's was clammy now.

"Samantha Parkington is most definitely *not* gay," Fran said haughtily. "Nellie, on the other hand . . ."

Ruby snorted. Fran's hand was still in hers, clammy and small and somehow perfect. How had this happened in one afternoon?

They spent the rest of the afternoon like that, walking around the quad, hands swinging. Ruby didn't notice the slight chill in the air left over from the winter. She didn't notice anything but Fran. Her chest felt like it was full of bubbles. In a really good way. Maybe she wasn't straight. Maybe she wouldn't stay a history major. But it probably didn't mean it was the end of the world.

Her phone buzzed against her thigh. With the hand not holding Fran's, she pulled it out to see she had a new email from her advisor.

"*Maybe* Molly is gay," Fran was saying. "I'm still on the fence when it comes to her."

Ruby studied the notification. If she opened it now, she'd have to face the future head-on, have to examine all of the paths available and try to pick one.

"I don't know," Fran said. "What do you think?" She met Ruby's eyes and smiled.

Here was Fran, solid and sure and stunning. Ruby barely knew her, but the lack of knowledge didn't scare her when it came to Fran. It wasn't terrifying. It was exciting. Ruby shoved her phone back in her pocket. She'd deal with the email later.

"Ruby?" Fran cocked her head to the side. "Don't tell me you're one of those people who's *obsessed* with Molly for some reason. I don't get it."

Ruby couldn't help but grin. Right now, she couldn't see herself writing a thesis about a specific time in history or working in an office, but she could see herself doing this. Holding Fran's hand and walking somewhere. That, at least, felt crystal clear.

Momo's Epic Rescue
By Boon Carmen

It's 7:29 a.m. when Eliza's enraged shriek echoes through her bedroom door into the hallway of our tiny apartment.

I allow myself one mouthful of cereal before the peaceful interlude of my breakfast is interrupted.

Eliza thunders out a minute later, shoving her phone in my face. "See what that bastard sent?"

That bastard is Dan Carter, Eliza's asshole boyfriend.

Maybe Dan's suggesting another break. They've had this weird on-off relationship that flicks both ways uselessly like a faulty light switch for quite a while now. I always have to pick up the pieces he breaks.

Right now, though, I can barely make out the blurry gray and blue chat bubbles hovering an inch away. "No."

She retreats slightly with a grumble. "How about now?"

Dan's text reads: *I can't do this anymore. It's over, Eliza. For good this time.* Beneath are the apt beginnings of Eliza's reply: *GO TO HELL—*

"How . . . articulate."

"That's not—" Eliza's hands curl into tiny fists of rage. "Sophie. He broke up with me. Over *text*." She paces back and forth, running a hand through her tangled blond hair. Her eyes are wild and bloodshot—I can't tell if it's because she's crying or if she just skipped straight past denial into murderous rage fresh out of hell. "I'm gonna kill him," she seethes.

I blink, not believing my ears. Their relationship had its fair share of ups and downs, but Eliza thought the world of Dan. Sure, he's a bit of a douche. But enough to kill? No way. This has to be her way of grieving.

Whatever's going on inside her head, it's not for me to judge—even if I'm relieved that Dan's out of the picture once and for all. Hopefully.

I don't tell Eliza that, of course. "We don't condone murder in this house," I tell her dutifully instead, reaching for my phone.

She scowls. "Don't tell me what I can't do."

"No, I mean you couldn't kill him even if you wanted to." I swipe onto Dan's Instagram page, showing Eliza his story. "He's at his family's beach house. Hosting 'the most epic party of spring break' with the booze-happy party boys of Kappa Zeta Epsilon and the university soccer team. Everyone's invited, apparently." I grimace. "Well, not us."

Eliza snatches my phone out of my hands. "Dan didn't block you? I can't see any of his socials!" She taps violently at my screen, her lower lip curling in distaste. "Of course he runs off to his cushy little palace before dumping me. He gets to wash his hands of me and enjoy spring break while I deal with *this*. You'd think he'd have the common decency to talk to me in person, at least. But *no*, he goes to the *beach house*." She drops my phone on the table, her eyes widening upon a sudden realization. "Oh my god. He has Momo."

After fifteen seconds of thoughtful chewing, Momo's identity jumps to the forefront of my consciousness.

I squint at Eliza. "Momo the red panda? The plush red panda?"

She's thoroughly panicked now, her breaths shallow and erratic. "WE HAVE TO RESCUE MOMO."

"It's an eight-hour drive," I point out.

"I'll drive."

"What about our spring break plans? We're supposed to watch *The Princess Bride* under a pile of blankets while scarfing down a never-ending flow of unhealthy snacks, remember?"

"I'll make it up to you," Eliza says, her eyes sparking with determination. "Come on, Soph, it'll be fun. A proper road trip, which is a way more authentic college spring break experience than staying in all week like we've done the past two years. Junior year can be the year we *finally* go on a real adventure. Just you and me. Eliza Young and Sophie Zhao—roommates turned best friends turned explorers of America's highways. Come to think of it, that's a pretty good premise for a series." She perks up in her seat, her eyes bright. "What do you say, Soph? Get in a car and drive to the edge of the country with me?"

Well . . . she does have a point. I haven't been in the United States that long. A road trip doesn't sound so bad. I could get off campus and have some fun like an actual tourist, even. The quintessential American college adventure.

As if she can sense my crumbling defenses, Eliza leans in with a devilish grin, lifting her car keys from the table with a cheery jingle. "And besides," she adds slyly, "once we get Momo back, watching all those movies will be so much cuddlier with that ball of fluff between us."

"Eliza," I sigh.

She flashes her dimples and grasps my hands. "Sophie."

I freeze, my mind emptying at her touch as my spoon clatters in my bowl. My breath catches, and I can almost swear my vocal cords elicit something that sounds an awful lot like a squeak. I want to slap myself, but Eliza's holding my hands, and I can't bring myself to pull away—so really, what I should do is just say yes, because I couldn't say no to her even if I wanted to.

She squeezes my fingers again, smiling that smile she knows I can't resist.

"Fine," I grumble. "For Momo."

Eliza squeals, her cheeks glowing and her eyes shining bright. "Thank you so much," she gushes, wrapping me in a bear hug. "I promise you won't regret this." She flounces back to her room, leaving me flustered.

"I'm regretting it already," I call after her once I retrieve my quivering voice from its hiding spot.

Her voice is muffled through the door. "You love me anyway!"

All of a sudden I'm glad she isn't there across the table. My cheeks burn, and my breath catches. I sit there like an idiot, staring after my best friend, roommate, and *oh, I don't know*, person I kinda sorta have feelings for.

Damn Eliza Young for knowing exactly which buttons to press.

· · · · ·

We've passed at least two state lines when Eliza interrupts the background noise of *Red (Taylor's Version)*. The album, not the song, because one doesn't simply listen to a single Taylor Swift song without going into a spiral begging for the rest.

"Are you mad at me?" she asks, her voice strangely muted.

I look up from my psych textbook as she quickly returns her gaze to the open road. "I could never be mad at you."

"You haven't said a word since we left UMB."

"I told you before that Dr. Moore loves torturing his students, didn't I?" I ask, holding my book up as the reason for my silence. I rub at my eyes, feeling a pulsing behind them. "I can bet my monthly salary he's gonna spring a surprise pop quiz once break is over. You know I don't study of my own free will."

Eliza shakes her head, her space buns bouncing energetically like bunny ears. "That's exactly why I can't believe you're studying."

"I have a scholarship to keep," I remind her, rubbing my throbbing temples. Serves me right for reading in a moving car, I guess.

"It's spring break. We should be relaxing." She turns to me slightly, her brow furrowed. "You're really not angry I roped you into an eight-hour road trip to rescue a plush toy?"

Well, when she puts it like that . . .

"I'm not mad." I mark my spot with a McDonald's receipt before shutting my textbook. A change in scenery would ease the motion sickness and give me a break from all those words. On the plus side, I get to talk to Eliza. Alone. I don't get to do that often on campus, considering, outside of Dan and me, she has a whole group of friends who play board games all the time and have weekly movie nights. Eliza's always either at their place or has them over at ours. They're nice—they often invite me to join them, but I rarely do because I'm not a group person. So the only time Eliza and I get to really hang out—just the two of us—is during rare moments, whether that's work at the bookshop, or late nights in our apartment.

Win-win for me, I suppose. She's all I've got, and I'm happy with what I have. It doesn't matter if it can't be more.

"Am I disappointed?" I prattle on, pretending to ponder her earlier question. "A little. Especially since I have to be trapped in your car for eight consecutive hours, but who's counting?"

Eliza swats at me. "Be serious, Soph. Really." She tries giving me a meaningful look, but her lips twitch as she struggles to hold back a laugh. "How do you feel?"

I can't tell her how I feel. Not really. But I can offer her a sliver of truth.

"I'm just glad I'm with you," I say, forcing an easy smile. That alone is enough to overshadow the irritation directed at Dan for ruining our plans. But since Eliza wants Momo back, we're getting Momo back. I pretend to be annoyed, but the truth is, I'm a little fond of that floofy fella, too.

She smiles back at me, perfectly oblivious to my inner turmoil. "I'm glad you're here too."

Before I can say anything, Eliza's phone rings, cutting through the chorus of "We Are Never Ever Getting Back Together (Taylor's Version)." I grab it and answer without bothering to look at the caller ID.

"Eliza's phone," I chirrup.

"Is it Dan?" Eliza asks, shooting me a sideways look. "If so, tell him he's in for an ass whooping when I get there—wait, don't tell him that. I don't want to give him a head start."

Even though they've broken up, he's always lurking somewhere in her subconscious. I could never get her to think about anyone else for long. Not even me.

I'd entirely forgotten about the person on the other line,

jumping at the sound of their confused voice through the tiny speaker pressed against my ear. "I beg your pardon?"

Oh, shit.

I slam my palm over the microphone. "It's your mother," I whisper to Eliza in a panic.

"Oh, *shit.*"

I quickly put Eliza's mother on speaker. "Hi, Mrs. Young!" I say too cheerfully, wincing at the sound of my voice.

She doesn't buy it for a second. "Who's getting an ass whooping?"

"Nobody, Mom!" Eliza shrieks.

"Eliza Young, tell me what you're doing right this instant," her mother commands through the phone's tiny speaker.

"Nothing suspicious," Eliza says immediately.

She's really not making things any better for herself, I think to myself, unable to hold back an affectionate smile. Classic Eliza.

To make matters worse, a car honks at us, speeding past in a blur. Eliza swerves out of the way with a curse, raising a hand to wave a rude gesture at the quickly disappearing vehicle.

"Are you driving?" her mother asks sharply. "Eliza, where are you? Shouldn't you be at the apartment with Sophie?"

Eliza groans. "Mom, you're breaking up," she shouts, making static noises through gritted teeth. "What—kssssh—Mom—"

"I can hear you just fine, Eliza—"

"Call you back!" Eliza shrieks, slamming her finger against the red icon on the screen to hang up on her own mother.

I stare at Eliza for a hot second, in awe and also in slight terror. "You've officially lost it," I tell her. If I'd done that with my mother, I'd be a fugitive.

"What did you expect me to do, tell the truth?" she shoots back, her chest heaving. "Oh my god, she's gonna kill me."

"Let me handle this," I tell her, using my phone to text her mom.

"Wait, what? What are you gonna tell her?" Eliza stares at me for so long that the car drifts out of lane, and it's only because of my shrill scream and the oncoming vehicle's honk that she jerks at the steering wheel, getting us back on track. She continues to stare, her hands firmly fixed at ten and two. "Well?" she presses.

I stare at Eliza, my heart galloping a thunderous beat—from fear of almost dying, and something else. "*Eyes on the road*," I get out.

She does as she's told, but I catch the way her eyes dart to me between seconds. "Sophie," she says breathlessly, "what are you going to say?"

"The truth." I twist in my seat and hold my phone up to take a selfie of us. "Say cheese."

Eliza automatically holds up two fingers in a peace sign with a perfect smile. "The *truth*?" she asks, her toothy grin frozen in place.

I take the picture and send it to her mother.

"With some omissions," I say reassuringly, patting her on the thigh. "Relax. Nothing about Dan. I'm saying plans have changed because you, being the awesome roommate that you are, finally convinced me to get out of the apartment, and that you're taking me on an all-American road trip of epic cultural proportions. I'm painting you as the unlikely saint—she'll be so shocked she won't be able to think of anything else to scold you about."

"Oh, thank god. I thought we were done for." She sighs in relief, the dimples returning to her cheeks when she grins at me. "Have I ever told you you're my favorite person in the world?"

"Flattery will get you nowhere. I'm only here for moral support."

"I thought you were doing this for Momo."

"I'm supporting Momo through the custody battle," I tell her, retrieving a packet of gummy bears from my bag. "It just so happens I'm also keeping you in check."

Eliza cackles, tipping her head back. I can't help but grin, my whole body loose and relaxed. I recline in my seat, appreciating the view—the way that stray lock of hair curls under her ear, how her cheeks flush from laughter, and the life that just surges in her every time she smiles.

God, she's beautiful.

"I knew I liked you for a reason," she says. "Choosing to live with you is by far the best decision I've ever made."

It's like a thousand butterflies erupt inside me. They flutter and swarm their way up my throat to the point of discomfort, and I just know that if I don't do something quick, I'll open my mouth and say something I can't take back.

So I kill the mood and think about Eliza almost killing us. Another thing to be mad at Dan for. "I can't believe I nearly died on a random road in America," I mutter into my phone. "I don't know how you got your license."

"Excuse me, would you like to drive the rest of the way?" she asks, a brow arched high.

"Moral support doesn't drive. Also, what maniac system drives on the right?"

Eliza doesn't even blink. "Anywhere that doesn't drive on the left."

Can't argue with that logic.

I scroll through Dan's Instagram profile again, chewing on a gummy bear while Eliza revels in her tiny victory. The party has come alive—there are people in the kitchen, the living room, the hot tub. Solo cups are in every picture—no doubt filled with alcohol courtesy of Kappa Zeta Epsilon's notorious drinking habits—and there's also a grainy video of someone hauling in a keg, much to everyone's cheers.

I think I recognize a girl from my lectures who's in one of UMB's sororities. A quick look at her tagged pictures tells me that she arrived with her fellow sorority members on a rented bus.

Huh. I guess Dan's party must be a bigger deal than I thought, if people are willing to rent a bus just to attend. I return to Dan's page, which is now filled with pictures of what look like his old high school friends and UMB soccer teammates.

Eliza clears her throat, interrupting my stealthy sleuthing. "What's he doing?" She tries to sound nonchalant, but her body movements give her away. Her fingers drum against the steering wheel, and her left leg bounces erratically.

I tap on his latest post. "Posing next to a giant inflatable swan." I don't mention the girls in bikinis on either side of him. If I want to survive this trip, I need her calm and tranquil. White lies are necessary for the greater good.

"Ugh." Her knuckles turn white. "I should've brought a needle. Come to think of it, why didn't I toss his shit out before we left? The dude had a freaking drawer in my room, Soph."

I lower my phone, adjusting my seat belt so I can face her properly. "Eliza."

"Yep."

"Can I ask you something?"

"Shoot."

"It's about Dan," I say slowly, watching her lips—*stop looking at her lips*—twist into a frown. "What did you see in him in the first place?"

Her jaw drops. "Et tu, Brute? Kicking me while I'm down?"

"No! No. I'm just . . . curious."

For several painful, stretched-out seconds, we ride in the quiet background music of Taylor Swift.

"I don't know," Eliza says at last.

I raise an eyebrow at her, biting off a gummy bear's head. "You were together for nine months."

"That's not what I meant. Look, I—when things were good, they were great." She shrugs, her voice taking on a melancholy tone. "We'd have dinner dates at Aesop's, go on these long drives. Just getting away from all the *noise*, you know? Kappa Zeta Epsilon can be so loud sometimes." Her voice trails off, and I watch her as she stares into the distance.

"But the bad parts . . . God, they were horrible. We were always arguing about the littlest things. Movies, sports, songs, hobbies— you name it, we couldn't agree on it. He'd always argue that his choices were superior to mine. And it's always me who has to compromise, to put aside my tastes to accommodate his.

"Dan would always make it up to me afterward, though. He's really good at that. And at least I always had you there to cheer me up at the end of the day." Eliza smiles softly at me. "You're always there," she murmurs, her gaze turning distant.

I never knew she felt that way. For as long as I've known her, she's always been this bright spot in my life—the one place I could go whenever things felt dark. I hadn't thought about how she might've needed some light of her own.

Eliza shrugs more energetically this time, her pensive mood lifting in an instant. "And besides, Dan's got that thing about him that just attracts everyone to him, you know? He's magnetic. Funny, charming . . . not to mention stupid hot."

"Emphasis on stupid," I mutter, watching Dan do a handstand

by the pool's slippery edge on his latest Instagram post. "It's a miracle he's survived this long."

Eliza barks a laugh, her shoulders shaking violently as she struggles to keep her hands steady on the steering wheel.

"Stop making me laugh, Soph," she gasps, placing a hand against her chest. "If you keep this up, I'm gonna ask you to sit in the back. I can't focus straight with you around."

I stare at her for a few heart-stopping moments, my mouth turning dry.

Eliza doesn't seem to notice how I've gone silent.

I wait for her to say something. Anything. My mind has run out of comprehensible thoughts, and all that's left is this little screensaver icon drifting in the vast emptiness of my head without a single corner in sight. I can't even focus on the decapitated gummy bear between my fingers that's getting stickier by the second.

"Hey, Sophie?"

I straighten in my seat. "Yeah?" I answer too quickly, and I kick myself for sounding so eager.

Eliza licks her lips. "Do you think I'm crazy?" she asks quietly. No matter how much I tilt and twist my neck, she won't look at me. "Driving over five hundred miles just to rescue a plush toy?"

I didn't expect her to ask me *that*.

"That depends. Do you want affirmation or common sense?"

I can't help but grin when she laughs.

"Sophie," she chastises, but she smiles at me all the same. "I just wanna know what my best friend thinks."

"Okay, okay. Just, give me a moment." I stare out the window, letting green wash over my vision. "So," I begin slowly, nibbling on the gummy bear, "your relationship just came to an abrupt end. This is you dealing with it."

"But it feels a bit much, don't you think?" she asks, pursing her lips. "I know I can come off as intense sometimes, but this feels like a whole new level, even for me. And you said it yourself, you're here to keep me and my emotions in check. Don't get me wrong, I'm glad you're here—there's no one I'd rather be with. You keep me grounded, and I love you for that. I just don't want you to feel like you have to baby me the whole time."

Don't think about how she said I love you, I tell myself. "I was joking when I said that," I say instead. "Eliza, I'm here because I want to, okay? And emotions are fine. I'd be concerned if you weren't hurt. Though I'm a little worried about the degree of anger you've been displaying, but that's not relevant here."

"You don't see this as the slightest bit excessive?" Eliza questions. "You, Sophie Zhao, voice of impeccable reason, don't see even the teensiest red flag?"

"Please don't tell me you're having second thoughts," I whine. "I didn't spend the past two and a half hours getting motion sickness just for you to turn back around."

She points an accusing finger at me. "I told you not to read in the car!"

"Not relevant. Look, if you need more motivation to go through with this, I'm happy to help. Dan Carter doesn't deserve to bask in the presence of the glorious Momo," I tell her. "You fought all the time. You were always breaking up and getting back together. He's a horrible texter. Never eats pizza crust, which might not seem that serious compared to the others, but trust me—it's a red flag. And he hates rom-coms." I cross my arms with a scowl. "He's such a dick. I'm seriously starting to question your taste in men."

Eliza rolls her eyes, giving me a lopsided smile. "You're lucky

I'm letting that slide because I like you so much." She looks back to the road. "But you're right."

"Say again?"

"You're right," she repeats, rolling her eyes good-naturedly. "Dan's a dick."

"A monumental dick," I tell her.

"So monumental they could erect one in his honor."

"That's if they can even get it up, though."

Eliza snorts. "And they say life imitates art."

· · · · ·

After almost six hours on the road, Eliza declares that she needs an urgent pee break, zooming into the next petrol station we come across. She practically sprints into the store, leaving me to fill the car on my own.

She waves me in once she's finished, tossing me the keys to the restroom when I enter.

"Get whatever you want after you're done," she tells me, digging through her pockets. "My treat." Eliza frowns. "As soon as I find my wallet."

The lady behind the counter watches us with an amused smile. She leans forward on her elbows, her eyes twinkling with interest.

I draw her wallet from my jacket and hand it over to Eliza. "You left this in the car."

She grins sheepishly. "Thanks."

I duck my head when I brush past, flashing a small smile at the nice lady at the counter.

"You girls on a road trip?" she asks Eliza. She seems like the kind of person who chats up customers to get interesting stories out of them. Goose bumps rise on my skin, and I feel the sudden urge to hide. The restroom sounds like the perfect place to do so.

Eliza hums under her breath. "Er. Sort of? We—"

The rest of her reply fades into the background as I walk deeper into the store. By the time I walk back out with an empty bladder, the two have become very chatty friends.

"This is Sophie, my best friend in the whole wide world," Eliza says. "Sophie, meet Amina. Amina, meet Sophie."

My hand rises limply to wave. "Hi."

Amina smiles warmly at me. She has nice nails—a mint green that complements her dark skin perfectly. "Nice to meet you, Sophie. Eliza tells me you're both from UMB. That's a long way from here."

My grin starts to peel off my face. "Yeah." I drift to the shelves, spotting a pack of citrus gummy bears.

Amina shifts her attention to Eliza. "Oh, you should stop by Talla's Diner right after your exit. You said you're going to the coast, right?"

Oh, look. The fridge has Jell-O cups. I gotta get some.

"Yep," Eliza replies easily.

"What's at the coast, anyway? Seems pretty urgent, if you're willing to drive over five hundred miles for it."

I knew it! I have to hand it to Amina—she sure knows how to pull a story out of someone.

"Um." Eliza pauses, possibly realizing this too late. "My ex-boyfriend's beach house."

Oh, Eliza.

Amina seems to have the same idea. "Seriously?"

Eliza gets defensive. "I'm just getting Momo back."

I spare a glance over my shoulder. Amina looks confused.

"Momo the red panda plush," Eliza elaborates.

"Girl, you're telling me you're willing to drive five hundred miles for a stuffed animal? Just because your ex has it? You need to go to the lost and found, because that's where your dignity is."

Eliza's voice is taut. "I'm getting Momo back."

Amina nods, unconvinced. "Sure. If that's what you keep telling yourself."

"Actually, we're going to vandalize his house."

Two heads swivel around to stare at me like I've lost it. For good reason. I hadn't even realized the words left my mouth until Eliza mouths, *What?*

Oh, well. I've already begun digging my grave. Might as well make it six feet deep.

"Eliza's being way too modest," I say, grabbing four Jell-O cups before shutting the fridge door. "By the way, do you have any eggs? Toilet paper's too expensive."

Amina blinks. Once. Twice. "Eggs?"

I mime throwing an egg, saying "*boom*" as a sound effect for a mini explosion.

Eliza stares at me wide-eyed.

Amina's flabbergasted look slowly shifts into awe. "Eggs," she echoes again. "Right. Um." She looks around, running a hand through her braids. "We have a whole carton, but they're not that fresh. Here." Amina reaches down under the counter to retrieve it—there's a dozen eggs in there.

It's my turn to blink. "I didn't think gas stations actually sold eggs."

Amina chuckles. "Welcome to the highway." She pushes the carton forward. "Here. On the house."

"Seriously?" I approach the counter cautiously, where Eliza has yet to take her eyes off me.

"I'm always a supporter of the occasional scorned woman who walks through these doors," Amina replies lightly. She takes the snacks from my arms to scan them. "That'll be twenty-five dollars for the rest."

I do the mental math, converting from dollars to ringgit by multiplying by four-point-something-something. *Holy shit, that's a lot.* Even after almost three years in the United States, I still do a double take at the price differences.

"Actually, I don't need that many Jell-O cups," I start, but Eliza thrusts her card past my face at Amina.

"It's all right," she says. "My treat, remember?"

Eliza pays and walks out the door with our—well, mostly my—snacks, wearing a stunned look. She's forgotten the eggs, though.

Amina doesn't say anything. She just nudges the egg carton forward with a knowing smile.

I can only laugh nervously as I grab the eggs and run after Eliza.

· · · · ·

Nothing particularly noteworthy happens for the rest of the ride.

Eliza's mother checks in every hour, and Eliza keeps inventing new stories (i.e., excuses) to fill an anthology of lies. I guess it's a good thing I decided to become roommates and eventually best friends with an English major. I should count my lucky stars that we were assigned the same shift at the university bookshop three years ago—but not so much because Eliza met Dan there, too. I've been playing the third wheel ever since.

We reach the beach house after sunset, the bass beat pumping through the base of my sneakers and vibrating against the soles of my feet. The party's colorful lights and lively chatter across the street are impossible to miss.

Eliza turns off the car engine, her hands drifting to remove her seat belt. But something stops her in her tracks, and she freezes.

"You can do this," I tell her.

"Can I, though?" She twists around to face me. "This is insane, Soph. I just drove five hundred miles over a plush toy."

I shrug. "Is it really about the plush toy?"

Eliza sighs, reaching up to tighten her droopy space buns. "Please don't psychoanalyze me."

"Just think about Dan's flaws again. He doesn't eat pizza crust. Doesn't like romantic comedies. Thought his taste was superior. Possesses the worst communication skills on earth. A possible dead zone, which might just explain his atrocious texting."

She laughs, the only clear thing amidst the muffled sounds of the party outside. "All the deal breakers of our relationship," she says to herself, smiling sadly.

I don't like it when she gets sad.

Eliza's bright. Vibrant. The kind of person who automatically brings life to the people around her.

"Let's go rescue Momo," I say abruptly, opening the car door into the liquor-fueled pandemonium of Dan's spring break party.

Eliza joins me soon after, bouncing beside me on the balls of her feet.

"Do you want me to go with you?" I ask.

"You don't like being around a lot of people," she replies, giving me a knowing look. "It's okay. Just wait for me here."

Eliza squeezes my hand once, then walks away. I watch until she disappears into the crowd of noisy young adults, feeling suddenly empty inside even as the party's volume goes up a notch.

Shrieks and shouts fill the house all the way down to the coastline, where people wave sparklers at each other in the darkness. A cheer rises not too far from me, and I tilt my head to the right just in time to see someone catapult into the pool in what might just be their birthday suit.

All this chaos makes me want to get in the car and drive away as fast as possible. The sooner, the better. I just need to wait for Eliza to return with Momo, and then we can run away together.

Oh, forget it. My best friend's entering enemy territory. I can't possibly let her go alone. We've spent the last eight hours on the road together—I'm going to be by her side to the end of it.

I retrieve the eggs from the backseat and rush after her, narrowly avoiding getting run over by some dude in a convertible. But the closer I get to the party, the more my heart thuds in my chest, and my brain starts whispering frantically in my head that *this is not a good idea in the slightest*.

But still I run, all the way to Dan's driveway. I stop next to his scarlet red Chevy.

This earns me a few weird looks, probably for holding a carton of eggs, but no one gives me grief over it.

This is America. I'm sure eggs aren't the weirdest things someone's ever brought to a party.

Eliza's in the belly of the beast. Any time now, she's going to emerge from the front door with Momo in her arms, and then we can get the hell out of here.

But nothing's going my way today, it seems.

She storms out of the front door carrying the three-foot-long fluffy red panda plush aptly named Momo. Behind her, Dan pushes his way through the crowd with a bottle in hand, shouting unintelligibly over the thumping bass. From a distance, I can see that he's wet all over, and it looks like he's just pulled on a pair of shorts—wait a minute, was that him catapulting naked into the pool?

Never mind about that. I look at Eliza again, and my heart lifts at the sight of her. Our mission to rescue Momo is officially a success, and now we can leave. I meet her halfway in the middle of the driveway, and she doesn't realize I'm standing right in front of her until I say her name.

She jumps a foot in the air, clutching Momo to her chest. "Sophie? What are you doing here?"

"Moral support," I say blankly, as if that wasn't clear.

Eliza laughs breathlessly. "Thanks, Soph, but we gotta get the hell out of here before Dan catches up."

I wince. "Too late."

She spins around, a venomous look taking hold of her features in an instant. "I want nothing to do with you," she snaps.

He holds his hands up drunkenly, a half-empty bottle of beer hanging loosely from his fingers. "You drove over, didn't you?"

Eliza's cheeks redden. She steps forward, eyes flashing. "Listen, Dan. Get it in your empty skull that your stupid face is the last thing I want to see. I have no interest in ever being in the same room as you again, much less breathing the same air you do. I came here for Momo."

Dan isn't of the right mind to be offended. This explains his bolder-than-usual streak of senselessness. "Oh, come on, Liz," he drawls. "It's a party. Chill out."

"Chill out?" Eliza echoes, her eyes practically bulging out of her eye sockets.

"No hard feelings?" Dan suggests, swaying drunkenly. "Join us, live a little. Hell, you're invited too, Sophie," he says, spotting me over Eliza's shoulder. He turns to Eliza again. "We can still be friends, right? We're adults."

Eliza continues to stare at him in silent fury, her cheeks an angry red by now. Any redder, and she'll be a tomato. "You've got to be kidding me," she finally says. "You dumped me over text, and you think we can just go back to being friends? What the hell do you take me for, a fucking doormat?"

"Do you want me to apologize?" he asks, painfully unaware of the impending nuclear meltdown. "Because I will, if that's what you want."

"You can shove your apologies right up your ass," Eliza tells him curtly. "I don't care. You're a waste of my time. You always have been. I should thank you for relieving me of my burden."

"Eliza," I say firmly. "Let's go."

"You want to know why I broke it off?" Dan asks, his eyes gaining some semblance of clarity. "Because you're never there. Not for any of my games, or anything with my friends. I'm so sick of you not participating with us every single time we get toget—"

An egg slams right onto his forehead, dripping runny yolk all over his shell-shocked—hah, egg pun!—face.

The party comes to a complete standstill. Even the music stops.

Eliza turns slowly to look at me, openmouthed, and that's when I realize everyone's staring at me now. Because I just threw a raw egg at Dan Carter's face.

I spot the telltale white cellphone lights in the dark that mean numerous people are recording us right now.

Oh, boy.

"We have to go," Eliza declares, hooking her arm through mine and pulling me away.

I look at her accusingly. "Oh, *now* you want to go?"

"*I* didn't throw a goddamn egg in his face! Quick, before he snaps out of it!" She tugs harder, dragging me to the road.

And that's when disaster strikes.

Eliza trips and falls. Which shouldn't really be a problem, except for the fact that our arms are linked, and the egg carton isn't covered when it flies out of my hands.

Everything happens in slow motion, in this weird bubble of time that only comes at the end of the world.

All the eggs land—crash, more like—unceremoniously onto the hood of Dan's car. The previously gleaming, beautiful, *clean* car.

I don't move from where I've landed on top of Eliza, simply staring at the gooey mess for a few heart-stopping moments. Momo is squished between our bodies.

"Oh, crap," Eliza breathes. Her hand is on my bare hip, a warm contrast to the cool spring air around us.

Dan has wiped enough egg from his face to finally see what happened to his car. Judging from his expression, you'd think I brutally murdered his entire family in front of him with a butcher's knife.

He screams. Actually, full on, screams.

"Time to go," Eliza yelps.

We run back to the car in a frenzy. I jump into the passenger seat, promptly surprised when I find the steering wheel in front of me.

"*FUCK!*" I scream as Eliza clambers into the actual passenger seat, tossing Momo behind us.

Why, why, why do Americans have to drive on the right—

"Just drive!" Eliza shrieks.

I do as I'm told, awkwardly twisting the key in the ignition as the engine roars to life. I don't know how I manage to not kill anyone getting out of Eliza's haphazard parallel parking, but I pull it off.

"*Gogogogogogogogogo,*" Eliza blabbers while I drive according to the speed limit. "Before he catches us!"

I jam my foot on the accelerator just as Dan Carter runs in front of the car, trying to stop us. *NO!* My foot fumbles between the accelerator and the brake moments before we slam right into him.

The car skids to a stop two seconds later, but two seconds too late.

We're surrounded by dozens of still-recording cameras, and possibly a dead body on the road before us. Pin-drop silence falls, interrupted by the mental monologue of my brain going *fuckfuck-fuckfuckfuckfuck—*

After a sufficient amount of time for everyone to accumulate enough evidence to convict me, Eliza clears her throat. "Did you just run over my ex?"

. . . . .

Dan's not dead. Thankfully. His arm is broken, that's all. At the very least, I won't be charged with manslaughter. As long as he lives through the night, I might be able to escape seeing the inside of a jail cell.

Eliza talks to him in his hospital room while I wait outside, carrying Momo for emotional support. I resist the urge to eavesdrop on their hushed conversation.

A nurse smiles at me. "Is the toy for a patient?" they ask.

I clutch Momo closer to my chest. "Um. No."

"Oh."

Eliza pokes her head out of the room. "Oh, hi, can I ask you something?"

The nurse nods brightly, eager to abandon me. "Yes."

While they talk, I tiptoe into Dan's room and peek over Momo's fluffy head.

"I can see you, Sophie," Dan says wryly. His voice is clear now, no longer sluggish from the alcohol.

I lower Momo from my face with an awkward smile. "Sorry for hitting your face with an egg. And spilling eggs on your car. *And* running you over."

He chuckles. "You don't have to worry. I won't be pressing charges," he tells me. "I probably deserved all that."

"You really did," I confess, my shoulders relaxing. My heart continues to beat a frantic rhythm in my chest, unassured despite his words. I'm surprised by how he's handling all this. To be honest, I thought his first move would be to threaten to sue my head off. Wonders never cease.

I can see that his cast has already received its first signature— Eliza's. There's a little heart drawn beside it. My stomach twists. "So, you and Eliza . . ."

Dan looks down at his cast. "Oh, no. We're not back together. This is . . ." He frowns. "An amicable split."

"I'm not sure the phone cameras will see it that way."

He winces at the memory. "If only there was a way to delete those videos from the collective consciousness."

If only. There's plenty of things I want to forget about tonight, especially how I nearly killed Dan Carter. I'm actually feeling bad about it, despite everything he's done to Eliza. If anything, I'm impressed at how Dan's taking this in stride.

I might have misjudged him a little—he's not as much of a dick as I thought he was, apparently. He now measures about a point and a half lower on the dick-o-meter.

"You've got mad driving skills," Dan offers. "One second later, and I'd be a pancake."

"I hit you," I point out.

"But you didn't kill me. That's a distinction in my book." His expression softens slightly, and he scratches his nose. "Um, I know I wasn't very mature, earlier. About . . . you know. But thank you."

"For what?"

Dan shrugs. "Being there for Eliza. I was an idiot. Dumping her over text was a dick move."

"Definitely," I agree.

"You should talk to her."

"About what?"

He raises his eyebrows at me. "You like her."

My jaw drops, and Momo nearly follows suit. "Wha—what?"

"Look, I like Eliza as much as the next person," Dan says, "but to sit in an enclosed space with her for eight hours? That takes a lot."

I shake my head slowly. "I don't know what you're talking about."

"She spends more time with you than with me," he continues. "Look, maybe one of the reasons our relationship didn't work out is, well . . . you. And I'm not saying you sabotaged us or anything," he says quickly, holding up a hand, "but Eliza's never been as invested in us as she is with you."

My raging heart skids to a stop. *What did he just say?*

"Talk to her," Dan tells me with a small smile.

232

I open my mouth to reply, but Eliza's head pops inside before I can say anything. My lower jaw slams upward and locks permanently.

"Hey, Soph, let's go." She turns to Dan, mirth glittering in her eyes. "Don't get run over by any more exes and their best friends."

He snorts. "Very funny."

"I should become a comedian," Eliza quips, hopping over and linking her arm through mine. She gives Momo a pat on the head. "Bye, Dan."

Dan lifts his uninjured arm to wave, smiling knowingly at us.

Eliza drags me out of the hospital in a matter of minutes, her face decidedly impassive.

Did she hear? I wonder. *Oh, no. This is going to be awkward, isn't it?*

"I've already booked a motel room for tonight," she says, opening the car door for me. "Hope you don't mind sharing a bed."

"As long as it's not a twin," I reply, tossing Momo into the passenger seat. "My butt's too big."

Eliza's cheeks flush in the cold spring night. "It's a queen size. And I like your butt just fine."

"I'll take that as a compliment."

Her hand shoots out, blocking me from entering the car. "I want to thank you," she murmurs.

I laugh nervously. "For what?"

"Being there," Eliza says, her eyes glowing in the streetlights. "You didn't need to. But you did it anyway."

My neck feels hot. So do my cheeks.

"You're my best friend," I say after a pregnant pause. "I'd do anything for you."

"Yeah?" Eliza grins. "Anything?"

"Listen, I landed Dan in the hospital for you," I tell her pointedly. "If that isn't an indicator how much I care, then I really don't know—"

"I overheard you and Dan. In the hospital room," she blurts.

Shit.

"I know how much you care," Eliza whispers into the silence between us. "Why didn't you say anything all this time?"

"Why do you think? This"—I alternate my fingers between us—"is good. I'm not going to ruin a perfectly good friendship."

"What were you going to do, wait for the end of the world?"

"I don't know! Maybe!"

Eliza nearly shouts at me. "Even if I liked you too?"

"Wait." I lean back slightly, my thoughts emptying. "What?"

"I just told you I liked your butt," she snaps. "Do I also have to tell you that I like you in general? Because I do. I've been trying to tell you all day. God, Sophie, sometimes you can be so . . ." She searches for the word, her gaze distant.

"Oblivious?" I offer.

"Dumb," she finishes.

Ouch. "You just broke up with Dan," I tell her. "You shouldn't be jumping into another relationship so quickly."

Eliza crosses her arms. "What do you propose, then?"

An ambulance siren whoops in the distance.

"You really like me?" I ask after a long pause. I'm smiling a mile wide at this point, but I can't stop.

She huffs, unable to hide a smile of her own. "Duh."

"One date." I lift a finger when she grins. "One date, and if we turn out to be absolutely horrible together, we go back to being friendly roommates."

"Very defeatist of you." Eliza steps forward with a playful grin, those dimples making a reappearance. "It's a good thing I'm more of an optimist myself."

"Mm-hmm." Our noses touch. "I'm sure you've thought about it all."

"There's a reason there's only one bed."

"Eliza."

She laughs, her breath intermingling with mine. "Shut up and kiss me, Sophie."

And that's how I get my first kiss. It's awkward and giggly, involving ten different kinds of contortions, but our lips finally meet at ten p.m. in the middle of a hospital parking lot, and it's not as bad as I worried it would be. It's magical, even.

I suppose I have Momo to thank for this. And Dan Carter, of all people.

Hell of a spring break road trip.

Begin Again
By Christina Li

The random number generator could have picked anyone.

If it had settled on any other number and any other name, Emma Zheng would have glanced across the room and given a small nod to whichever partner she was assigned to for the final project in her film seminar, and then gone about her day. Maybe they'd exchange emails. Maybe they'd frantically message each other the day before the final was due, and then they'd slap together a hasty ten-minute movie. And then she'd fulfill the graduation requirement for taking a creative arts class—Professor Kwon never gave lower than an A minus—and, then, school would be done.

As in, done done. She wouldn't stock up on spiral-bound notebooks or blow through a pack of mechanical pencils or stay up late on a Sunday night cramming for an eight a.m. Monday final. In five weeks, she'd sit in the sweltering sun and fling her cap into the air, and then, it was onward, without a look back, from Milbridge to Manhattan.

"I'm assigning you random partners," Professor Kwon said,

leaning over the stand from where she lectured about movies in FILMSTUD 187: Film Narratives, "because I know most of you are seniors. And I want you to get to know one more person before you graduate."

It could have landed on any other person.

Instead, the random number generator picked the one across the room whose presence made Emma's heart tip into her throat.

· · · · ·

It was three weeks before graduation when Valerie Wu got around to responding to Em.

The email had been sitting in her inbox for a week, and she'd been meaning to open it up. But each day the previous week, Val tended to more urgent things, big and small. On Monday, she sat on the futon in her friend Violet's room and consoled her for two hours as Violet recounted her breakup at The Last Drop. Like a lot of graduation breakups, it was amicable, and inevitable, and still, it hurt like hell.

It harkened back to Val's own breakup, three months ago, in the corner of The Last Drop, practically shouting to be heard over the Wednesday night live jazz set. (It didn't help that they were sitting next to the wall where people posted their meet-cutes from The Last Drop. In Val's experience, everyone always somehow ended up breaking up there. At least the whipped cream hot chocolate offered slight consolation.)

On Tuesday, she picked up her cap and gown. On Wednesday, she mediated a fight between two of her mutual friends who had been friends all the way back, since freshman orientation, and then, suddenly, weren't talking anymore, weeks before graduation. On

Thursday, she sat in the registrar's office for hours as she convinced them painstakingly that her philosophy class could, in fact, count for her science requirement that was sorely lacking. "It's a science of thought," she said, bringing back her high school debate voice. "Please, if this doesn't count, then I can't graduate on time. Because of this one class. And Professor Lorimer signed off on it." And on Friday, she ran around campus giving away her LSAT practice books, making a pit stop at her old freshman dorm, and once more thought about the decision that had been brewing in her for months.

So it was kind of a relief, finally, when she was able to get a moment's rest on Saturday and sit in front of her email, trying to catch up on an overflowing inbox, with the small fan at full blast in her face. Because the truth was, she had been thinking about this all week. It hummed in the back of her mind, always present, for some reason.

A film project. With Emma Zheng.

Emma, with her heart-shaped face and her calm voice, flitting in and out of Val's sight throughout the years. She was an extra in the play Val directed sophomore year, and then sat across the table from her a week after the show wrapped, for a project conducted for one of Violet's psych classes, asking questions adapted from the *New York Times'* 36 questions for love—but this time for friendship. And there were other moments, too: a drunken conversation sitting on the steps outside one of their friends' apartments during a Halloween party, cut short when Val's then-boyfriend, Dev, came out to check on her and she went back in with him. And then just months ago, when they reached for the same book on the top shelf of the campus bookstore and Emma's cool fingers brushed Val's.

"Oh, sorry," Emma had said, taking a step back. "You had it first."

Val glanced up. "You're taking Film Narratives, too?" The film minor was small, and Val hadn't seen her in any of the classes.

Emma shrugged. "Yeah. Have to fulfill my arts requirement."

"Ooooh," Val said. "Well, you picked the right class. I think. Everyone loves Nancy Kwon. She's chill." She grinned and held the textbook out. "Here, take it. I know people who have taken this class. I'll get a copy from them."

And Em had given her a small smile. A smile that Val found herself thinking about right now.

Hey, the email opened up. It's Em from class. Any chance you might be free this week to brainstorm our final? I'm pretty much down whenever, just let me know.

Yes ofc, Val hurriedly typed back. So so sorry for the late response! How about this afternoon or tomorrow?

Val leaned back and peeled her hair off the nape of her neck and into a bun. She looked at the calendar on the wall. Twenty days left until graduation.

Moments later, her inbox dinged.

Tomorrow works for me. Meet at the tables outside of the bookstore?

· · · · ·

Em was leaning over the tables near the bookstore and trying to figure out how to Google Translate a coming out speech when she spotted Val across the quad.

It wasn't that she didn't know Mandarin. She'd grown up speaking it at mealtimes to her parents and to her extended family over the phone, with the hum of a Chinese TV channel in the background. But she didn't know the exact words for what she was about to say, because she'd never once heard them in passing or in conversation. All she knew right now were the words in Mandarin for *I hope you accept me.*

Was that enough? Could it be? Em could imagine her mother's pinched expression and the words that were sure to follow: *Are you sure?* and *Why?*

Em didn't know if she had the answer for either. All she knew was that she had to say it the weekend of graduation, or at least in the following week. If they were cool with it, fine. If they weren't— well, at least she'd be moving into a new city.

Or you could just, you know, not say it, ever. Historians will say you had really good friends.

Em didn't have time to think about it more, because Val dropped her tote bag into the empty chair and pushed her sleeves up. She set her coffee on the table. And then she glanced up with a small smile that scattered the rest of Em's thoughts. "Hey. Sorry for being late. But I started a Google Doc of ideas and shared it with you, if that's okay." She talked a million miles a minute, just like when she was directing her play sophomore year. She took a sip of her iced coffee.

"I read through them," Em said. "They all sound great. I like the one about the farewell film throughout campus." Val was the film expert, after all.

"Sweet," Val said. She fiddled with a pen in her right hand. She never stayed still. "I love that one. I was thinking, you know how there's always a graduation parade through campus? I was thinking we put a creative spin on that and film places throughout campus. Like start with Desai, and then pan to different places as we grow through the years, including the World's Tiniest Wishing Bridge. Like a farewell tour or something."

"I like that," Em said. She paused, and then offered, "And maybe we could add some off-campus places, too."

Val tilted her head to the side. "Oh, definitely. We can add iconic spots like Cinema City . . ." Her eyebrows knit together. "I'm trying to figure out how to make it all cohesive, though. There's a lot of places for a ten-minute film."

"Ah," Em said. She shrugged. "Never mind. We don't have to film off campus."

"Unless . . ." Val drummed her fingers on her laptop. Em knew it as her thinking face, from when she was mulling over stage directions during the rehearsals for the play, and when she glanced down when they were partnered for that psych project. *Would you like to be famous?* was the question. *And if so, in what way?* Val had thought long and hard about that one, subconsciously tapping her boots on the floor. *I don't think I want to be famous, really. But I want my work to be known.* She'd locked eyes with Em then, and the room was quiet. *Does that make sense? Is that possible?*

"Oh," Val said. Her eyes met Em's now, and they lit up. "You know what? Scratch that. You're totally right. We start on campus, and then we go off campus. And film through Milbridge. That's where the movie should be."

She grinned, and it was the same smile that Em had seen at the beginning of the semester, in that very same bookstore, when they reached for the same textbook. A flicker of hope lit up in Em's chest.

Who was she kidding? It started way before then.

· · · · ·

She really should have become friends with Em earlier.

Halloween would have been the time. How many friends had

drunk Val made? She'd lost count by now. An effervescent compliment in the bathroom had turned into a once-stranger pulling her onto the table to dance with her at a party that hadn't seemed very fun until that moment. A pizza trip after her show's after-party stretched into a four a.m. campus tour when she became friendly with someone she'd met at the party—well, more than just friendly, but that was a story for later, and that person still glanced her way when she passed Val on campus.

The point was, Val was good at making friends. And even more so when she was two Smirnoff Ices in. And if Dev hadn't interrupted their conversation outside of Violet and Mina's joint Halloween party, she and Em might have even gone on to follow each other on social media. Val could have liked some of her tweets. They might have met up at other parties. There was something about Em's low laugh, her tentative smile, the way she always seemed cool and unflappable, and, well, nice.

Well, Val could do that all now. This film was her chance. Right? A chance to finish the conversation they started all those months ago, when the road before graduation was a small eternity away. When they could still tip their heads back in the cool air and pretend that they had all the time they needed.

· · · · ·

Em made her way around a group of grinning seniors on the quad, arms around each other.

She heard the click of the camera follow, and then they eased from each other.

Golden hour. It explained why she nearly ran into one group after another, clustered across the quad, even on a Wednesday late afternoon. She'd taken her own pictures a couple of hours earlier, with Lily and Julian and Nate. It had taken half an hour longer than she'd predicted: Nate couldn't find the right shoes and came late, and Lily had to pause after every shot because people kept coming up to say hi to her—people from her clubs, a former freshman that she'd been an orientation leader for, her boyfriend's group of friends. Em sidestepped a spray of champagne as she hurried from lab to the school gates.

Val was there already, setting up her tripod. "Hey," she said, glancing up.

"Sorry," Em rushed, taking the script out of her backpack. She'd scanned the lines the day before, marveled at how intentional Val's direction was. "I was picking up my materials from the lab, and then it took forever to print, and then . . ."

"No worries," Val said. "I love your lip color."

"Oh, right," Em said. She touched her face. "Thanks. I was taking grad pictures earlier, too. I keep forgetting I have shit on my face and accidentally rubbing it off."

Val smacked her head with her palm. "I really need to get on that. I've been trying to coordinate grad pics with my friends for weeks, but they seem to have a knack for scheduling boozy brunches and breakdowns instead." She glanced up. "Well, it looks good on you," she said, her gaze lingering for just long enough to jump-start Em's pulse. "Anyway." She turned back to the camera and tapped it with pristine white nails. "I was thinking we start here. Catch the sun going over the rooftops of the buildings. And have the shot pan to you—" She gestured to Em. "As you head out the gates."

"Wait," Em said, "I'm the girl in the script?"

"Yes?" Val said, her eyes wide. "Oh, is that okay? I mean, if you don't want to, we can totally do something else."

"I don't mind," Em said. The subject of a movie? She hadn't been anything more than a stage extra before. "I just thought that you'd be in it because you . . ." She looked at Val shielding her eyes against the sun, her hair done up effortlessly, her dress swaying in the breeze. *Seemed like more of a main character.* "Would know what you're doing."

"Nah, I'm more comfortable behind a camera," Val said. "Plus, I've acted in enough class projects this semester. I'd love to have you star in this one. If you're cool with that?"

Em paused. Her eyes met Val's hopeful expression, and her heart thudded. "Yeah," Em said. "I am."

"Perfect." Val peered from behind the camera. "Okay, this angle looks great. And then . . ." She paused. "Wait. Sorry. Stay still, and I'm just going to fix your hair a bit."

Em stayed perfectly still. Val came over, eyes fixed on Em, and her hand tucked a strand of hair over Em's shoulder. Em glanced toward the campus quad, where everyone was still taking their pictures, pretending it was the setting sun that warmed her cheeks.

• • • • •

Val loved this.

She loved crafting the perfect shot behind a camera lens. Loved playing with the settings and seeing the town lights soften in a hazy burst of colors before she sharpened the focus. Loved catching the small moments in frame; the breeze that ruffled Em's sleeve as she looked toward Milbridge, the flowers in bloom, the buildings that rose up behind her.

"Oh, that looks amazing," Em said, peering over Val's shoulder at the golden hour shot. "You make everything look good."

"Hey, you're the one carrying this," Val said. "Oscar-worthy acting, dare I say. You always were really good at acting."

Em smiled at the ground, and looked up. "Even as an extra in your play?"

"Yeah," Val said. "You were."

"You directed another play this year, right?" Em asked.

"Yeah. Co-directed with Rin Takagi. I kinda wished I saw you at auditions."

"Right," Em said softly. "I remember seeing flyers for it around campus. I uh . . . really should have auditioned. Guess I just chickened out." She cleared her throat and glanced up. "Should we move to the next scene?"

Filming felt more natural than anything as they made their way from Aesop's Café to Cinema City to film. And so when Val thought of what lay at the end of summer—stuffy classrooms and heavy textbooks and a crowd of nervous students and late nights studying at law school—her shoulders dropped with a sigh.

What had happened? That was what she'd always wanted. All signs had pointed to this. Her overflowing bookshelf at home. All the times people had told her that she would be a good lawyer at dinner parties because it was a nice way of telling her that she was argumentative. The thrill at high school debate tournaments. How she'd loved Professor Felt's Philosophy and Moral Justice class, aced it even, when everyone else was cowed by Felt's cold calls and barely emerged with B pluses. When she'd wrapped up her LSATs and gotten her acceptance letters, narrowed down on the law school that she felt like would best define the next three years of her life, a wave of relief had washed over her. But now, when she looked at her horizon contracting to the end of summer, she felt her heart constricting.

All because she had an offer to help make a film in New York from a friend at a film festival.

Wasn't film just supposed to stay a hobby? Something that a minor and a couple of college classes satisfied? So why was Val still so torn up about this? Why did the thought of packing away her cameras fill her with dread?

"Should I position myself further back?" Em said, bringing Val's thoughts back to the shot in front of her. She paused over the Cinema City ticket counter. "Or should I . . ."

"No," Val said. "You're perfect where you are. Just look down at the tickets, and then up at the marquee." Golden hour had melted away into dusk by then, and even in the dim light Val could make out the wistfulness in Em's eyes. She was such a natural. Or maybe she really was nostalgic over the Monday matinee. "And . . . cut."

Em looked up. "How does it look?"

"Oh, the lighting is superb," Val said, clicking through the frames. She looked up. "Is it weird that I miss college already, even though we're still, like, fully here?"

Em shook her head. "No, this really does feel like a throwback." She glanced up. "To all the Sunday night films and the two awkward first dates I've had here: you will be missed."

Val laughed. "Don't even get me started on the iconic Cinema City dates." Somehow, that was the universal Milbridge experience; you'd get coffee at The Last Drop, or, if it was the second date, a panini at Aesop's Café. You'd get some ice cream, maybe. And then you'd meander over to Cinema City and get a huge bucket of popcorn or maybe a slushie. "Once, I came here with a guy who tried to impress me by choosing an A24 horror film. He spent the whole two hours hiding in his sweatshirt." It was awkward—but, then again, Val had her fair share of laughable moments. Namely, the time she tagged along to a late Friday movie with Violet and another friend, only to find out halfway through the preview trailers that, well, Val was the oblivious third wheel. And she had her share of good times at Cinema City, too. "Every year before winter break, after all our finals were done, my friends and I would get wine-drunk and come watch a movie," she said. "It was our holiday tradition."

She could picture it now; Dylan would always try to get a snowball fight started. Val would comment on how cold it was, and someone would make a California joke. Violet would accidentally buy too many Junior Mints. Mina would try to smuggle in a croissant from The Last Drop. And they'd watch the oldest movie in the queue, so they'd almost always get the theater to themselves.

"That's wholesome," Em said.

Val shook her head. "I'd hardly call a bunch of twentysome-things trying not to puke into their popcorn buckets wholesome. But it was a hoot and a half."

"I mean, it sounds like a good tradition," Em said. "My friends and I would always go to a movie at the beginning of each semester. But then my friend Nate got a projector and a futon, so we mostly just bother him now when we want to watch stuff. We put string lights and draped blankets around it, so it's more like an elaborate fleece cave."

"Now, that's the cutest shit I've ever heard," Val said. "Save me a spot next time."

"Will do," Em said, and grinned, and it was funny and sad, because both of them knew that there wouldn't really be a next time. She cleared her throat. "Should we move to The Last Drop?"

Val could make out the glow of the windows down the street. "Yeah, let's do that." She glanced down at her phone. "I think one of my friends is actually in there, too." She tapped out a text to Violet.

As they made their way there, she caught herself staring at the way the setting light played with the highlighter on Em's cheekbones, so much so that she almost tripped on the curb. Em glanced back. "You good?"

"Oh, me? Yeah—yes." Val stopped in front of The Last Drop. "You mind if I go in there to say hi?"

"Not at all," Em said. "I'll grab a coffee."

Val's pocket buzzed with a text. Grinning, she headed into the coffee shop after Em.

· · · · ·

Em glanced over her shoulder at Val as she paid for the two cups of coffee at the counter.

She was leaning over the table, talking to what looked like her friend. Violet, maybe? Em remembered seeing her jean jacket and black braids around campus tables and in the library. Em caught Val's eye and held up the two coffee cups. And then she nodded toward the door and smiled, as if to say, *Take your time. I'll be outside.*

And then she was stepping into the cool dusk air, staring at the streetlights of Milbridge. A bus rumbled down the street. On the other side, peals of laughter floated over from a group of what looked like college students. Em smiled. She remembered tagging along with different groups her freshman year, before she found Lily and they dragged each other, one shitty problem set after another, through the differential calculus class that was a prerequisite for their product design classes. And then, somehow, they went from complaining about tests to hanging out on Friday nights, and their friendship was solidified when she went with Lily to get a tattoo and they split a burrito after. And then they met Julian and Nate in the tiny communal kitchen of Desai, and that was it. But now it was about to be graduation, and then Julian was moving back to California, while Nate headed to Portland. At least she would have Lily around in New York.

She really was getting ahead of herself. She still had all of two weeks.

But it was all ending soon. Faster than she'd thought it would. It felt like yesterday when her friends all attempted the Fabled Feast challenge in Aesop's Café for the sixth time in August, because nothing beat the hunger and jaded determination of seniors who had just finished moving in for the final time. In September, when she signed her job offer. In November, when they gathered in Nate's room and scrambled to sign up for classes for the last time and Em chose the film class because she had heard about it somewhere, realizing only weeks later that it was Val who had told her about it. In December, when she swore she was pulling her last all-nighter to turn in a final project on time. But then suddenly, she was hurtling toward graduation, like time itself warped.

Em couldn't help herself from glancing into The Last Drop. Violet was leaning over to say something, her eyebrow raised; Val's head tipped back in laughter as she shot back a response, and Em felt a flutter in her chest.

If everything was coming to a close, why did Em feel like she was waiting for something to start?

In a braver world, Em would step up to Val. *I like you. I've liked you since Halloween.* To hell with bad timing, with the fact that they would never see each other after graduation, that they didn't have any reason for staying in touch. Em would release the words into the night. Hadn't this been the kind of person she was trying, resolving, to work herself toward? The kind of person that made stuff happen. The kind of person who wouldn't keep quiet and fold her thoughts up into tiny pieces until she could slot them in the back of her mind.

But in this universe, Em simply shoved her hands in her pockets and jumped when the door opened, the jingle of the doorbell catching her off guard.

"Sorry about that," Val said, stepping out. "My friend and I were having a nice panic session in there."

Em handed her a coffee. "Everything okay?"

"Oh, I mean, it's just the usual. Neither of us know what the fuck we're doing after graduation. It's the Violet and Val depression show. We encore a lot."

"I thought you were going to law school," Em said. "Right? In Chicago. I remember you telling me about it at your friend's Halloween party."

"Right," Val said. She tilted her head. "You remember?"

Em shrugged, trying to feign a casual smile. "I have a good memory."

Val exhaled into the night and crossed her arms. "Well, law school was . . . is . . . the plan."

"But?"

She met Em's eyes. "I got an offer to make an indie film in New York."

Instinctively, Em's heart leapt. "Oh."

"Yeah," Val said. "And I've been thinking, I mean, I haven't ever fathomed a career in film, so what's the point? I might as well get my life started and go to law school already. But the thing is, I want to go to New York and make the film. It sounds like . . . an experience I want. Even if nothing comes of it. And so I have this gut feeling telling me to defer law school, and my brain tells me to ignore it, and so they've been having a healthy argument over the last few months."

Val in New York. Em tried to keep her expression neutral, even though every part of her thrilled at the possibility of them existing in the same place again. "I'm sure you'll figure it out," she said. "I mean, the movie sounds exciting. And you can go to law school after that anyway. And . . . you are really good at making films. And directing."

"Really?"

"Yeah," Em said. Val's gaze was intense. Em's first instinct was to look down, but instead she blurted out, "It's like a light comes on in your eyes. And I like the idea of doing something just because it makes you happy." Her cheeks felt warm. There. She'd said something. But maybe she'd said too much. "But yeah. I get it. Just wanting to get started. Both decisions are valid. I . . . just think you should give film a chance, that's all."

"Thanks," Val said. She took a long sip of coffee and tilted her head. "So, what's your big plan after graduation? It's okay if you don't have one. Violet and I will gladly welcome you into our dysfunctional group."

Em laughed. "I'm going to be working. At a design firm in New York."

"You really are put together," Val said, shaking her head in admiration. "But also, New York?" She raised her eyebrows, and the corners of her mouth tilted up into a smile. "Man, maybe I really should go, too."

Em's mind froze on the words. Does she—did she mean—?

But Val was already turning away, bringing the camera up. "Should we get a shot here, before the place closes? You can sit at the tables, and I'll film from the outside. I really like the glow of the lighting." She glanced back. "Oh, by the way, did I tell you about how I got broken up with here?"

"Do tell," Em said.

"It was on a Wednesday during jazz night, the week before Valentine's Day," Val said. "I mean, who the fuck gets broken up to live jazz?"

· · · · ·

Em was more perceptive than Val had given her credit for.

It's like a light comes on in your eyes, she'd said. When had anyone said that to her? The best praise she'd gotten from a film class was Professor Sorkin, saying, "You have a knack for this." And her parents had been proud of her—they'd watched all of the films that she posted on her website and sent her effusive thumbs-up emojis, which was honestly pretty great as far as feedback from Asian parents went.

And yet here was a practical stranger who was making her think about throwing all her future plans up in the air and heading to New York.

A practical stranger who looked beautiful in the light of the coffee shop, eyes searching the room, and then glancing back down at her computer. Em ran her hands through her hair, and it tumbled down gracefully over her shoulders. And suddenly, Val wanted to know more about her. She wished she had weeks, months, to invite her to parties and to text about the film class and to spend time with her. She wished it were the beginning of the semester instead of the end.

She wished for more time.

That was what she always wanted. More time to decide. There were so many reasons. She wanted more time to peer down the fork in her path, to get her shit together, to have the time to put together a convincing argument to her parents to defer law school (and a convincing argument for herself, really), to send off the year with the friends she loved. But this night, when she wished for more time, it was because of Em.

· · · · ·

"One last place," Val said, as the dusk deepened into night. "We should go to the tiny bridge."

There was a creek that ran through campus, toward Pitfall Lake. It was narrow enough to hop over, really, but still, there was a tiny bridge that joined the two ends of the sidewalk. It had become the wishing bridge over the years—campus stories said that if you stood at the bridge and made a wish, it would come true. A sign was posted at the bridge: PENNIES NOT REQUIRED. During finals week, the line stretched around to the street.

Val held her camera up steadily. Em watched her focus on the lights and the buses, on the crowds on the sidewalk as people left dinner. Eventually, they came to the tiny bridge. Val glanced at her. "What would you usually wish for?"

Em shrugged. She remembered just what she wished for two weeks ago, when she came to the bridge, but she didn't say it. "You know. Good grades. Stuff like that. You?"

"Yeah, pretty much the same. Good grades. Law school. Crushes. The usual."

Em smiled, because she couldn't imagine Val needing luck for the last bit.

Val set up her camera, and it was quiet while she worked. Em stared at her feet, thinking hard. Wishing again. Time and time again, she wished for the same thing: for the conversation with her parents to be quick and painless. Supportive, even, maybe, but that was less likely.

But this time, she didn't just wish for that. She knew what she was going to do. What she was going to tell her parents. Maybe it was the fact that the final days of college were descending upon them. There was a kind of curious confidence, a new assuredness that was settling over Em. Instead, this time she peeked over at Val and wished for something new.

"All right," Val said. "And that's a wrap. I think we have all the scenes we need. And then I can put it together in Final Cut and we can knock Professor Kwon's socks off." She looked over at Em and grinned. "Thank you, actress extraordinaire. You're a natural."

"Hey, you're the pro filmmaker," Em said. "It's all you."

They lingered at the bridge. Val started to say something, and then closed her mouth.

"What?" Em said.

"I was just thinking . . ." Val said. "I wish there was more time to do everything. All this time during these past years I was just try-ing to get through things to graduate. And now I'm actually here. And I wish I'd done more?"

Em exhaled. "What do you wish you'd done?"

"I mean, I guess I'm pretty happy with the way things turned out, because I couldn't do everything, right? Finite time constraints and all that. But I don't know. I always wish I'd gotten to know more people. Or taken more cool classes." She glanced up at Em. "Is there anything you . . . wish you'd done?"

Em's heart was pounding in her chest. She put her hands in her pockets. Somehow, in the clear night air, it was easier to tell the truth. "I wish . . ." She stared at her shoes. "I wish I'd come out to my family earlier. I've wanted to for the longest time. I mean, I will. I told myself I'd tell them before graduation. But I've known for years and I wish I hadn't waited this long. I always just hold back and overthink things and end up chickening out, with literally everything I do in my life. I wish I just, you know, *did things*." *I wish I knew how to tell you I like you,* she thought. *I wish I had the guts to.*

"Yeah," Val said softly. "Telling family's a big step."

"I guess so," Em said. She cleared her throat and steadied her voice. "And I know things in my life are lined up, but I feel like it won't properly start until I've told them. For some reason."

She looked up. Val was looking at her. She said, softly, "Yeah. It took me years to come out to my family, too. But I knew I wanted to tell them."

"And how did they react?"

"Better than I thought they would." Val gave a sly smile. "I mean, it took multiple conversations. But they got there. They support me now in their own way. And I hope yours do, too. It's what you deserve."

Em exhaled. "I hope," she said.

"Let me know how it goes. If you tell them."

Em smiled. "I will. When I do." She turned to Val. "And let me know if you end up taking the film job. Law school seems cool. But I, uh. Really hope to see you in New York."

Val stared out for a moment. And then she seemed to square her shoulders, and she turned to Em. "I think I made up my mind already, actually. I think I'm going to defer law school for a year. I'm going to go make the film. Maybe we'll meet at another Halloween party or something."

Em's heart soared in her chest. Somehow, in the clear night, everything seemed so sure. This was it. Finally, she threw caution to the wind. She blurted out, "Do you . . . want my number or something? So we can hang out?"

Her heart thrummed in her chest. Maybe there was hope that something could start here, after all.

Val looked up, and a slow grin spread over her face. "Yeah," she said softly. "I'd love that."

· · · · ·

Some things didn't just end at a Halloween party. Or a bookstore. Or at graduation.

As Val walked home that night, her head swimming with the decision she'd just made, she didn't feel like her future was narrowing anymore to a predetermined, fated point. Instead, she listened to Em's low laugh and to the sounds of students talking from across the street. And when Em handed back over the filming props at the end of the night, their hands brushed, just like that time in the bookstore. Except for this time, Em's hand lingered for a moment more, and Val let her.

She and Em parted ways, and Val crossed the campus back to her apartment. The quad was quieter now. No one was taking graduation pictures anymore. A pair of friends sat on the benches, looking up, their laughter drifting across the quad.

Her phone buzzed in her pocket, and her heart trilled. She could picture it now. She and Em sitting in a café together. Em's soft smile. The two of them at Violet and Mina's next party, talking into the night. Holding hands on the way home.

She looked at her phone's calendar, which was counting down the days until graduation. But she didn't feel like counting down anymore.

She had all the time in the world.

SUMMER

Catch You on the Quad
By Oyin

III.

Imagine for a moment
        leaves swirling on
lazy breezes
        a campus preparing
bittersweet goodbyes of
        Great houses that will soon be
almost-empty forts
        energetic anticipation while filling
suitcases and storage
        bins with fairy lights Polaroids T-shirts proudly proclaiming them
in the UMB army
        Class of 23 items on the menu at Aesop's
Café of 24 hours left
        to try to embrace, of 25 meal points remaining for some
and so on and so on
        the campus watching as it has done
in the background;
        imagine the calling of names
balloons in sweaty hands
        and tears held in
eyes focused on the processional
        the shifting from sitting to
standing waving some even
        smiling because after years of
crying and courting and
        clapping for others
cheering those in gowns caps on
        their moment is now
walking across the stage
        across the campus to degrees
across the soon-to-be-empty quad
        to cars or planes or trains
to summer.

College Advice: From Studying to Connecting (and More)

"Welcome to university! Believe in the power of your potential, make all the memories you can, and live every moment to its best and brightest extent. You're finally exactly where you're supposed to be."

—ANANYA DEVARAJAN, CLASS OF 2023

. . . . .

"Make good friends, and you'll figure out the rest. Dining hall cereal is not dinner. If your heart gets broken, you'll find a way to stitch it back together."

—JAKE MAIA ARLOW, CLASS OF 2019

"Here's to a great college experience! If you choose university as part of your life journey, I hope it treats you wonderfully. Meet new people, try to learn something about yourself and the world around you, get involved in your community, participate in silly social events, and *go to office hours*!"

—AASHNA AVACHAT, CLASS OF 2020

. . . . .

"If you're living in a new city or town, go off campus and explore the local area as much as possible. In retrospect, it is so gratifying to feel like you authentically lived in a place."

—MICHAEL WATERS, CLASS OF 2020

"Enjoy this chapter of your life! Through all the chaotic ups and downs, don't forget to believe in yourself and appreciate that you've made it this far!"

—RACQUEL MARIE, CLASS OF 2020

· · · · ·

"Don't be afraid to follow your heart, even if that means stepping off the path that you thought was for you! There's time to grow and figure things out, so be present and enjoy all the little moments that make up the college experience!"

—LAILA SABREEN, CLASS OF 2023

"Your college experience is yours and only yours. Prioritize self-care, surround yourself with uplifting people, and don't fall into the trap of comparison. Here's to a transformative time!"

—ARUSHI AVACHAT, CLASS OF 2024

. . . . .

"This is the best time to explore everything—who you are, what you like, what you don't. Don't be trapped by the idea you had of yourself. It's okay to become someone new."

—JOELLE WELLINGTON, CLASS OF 2020

"Don't be afraid to make friends outside of campus, especially older friends, if you can! They can help give advice about school, jobs, and relationships, because they've been through all of it before. It also helps you form a community outside of the school and with the wider community."

—Camryn Garrett, Class of 2022

· · · · ·

"Welcome to college! These are the years of endless possibilities filled with opportunities for you to reach for the stars! Chase your dreams, and never be afraid of the soaring heights you can achieve."

—Boon Carmen, Class of 2023

"Things are always in flux during college: don't be afraid to explore new things, get acquainted with new people, and take all kinds of classes that interest you!"

—CHRISTINA LI, CLASS OF 2021

. . . . .

"Participate in class (one comment/question during each session can go a long way), attend club meetings and events (a great way to meet people), find truths in being fearless (or lonely or stressed). After years of clapping for others . . . your moment is now. You got this!"

—OYIN, CLASS OF 2019

Acknowledgments

This book would not have been possible without the guidance and support of Laurel Symonds and The Bent Agency. Thank you, Laurel, for believing in this anthology from the start, and for every effort you took for *Study Break*. Enormous thanks to you and The Bent Agency for all that you do for authors and our dreams.

To Foyinsi Adegbonmire: *Study Break* would still be a Google document titled "Anthology Proposal," if not for you. Thank you for your vision, passion, and dedication for this project, and for your excitement for more fiction set in college.

Thank you to Liz Szabla and the rest of the Feiwel & Friends team for making Milbridge a reality: Jean Feiwel, Kim Waymer, and Helen Seachrist.

Thank you to artist Mlle Belamour and designer Kerri Resnick for bringing UMB and its students to life with this beautiful cover. We are so lucky to have your artistry represent our stories. The cover is everything we could have imagined and more.

To Ananya Devarajan and Camryn Garrett, for your tweets and for the initial *Study Break* group chat, and to everyone who participated in brainstorming there and beyond.

To Ahmad Ali, for the title. To all our friends, parents, and family who supported each of us.

Thank you to every contributor: Jake, Ananya, Michael, Racquel, Laila, Arushi, Joelle, Camryn, Carmen, Christina, and Oyin, for your stories and poetry, which made this world possible, and to the contributors' agents, who supported the journey.

Thank you as well to every author who submitted a story to our open call; we appreciate you very much.

And finally, a huge thanks to you, the reader, for making room on your shelf for books like ours.

About the Contributors

Manasi Patel

Ananya Devarajan is an undergraduate at the University of California, Irvine, pursuing a major in neurobiology with a minor in English. Like the majority of her characters, she is a second-generation Indian American young adult. Her love for storytelling began on Wattpad, where she grew her audience as a featured author, and she later went on to win first place in TeenPit 2019. Now Ananya writes young adult romance novels featuring dynamic Indian teenagers, lighthearted drama, and swoonworthy banter. Her debut novel, *Kismat Connection*, is slated for publication in Summer 2023 by Inkyard Press/HarperCollins, and you can learn more about her and her stories on Twitter and Instagram under the handle @ananyad12.

Torrin Nelson

Jake Maia Arlow (she/they) is a podcast producer, writer, and bagel connoisseur. They are the author of the middle grade novel *Almost Flying* and the young adult novel *How to Excavate a Heart*. She studied evolutionary biology and creative writing (not as different as you might think) at Barnard College, and lives with her girlfriend and their loud cat in the Pacific Northwest.

Emily Zeng

Aashna Avachat is a YA author and editorial assistant with a love for hope-filled stories. She graduated from the University of California, Berkeley, in spring 2020 with a BA in English and is currently a 1L at Harvard Law School. She is passionate about amplifying marginalized voices in publishing and increasing space for readers to see themselves in book pages. When she's not writing, she's probably reading on a sunny patch of grass, going on long walks to grocery stores, or being cozy with one of her many foster kittens. You can find her on Twitter: @AashnaAvachat.

Michael Waters is a journalist who has written for *The New Yorker*, *The Atlantic*, *Wired*, and other publications about everything from queer history to the death-care industry. You can find him on Twitter at @michaelwwaters.

Racquel Marie grew up in Southern California, where her passion for storytelling of all kinds was encouraged by her friends and big family. She received a BA in English with an emphasis in creative writing and a minor in gender and sexuality studies from the University of California, Irvine. Racquel primarily writes YA contemporaries starring queer Latine characters like herself and is the author of *Ophelia After All* and *You Don't Have a Shot*. When not writing or reading, she loves practicing beauty and special effects makeup, watching and producing YouTube videos, and teaching herself to play ukulele in spite of her extremely long nails. You can learn more about her writing and love of books through her Twitter, @blondewithab00k.

Nohelia Valentin

Laila Sabreen is a young adult contemporary writer who was raised in the Washington, DC area. She currently attends Emory University, where she is double majoring in sociology and English. Her love of writing began as a love of reading, which started when she used to take weekly trips to her local library. There she fell in love with the Angelina Ballerina series, so much so that she started to write Angelina Ballerina fanfiction at the age of five (though she did not know it was fanfiction at the time). Her debut YA contemporary novel is *You Truly Assumed*. When she isn't writing, she can be found working on essays, creating playlists that are way too long, and watching *This Is Us*.

Nura Esmailizadeh

Arushi Avachat studies English and political science at University of California, Los Angeles. She loves dark chocolate, Bollywood dramas, and California winters. You can reach her on Instagram at @arushi.24 and on Twitter at @arushiavachat.

Minnie Yang

Joelle Wellington grew up in Brooklyn, New York, where her childhood was spent wandering the main branch of the Brooklyn Public Library. Her debut novel *Their Vicious Games* is slated for publication in Summer 2023 by Simon & Schuster Books for Young Readers. When she isn't writing, she's reading and when she's not doing that, she's attempting to bake bread with varying degrees of success or strengthening her encyclopedia-like pop culture knowledge. You can find her on Twitter at @joelle_welling.

Louisa Wells

Camryn Garrett was born and raised in New York. In 2019, she was named one of *Teen Vogue*'s 21 Under 21 and a Glamour College Woman of the Year. Her first novel, *Full Disclosure*, received rave reviews from outlets such as *Entertainment Weekly*, the *Today Show*, and the *Guardian*, which called it a "warm, funny and thoughtfully sex-positive, an impressive debut from a writer still in her teens." Her second novel, *Off the Record*, was released in 2021 and received three starred reviews. Camryn is also interested in film and is a student at NYU's Tisch School of the Arts. You can find her on Twitter at @dancingofpens, tweeting from a laptop named Stevie.

Boon Loy

Boon Carmen is an undergraduate at the University of Nottingham Malaysia, studying psychology. She was born and raised in Malaysia, where she cultivated a healthy appetite for YA novels and all kinds of cuisines. When she's not writing about chaotic girls and fantastical worlds, she can be found (or not—you need to look really hard) with her nose in a fantasy book or lurking on Instagram.

Bryan Aldana

Christina Li graduated from Stanford with degrees in economics and public policy. In her spare time, she is dreaming up characters and stories for children and young adults. She is also the author of *Clues to the Universe*, out from HarperCollins.

Ashé Davis

Oyin's love of storytelling led to pursuing bachelor's and master's degrees in creative writing and literature. When not working as an editor or thinking about her very large TBR pile, she can be found obsessing over bullet journaling or watching Black sitcoms from the '90s/early 2000s and fictional crime shows.

Thank you for reading this Feiwel & Friends book. The friends who made *Study Break* possible are:

Jean Feiwel, Publisher
Liz Szabla, VP, Associate Publisher
Rich Deas, Senior Creative Director
Holly West, Senior Editor
Anna Roberto, Senior Editor
Kat Brzozowski, Senior Editor
Dawn Ryan, Executive Managing Editor
Kim Waymer, Senior Production Manager
Emily Settle, Editor
Rachel Diebel, Associate Editor
Foyinsi Adegbonmire, Associate Editor
Brittany Groves, Assistant Editor
Elizabeth Clark, VP, Senior Creative Director
Michelle Gengaro, Designer
Helen Seachrist, Senior Production Editor

Follow us on Facebook or visit us online at mackids.com.
Our books are friends for life.